BRO CODE HELL

Hellman Brothers #2

MARIKA RAY

Bro Code Hell

Copyright © 2022 by Marika Ray

First Edition: July 21, 2022

Ebook ISBN: 978-1-950141-45-6
Print ISBN: 978-1-950141-46-3

BRO CODE HELL

Living with my older brother's best friend wasn't even my worst idea lately.

Keeping it a secret from my brother was on the list too. Oh, and actually falling (literally) for Blaze Hellman—when every frown clearly said to stay away—was most definitely at the top of the list.

I was kind of a genius normally. I'd managed to graduate early and was about to open my own veterinary clinic in my hometown of Hell. I clearly had my life together.

Until Blaze came back to town, moving slower than a sloth on crutches, more wounded emotionally than physically. We ended up bonding over stray dogs, exes from hell, and oddly enough, shared grief.

But helping him get his life back together could cost me my heart...and destroy his friendship with my brother. Will the heat between us create a situation that breaks all the bro codes?

CHAPTER ONE

laze

"BLAZE, honey, do you need help getting your pants on?"

My eyes popped open, the pain already blooming behind my eyeballs. It was nothing compared to the pain that pulsed out a steady beat from my right leg, but the headache had joined in due to the nightmare I'd had several times already since moving back home to Auburn Hill, aka Hell.

"Just a second, Mom," I croaked.

Not exactly the way a grown man wants to be woken up. If my brothers were here, they'd tease me mercilessly about my mommy needing to put my pants on for me. Sure, I'd broken my leg in multiple places and had several surgeries to set it properly, but brothers didn't care about pesky details like that.

I ran a hand over my face, surprised to find a healthy dose of whiskers there. Now that I thought about it, I couldn't remember the last time I'd shaved. I gave my armpit a little sniff before lowering my arm. Fuck. Or showered.

Wallowing was a funny thing. I'd had every right to wallow in misery when I found myself waking up in the hospital with my arm in a sling, a bandage around my ribs, and my leg in a full-length cast, but most of that had healed to a point I could get around with the help of crutches. Except the wallowing had increased the more I healed. Maybe it was being back in Hell. Or living with Mom again and her incessant drama-filled fluttering. Or maybe because my future looked like some long dark hallway of nothing. Whatever the reason, I'd perfected the art of the wallow.

The door to my old bedroom flew open. When I first moved back in with Mom over a month ago, I'd slept nude like I always did. I'd learned real damn quick to always have boxers on. Nikki Hellman respected closed doors as much as she respected keeping quiet on a juicy bit of gossip. Boundaries weren't a thing when it came to Nikki and her boys.

"Jeez, Ma. You ever think of knocking?"

She put her hands on her ample hips, striking a pissed-off pose she'd probably learned back when she was the reigning county beauty pageant queen. The pattern on her blouse reminded me of some drapes I'd seen in one of those snooty hotels down in Los Angeles. Her patent leather Air Jordans were pretty sweet though. I knew a few kids in my old neighborhood who would have done some shady shit to get a pair of those.

"I don't need to knock on my own damn door, now do I, Blaze Hellman?" She rushed over and swatted at my good leg under the covers. "I even yelled through the door first. Why would I knock?"

I shrugged, knowing this was a losing battle but still unable to let it go. Perhaps this was a sign my wallow hadn't yet reached rock bottom. I was still willing to fight for my privacy.

"I'd hate for you to walk in and get an eye full."

Mom snorted and rolled her eyes. "As if you have anything I haven't seen before. I wiped your ass, young man."

I hooked two hands under my bad knee and swung my legs over the side of the bed, making her jump back so she didn't get hit by the human windshield wipers. "I'd like to think I've grown and changed a bit since then."

"Are we really going to talk about that? Really?" Mom got busy darting across the room, grabbing a pair of sweats off the floor, giving them a sniff and then making a face. She grabbed another pair off the back of the chair in front of the rickety desk that held all my trophies from high school, and this time, the sniff led to a shrug instead of a grimace. Guess I did have at least one clean pair left. "If we don't hurry it up, you'll be late to your first day of physical therapy."

Mom liked to pretend to be all drama all the time, but she was unflappable. You didn't raise five boys as a single mom without building a tough outer layer that wasn't fazed by dick talk. I remember one summer us boys literally measured our dicks to see whose was the longest. Stupid, yeah, but that was boys for you. Mom found us, right when we crowned me the winner of that contest. She'd blistered our ears for what felt like hours, discussing how the size of the tool didn't matter if you didn't know how to use it. Turned out, that was solid advice.

Mom crouched down in front of me, her knees popping like the Fourth of fucking July. I grimaced, feeling like an absolute asshole for making my mom squat down to help me put my pants on.

"Mom, let me try. My shoulder's feeling much better."

It wasn't, but a man had to draw the line somewhere. I gently took the pants from her hands and leaned down to hook them over my right foot. With the immobilizer brace on—I'd gotten the cast off yesterday—I still couldn't bend my knee, which made putting on pants a test of my hamstring flexibility. Normally, it was pretty good, but over a month on bed rest had done a number on me. My shoulder screamed but I ignored it with even breaths and clenching my jaw for all it was worth. The pants snagged on my toes and I gave them a tug. They slid up my leg and then got caught on the brace.

Mom patted me on the shoulder and bent down to pull them over the brace. "It's okay to ask for help, you know."

I grunted and got the other leg in the pants. "I'm here, aren't I?"

I pushed off the bed with my good leg and stood there finding my balance before pulling the pants up the rest of the way. Mom threw a T-shirt at me and I pulled that over my head. My shoulder didn't like that movement either, but tough titties. I wasn't going to let my mommy dress me completely. A few passes of my hands over my hair and I was ready to go.

Mom looked at the top of my head, her nostrils doing that thing she did when she wasn't happy about something, but wasn't going to say anything. Her nostrils did all the talking for her.

"It's as good as it's going to get for today," I grumbled, wondering for the thousandth time when my best friend, Ben, was going to get back in town. He said I could move in with him as soon as this latest work project of his was buttoned up.

We made it just in time for my therapy session. Mom dropped me off and got coffee down the street, thank God, and I spent the hour grimacing through the nastiest stretches I'd ever been put through. I was an avid exerciser, lifting heavy weights and running miles every single day. One had to be in top shape to work as a stunt double in Hollywood. But the pain of physical therapy was on a whole other level. When Mom came back to pick me up, I was drenched in sweat.

I made it out to the car on crutches, folding myself inside the vehicle and storing my crutches without Mom's help. I felt a little bit like I'd just climbed Mt. Everest and survived to tell the tale. Mom shot me a wink and handed me a black iced coffee.

"To celebrate, I had them give you the nitro coffee."

I frowned. "Hell has nitro coffee now?" That was the type of shit LA would have, but I didn't expect it in my tiny hometown.

Nikki turned the wheel and headed home. "Some things have changed since you've been gone, honey."

I nodded, staring out the window like I was seeing the town for the first time. In a way I was, seeing new shops, freshly painted curbs, trees that had grown, and people who'd moved to town since I'd been away. A cop car had pulled over a light blue boat-like Cadillac just past the roundabout up ahead. My gut clenched and I had to crane my neck to the side to see who the cop was. Dark brown hair pulled back in a bun, smooth olive skin, and a mouth that could mesmerize a man.

Fuck.

My ex. Dani.

I scooted down in the seat and ducked, hoping I'd somehow turned invisible. Mom headed into the roundabout and glanced over at me.

"What the hell are you doing?"

"Just. Keep. Driving," I said from somewhere below the dash.

She shook her head, but did her job, getting us through the roundabout and on our way into the residential area. See? Unflappable. When I felt like the coast was as clear as it could be, I sat back up, heart hammering.

"I'm not even going to ask."

I nodded. "Good. I wasn't going to tell you."

"You're impossible, you know."

"Still gotta love me."

"You know I do."

My phone rang, interrupting just as Mom opened up her mouth to ask me something else I probably wasn't going to tell her. This was a game we'd played my whole life. She swore I didn't tell her anything, and I swore she was nosy as shit.

I just didn't understand the human obsession with sharing. In third grade, when the teacher had asked us to bring something to share with the class about our summer, I'd written an essay instead on why being forced to share personal details was a violation of my privacy. In best-friend solidarity, Ben had backed me up and written an essay on why the phrase "sharing is caring" was actually bullshit made up by overly nosy people.

Speaking of the best friends the world had to offer, Ben was calling. "Hey, man. Tell me you're in Hell."

His deep chuckle gave me one solid reason to be happy I was back in my hometown. I'd missed him living hundreds of miles away.

"My flight just landed, yeah. Should be at my place in an hour."

Relief swept through me and I almost didn't mind the fact that my leg felt like a heartbeat, pulsing out waves of pain. An airport announcement blared through the background and I waited it out until I spoke again.

"Is it too soon to ask if I can move in tonight?"

Mom let out a squawk right as another announcement started up. Ben responded, but I couldn't quite make out what he said. The announcement stopped and Mom got the car parked in the driveway, a frown directed my way. Not sure why she was put out. I'd explained right from the beginning I was only staying with her until Ben was back in town.

"Ah shit. I have to go. They've moved our flight to a different baggage claim." Ben sounded stressed. And tired. Two emotions I understood all too well.

"Okay, drive safe and I'll see you shortly."

We hung up and I turned to Mom. "Why are you mad at me?"

Her nostrils were doing their thing. "Your tone of voice."

I scrubbed a hand over the headache that just wouldn't quit. "My tone of voice? You have to spell it out for me."

Mom looked away and shrugged. Looked a lot like she was gearing up for an award-winning performance. "You just seemed quite happy to move in with Ben. Your tone of voice suggested that staying with your mother while I nursed you back to health was some kind of hardship for you."

Jesus. "That's not true at all, Mom. But I am a grown man and would prefer to stay with my best friend. Who is also a grown man."

Mom sniffed so hard I worried she'd suck up all the oxygen left in the car. "It's all in the tone, Blaze. It's all in the tone."

And with that, she hefted herself out of the car and climbed the stairs, pausing with her back to me. I opened my own door and nearly chuckled when she called over her shoulder, "Are you getting out or what?"

I bit back a grin. She was mad at me, but she wasn't going to go inside and abandon me while I tried to get myself in the house. She still loved me.

I pivoted, placing my crutches where I needed them, and pushed myself up to standing with considerable effort. Letting out my own award-winning moan, I gave Nikki Hellman a taste of her own medicine.

"I don't know if I can make it up the stairs. PT just wore me out."

She spun around with a worried look on her face and hustled back down the stairs to grab my arm. "Well, you poor thing. Let's get you inside and set up on the couch. I'll get some ice and make you a grilled cheese sandwich. Your favorite."

I let her mother hen me until my belly was full and my knee pain was down to a seven out of ten. Then I got up, hobbled to my room and packed my shit. She gave me looks all the way to Ben's house, trying to make me feel guilty. Under normal circumstances, I would feel bad for disappointing her, but she'd walked in on my shower one too many times in the last three weeks with a towel or soap or some other such thing that just couldn't wait. Seriously, the topic of boundaries was something I'd have to sit her down and talk about when I wasn't either dealing with pain that made me crazy, or woozy from pain meds that made my brain mush.

"Is he even home?" Mom parked at the curb outside Ben's house, peering up at the dark windows.

I opened my door and once again geared up for having to get out of a vehicle with one good leg and one good arm. "He will be shortly, don't worry."

Mom got my bag of clothes out of the back and made sure I made it up the steps to Ben's front door. I hobbled over to one of two pots that sat on his porch with dirt in them, but no plants. I tilted it and immediately found his front door key.

"Well, that's safe," Mom said wryly. "Also, where the hell are his plants?"

I got the door open and turned to give Mom a hug. "Not everyone has a green thumb like you. Plus, he's not home much due to his company."

Mom stiffened. "Then why are you staying with him? Who's going to help you?"

I patted her back and then set her away from me with my hands on her shoulders. "He'll be home long enough to help me heal. And I won't always be this helpless. Just trust me, Ma."

She bit her lip and studied me for a long moment. "I just worry about my boys, you especially."

"Bones heal, Mom."

She patted my cheek. "I'm not talking about your accident." Then she stepped back and skipped down the steps to her car.

"Might want to wash those clothes before Ben gets home, takes one inhale, and kicks you out," she called over her shoulder.

I shook my head and closed the door. The silence welcomed me, making me feel right at home. I loved my mother, but the woman was a talker. How she'd birthed me was a mystery, considering we were so different. Using my good leg, I kicked my bag into the house, hobbling behind on my crutches until I had to kick it again. I made it all the way to the guest room down the hall in this manner proving that I could take care of myself just fine, thank you very much.

Ben's place was dark and a little bit cold. He liked to turn the heat down whenever he left for an extended period of time. He'd bought this little two-bedroom, one-bath house when his gaming app first took off. At the time, I was still living here in Auburn Hill, working as a police officer. Ben's app had exploded soon after, earning him a cool million dollars that first year and even more in the most recent years. He could have bought one of the nicest homes in Hell, but he'd stayed here, preferring simplicity.

The guest bedroom had a queen-sized bed shoved against one wall, a navy-blue comforter draped over it, and green drapes. Not one item decorated the pale gray walls, but there was another pot in the corner where a plant lived out its very short life in Ben's care. The dirt that remained even looked a little lonely. The room wasn't anything special, but it looked like paradise to me.

I kept going down the hallway to the laundry room that was basically just a breezeway before you were in the garage. Tossing the entire contents of my bag into the washing machine, I poured in the soap and slammed the door shut. Then I stripped the T-shirt and sweatpants off too, threw them in and started it. These boxers would just have to do for one more night. Ben wouldn't care.

The guest room bed called to me and I answered. I lay down under the comforter, stacked my hands behind my head, and listened to the glorious silence. I was out within seconds.

CHAPTER TWO

nnie

"WHAT DO you want to do today?" I heard Grandma Donna ask her new boyfriend, Juan Carlos, in the kitchen.

"Juan Carlos plans on—doing you," he said back in what could be construed as a seductive manner if it wasn't for the phlegm clearing in the middle of it. And if it wasn't for the man referencing himself in third person.

I swung into the kitchen, finding them smooching over by the coffee pot. If I didn't need the caffeine so badly before I started my day—and didn't want to part with the cash to pick up a coffee in town—I would have avoided this display of affection. Juan was only wearing a pair of boxers with beagle faces on it, proving that not just women had to worry about the inevitable breast sag as we aged.

"Jesus," I grumbled, putting a hand over my eyes so my vision was limited to the old laminate flooring Grandma Donna had had for longer than I was alive. "Can y'all keep it rated-G just long enough for me to get out of here?"

Grandma Donna snorted, but based on where her slippered feet moved, I was fairly certain she and Juan were no longer pressed together. "You are a grown woman, Annie, darlin'. A little good-morning kiss shouldn't be a problem."

I grabbed my favorite travel mug and filled it with the steaming hot coffee, pausing to pour in some cream before screwing on the lid. A mug appeared in my field of vision, a hand with hairy knuckles attached. I poured Juan a cup of coffee too, because Grandma had raised me to have manners. A full-body shiver overtook me just thinking back on the sounds I'd awoken to last night. Buying earplugs was on the top of my to-do list today.

"Sounded like a hell of a lot more than a good-morning kiss last night," I grumbled.

Juan barked out a laugh and then that smooching sound was back. Dear God, I was getting sick. Grandma Donna had had boyfriends before, but I think her recent decline into menopause had altered something in her chemically. Where most menopausal women bemoaned a lack of sex drive entirely, Grandma Donna had swerved the other way. She was like a dog in heat, searching out the nearest male to rub up against.

"Okay. I'm outta here. Have a great day, Juan. Grandma." I backed out of the room, eyes still cast to the floor, hoping to get out of the house without seeing something that would haunt me the rest of the day.

"It's Juan Carlos, darlin'. He's from Spain and they like their two names there," Grandma called after me.

I rolled my eyes. Juan had been born in Fresno, but if he wanted to pretend he was legitimately from Spain, who was I to burst his Latin bubble? "Sorry, Juan Carlos!"

The screen door slammed shut behind me and I let out the breath I'd been holding. The sun was just rising in the east, setting all the leaves to glowing as they swung from the trees in the morning breeze. Houses on this street were all one story, redone over the years to keep them vibrant and in style.

I'd lived here in Auburn Hill, aka Hell, my whole life. Minus the four years I'd been away at college. Those handful of years were enough to confirm that I never wanted to leave Hell. It was my home, and it would soon be the home of my new veterinary clinic. If I got my ass in gear and got the place ready to open, that is.

I rushed down the porch steps and into my 1979 gold Firebird that had been my father's. My parents had died when I was just a baby. I didn't even remember them, so having my dad's car was one of the ways I kept them close to me.

The leather seats were freezing and the engine took a few cranks before it turned over, but the musty smell of an old car was worth the hassle. My older brother, Ben, had begged me to sell the damn thing and buy something reliable so he didn't have to worry about me, but I wouldn't hear of it. Besides, the backfires were kind of charming. I liked the way they announced my arrival into town. A conversation starter, if you will.

Speaking of, the parking was sparse on Main Street at this time of day. There was already a line outside Coffee, the local coffee shop here in town. Everyone parked in front of my storefront three shops down, but I was just fine with that as it gave me some foot traffic. I'd been updating the sign in my front window with my opening date and services that would be offered. Everyone in town knew they could take their pets to me soon, and not that place in Blueball that was so negligent I almost wanted to call the Better Business Bureau on them. Besides, as soon as my shop was officially open, I'd have two dedicated parking spaces out front. I'd made sure that was in my lease before signing.

"Good morning, Annie!" called Poppy from one of the tables set up outside Coffee. She lived just down the street from me. She was also one of Grandma Donna's frenemies. The two went at it like drunk spring breakers on a reality show, but secretly, I thought they were very similar. Not that I'd ever say that to Grandma Donna.

I waved back with a bright smile as I tried to get my key in the lock of my front door. It was nice to see Poppy enjoying her retirement from the postal service. James was a much more efficient deliverer of mail, though he did it quietly. And without spreading gossip. In a weird sort of way, I kind of missed how nosy Poppy was in her prime as she came by all our houses.

The door finally gave with a pop, flinging me into the empty space that would soon be my thriving vet clinic. I added *fix front door* to the growing to-do list in my head.

First on that list? Calling Ben, my brother. That idea had come to me on the car ride over here, pushing earplugs to a contingency to-do list. If Ben would let me move in with him, I could avoid early morning kisses between Grandma Donna and Juan Carlos. And especially the midnight groans of "Hold on, baby! My hamstring locked up!"

Seriously. No one under forty should have to listen to geriatric sex. It kind of ruined it for me, thinking that was in my future. Then again, I could only hope some kind of sex was in my future. Encounters in that department had been somewhat nonexistent since I moved back to Hell.

I put my coffee and purse on the front counter where we'd check in new patients. I'd gotten the walls mostly painted, and the front counter up. Now I needed cabinets and tables in the exam rooms and chairs in the waiting room. Oh, and decoration, like paintings and plants. It looked like a hospital in here and that just wouldn't do. I wanted my furry friends to feel comfortable in my clinic. The humans too.

Pulling my phone out of my purse, I hit Ben's contact and waited while it rang. I thought it was going to voicemail when he finally picked up, out of breath.

"Hey, Annie."

"Benji! How are you? Are you home?"

His chuckle was more exhausted than humor. "No, not yet. I am at the airport though. About to board my flight home if I get to my gate before they leave."

I put my thumb up to my mouth, chewing on the nail. A disgusting habit, I knew, but it happened every time I got stressed. My nails during finals week in college had been downright bloody.

"I'll be quick, then. Any chance you can let me take the guest room at your house for a little while? I'm having some issues at Grandma Donna's."

The airport announcer squawked in my ear and I had to pull the phone away from my head. We both waited until that was over.

"I'm not sure I—"

The announcer started talking again, and this time, Ben tried to talk over them. "Let's talk again when I land, okay?"

He said something else, but I couldn't make it out.

"Can I call you tonight?" I shouted, voice bouncing off the empty walls of my clinic.

Ben said something and then I heard, "sure."

"Okay, talk then!" I hung up, dancing a little jig on the new vinyl plank floors that looked like real wood. Real wood floors in a vet clinic were a hard no. Have you ever tried to clean up pee that soaked into wood?

I danced over to put my phone back in my purse. Things were looking up. I'd chat with him tonight and convince him this was a good thing. I'd move in. Ben would lecture me on taking on too much with opening this clinic so soon after I graduated. I'd assure him I was up for the task and we'd cohabitate in peace until I got the clinic up and running. Then I could move out on my own. No older brother helping me. No geriatric sex keeping me up at night. It would be great.

I turned in a circle, looking at my clinic and giving myself a second to just dream. To envision what my life would look like in a few short months. It had been my dream to take care of animals and make a decent living. One where I could take care of myself.

Grandma Donna had never hinted at being put out by the

responsibility she took on by raising me and Ben. She'd been lost in grief when our parents died, but she stepped right up and became the parent we needed. The woman deserved sainthood. But even so, some small part of me knew that hadn't been what she'd planned for her life. I knew raising us was a burden. And yes, she took it on cheerfully, but you could not convince me we weren't a burden.

Ben and I had been tested early on, the results showing we both had higher IQs than most kids our age. Ben especially. He'd been building his gaming app in high school, launched it the day of graduation, and was now a millionaire. I, on the other hand, was a little bit of a late bloomer. I didn't have millions in the bank yet, just a master's degree and my veterinary license at age twenty-three. I had some catching up to do if Ben was my gauge of success.

It took me all day, and I was one sweaty mess of a girl when I was done, but the cabinets had been moved into both exam rooms. I was ready for the countertop people to install. And I needed to call Charlie, the woodworker we all used here in Hell. He'd said he could make a metal stall for the back exam room, the one I'd use for medium-sized farm animals. I wasn't set up for cows and horses, but goats and pigs were welcome.

I shut off the country music that had been blaring, my stomach letting out a fierce growl. I realized I hadn't even stopped for lunch. The Forty-Diner and their tuna melt was sounding good right about now. I could grab that to go, head home for a shower, and then start packing my bags. I planned to move into Ben's place tomorrow morning after I convinced him I'd be the perfect roommate.

The sun had set by the time I limped out of my Firebird and the porch steps looked quite daunting in my tired condition. Only the smell of melted cheese, butter, and bread from the takeout box in my hand was keeping me going at this point. I'd just opened the front door when I heard the familiar masculine voice that would haunt my nightmares.

"These assless chaps are pinching Juan Carlos's balls, baby. Can you pull them loose?"

I gagged, backing out again and practically running for my car. I had to practice deep breathing from the safety of behind the wheel, windows rolled up. Thank God for my friend Addy's yoga classes that taught me how to control my mind and not letting it wander. I needed superhuman strength to push that scene out of my brain. Eventually, I was able to open my eyes again and eat my dinner.

When all the lights went out in the house, I crept back to the front door. I pressed my ear up against the wood and held my breath. No voices. No grunts. No movement of any kind. The coast was clear.

I walked on tiptoes to my room, wishing I'd remembered to put earplugs back on the to-do list, just in case they caught a second wind at some point in the night.

"Just one more day," I whispered to myself in encouragement. I threw down my stuff and took the world's shortest shower. When I had pajamas on and my wet hair was twisted in a towel perched on the top of my head, I called Ben back.

The jerk didn't answer, but he was probably already asleep. The guy liked his early bedtime, especially when he'd been out of town traveling for work. That was okay. I'd just show up on his doorstep with my bags. He couldn't turn away his own little sister if I gave him the puppy dog eyes, right?

CHAPTER THREE

laze

A KNOCK PULLED me from the same nightmare that had replayed like a brain virus every single night since I'd been back in Hell. I blinked my eyes open and tried to clear away the face that taunted me.

"You awake, Blaze?" Ben's voice came through the door, reminding me where I was.

"Yeah, come on in," I croaked, sitting up and rubbing the sleep from my face. A soft beam of early morning sun filtered in through the curtains.

Ben poked his head in the door and then came in, already dressed in slacks and a button-down shirt. His eyes looked tired behind the thick black rim of his glasses, but he gave me the goofy grin I remembered.

"Hey, brother. Glad to have you back home." He came over and sat on the edge of the bed.

"I could say the same for you. You've been gone quite a bit?"

Ben sighed. "Yeah. This latest app game is trying to kill me."

"Is that why you're in formal attire? Headed to your own funeral?"

The goofy grin was back. "Not yet, I hope. But I do have to leave again. I have a flight in two hours."

I sat up straighter. "Already? I was hoping you'd be home for a little bit and we could catch up."

"I know, I'm sorry. I was hoping so too, but I got a call late last night that the app crashed again, and with the launch a few weeks away, the board is freaking out it won't be ready."

Seemed weird to be so stressed about a game on a phone, but I knew his business was worth millions already. I was happy for him. Ben had always been brilliant. He was also one of the nicest guys you'd ever meet, so I was happy he'd found success. Even if it did highlight my own failures when it came to a career.

Ben's gaze focused on a spot in the corner of the room. "Can I be honest with you?"

"I'd prefer honesty, yeah."

He rolled his shoulders back and blew out a deep breath. "I think I might sell the company. Retire. Be done. Live the rest of my life in T-shirts with holes, lying on the couch watching reruns. Never see the inside of an airplane again, unless I'm traveling to some exotic locale for vacation."

That was news to me. Ben had been obsessed with gaming since we were kids. Coding his own app had been his dream. Retiring at twenty-six just seemed a bit premature, but then again, I'd been gone. I hadn't been here to see how much stress he was under.

I clapped him on the shoulder. "Man, I'm sorry. If you're talking retirement, you must be dealing with a lot, and I haven't been here to help out." Here I was asking him for a place to stay and for him to be my nursemaid on top of everything he was dealing with. What an asshole of a friend I was.

"It's fine. You know I don't really talk about stuff anyway. Even if you'd been here, I would have said everything was fine."

I nodded. "Sounds familiar. Probably why we're friends."

Ben's head lifted, the sunlight hitting his hair at just the right angle to show the red peeking through. "Best friends, right?"

I held out my hand and we did our secret handshake, the one we'd made up when we were eight years old. "BFFs. Isn't that what the girls say?"

Ben grinned. "I wouldn't know. I don't hang out with many girls."

Typical Ben. So focused on his gaming he didn't pay attention to the outside world. I slugged him in the arm. "And that right there is why you're stressed. Get yourself a woman or two and I'm sure the stress will be gone. A good roll in the hay will change your perspective."

Ben didn't seem so sure. "And what about you? Got women just parading through your room these days?"

I scoffed. "Yeah. The arm sling and knee brace is a real turn-on for women. Oh, and don't forget living with my mother. Damn. The women were comin' on so thick I had to beat them back with my crutches."

Ben laughed, the same boyish chuckle I remembered from our youth. "Well, you're welcome to stay here at my place while I'm gone. Maybe you can find a woman or two without your mommy around."

"Fuck off."

He and I just grinned at each other.

"It's good to be back," I said quietly, actually meaning it for once. "Things have kind of blown up in my life and it's nice to know I still have my best friend."

Ben stood. "Let me get this damn app launched and then I can enjoy you being back too. After this, I plan to take some time off. We can get into some trouble together like old times."

I snorted. I'd been the one to drag Ben into trouble when we were young. Ben had been the voice of reason trying to hold me back from doing something stupid. He rarely succeeded.

"You better hurry back or trouble will find me on its own."

"Don't I know it," he said over his shoulder as he left the

room. "Oh, and I put the spare key back under the pot and left you my house key on the kitchen counter."

I got out of bed and went to put pants on, forgetting they were all in the washer. Whatever. Boxers would have to do. I grabbed my crutches and hobbled out to the kitchen to see Ben dragging a small suitcase behind him on four wheels.

"I'll water the plants and feed the cat, honey."

Ben paused before shooting me a grin. "Your mom will probably be over with plants before I'm back, but the cat might be a stretch."

"Thanks again, man. I really appreciate you letting me stay here."

He got his suitcase out the door, the cool morning air rushing in and making me shiver. "Thanks for watching the place. I'll call you when I have an idea on when I'll be back."

And with that, he was gone. No way in hell was I going to let Mom know I didn't have Ben around to help me like I planned on. She'd have me moving back in with her before my load of laundry dried. I'd be fine on my own. Independence might be what I needed to pull myself out of my epic wallow.

With some maneuvering, I got my load of clothes in the dryer and turned on the hot water in the shower. I was tired of smelling myself. The doctor said I could take the brace off for bathing, so I ripped all the bands of Velcro and took the damn thing off my leg. The scars along my thigh were bright red, obviously still in a massive healing phase. Beyond the scars, my leg didn't look like mine. It had shrunk in just the last month or so, the muscle I'd spent years building wasting away from lack of use.

I looked up and flexed in the mirror over the sink, satisfied that my upper body looked decent. All the pulling myself out of beds and chairs and using crutches had helped me keep my muscle there.

"You still got it," I told my reflection. I even shot myself a wink.

I turned to get in the shower and realized there wasn't a towel on the rod. "Dammit."

I grabbed my crutches and hobbled out of the bathroom and down the hallway to the linen closet. As I went, I saw a picture of Ben on the wall from when he was four, the last picture they'd taken as a family before his parents died. Annie was also in the picture, just an infant in her mother's arms. It was crazy how much Ben looked like his father now that he was a grown man. Although he still had a hint of red in his hair that was from his mother.

And speaking of Annie, I should have asked Ben how she was doing. All this wallowing in my own injury had made me forget basic manners. I needed to pull my head out of my ass and notice the people around me. Shit, I was more like Ben than I thought. Annie had been our little shadow growing up and I hadn't even asked how she was doing. Or where she lived. Last I talked to Ben about her, she'd been away at college still, our connection having been broken when I left Auburn Hill with an attitude and something to prove.

Towel slung over my shoulder, I hobbled back to the bathroom. My phone dinged on the sink counter where I'd left it. Unlocking the screen, I saw it was just a text from one of my brothers in the group chat they kept going and I read occasionally.

Daxon: Congrats on moving out of Mommy's house, bro!

Callan: You moved out, Blaze? Are you at Ben's?

I rolled my eyes. My four brothers acted like girls sometimes, always pissed off when they found out something through the gossip mill instead of directly from my mouth. Last I checked, I didn't need to update them on my every move.

Me: Of course I moved out. That was the plan all along.

Ethan: Dude, I would have stayed for the grilled cheese. No one makes it like Mom.

Daxon: Ahh, little Ethan wants his mommy. Why don't you move in with her, then?

Ethan: Because little Ethan has too many women knocking down my door. I can't live with my mommy.

Ace: Since when?

Daxon: hahaha...burn, Ethan.

I turned the phone off. I didn't have time for their juvenile bullshit. They spent more hours texting than actually working. Not that I was doing a lot of working these days since I'd been let go. You use worker's compensation one time for a legitimate accident and suddenly you're a pariah in the movie business. Not that I was going to let my mind go there. Not today, Satan.

Crutches stowed next to the shower door, I used the wall to help step into the shower, putting a bit of pressure on my bad leg. The whole right side of my body ached, but I managed it. The hot water hit my chest and I let out a moan of relief. Today felt like a new beginning. A chance to push myself out of the wallowing I'd been doing and get my life together. Starting with a damn shower.

I'd just washed the shampoo from my hair when I heard a noise that sounded an awful lot like the front door slamming. It could have been Ben coming back for something he forgot, but he didn't slam doors. He was a quiet guy, preferring silence like me. And if it wasn't Ben, it could be an intruder, thinking the house was empty again. My old instincts from being a police officer kicked in.

I left the shower running, but pulled the door open. I used the wall to carefully step out of the shower and grabbed the closest thing to me as a weapon: one of my crutches. I hobbled on one crutch to the door, my hand reaching out slowly to grab the doorknob. The thing slipped beneath my wet fingertips and suddenly the door was swinging open, nearly clipping me in the face before I could step back.

Pain lit up my right leg as I shifted and a blur of color ran straight into me. My arms cartwheeled to help me stay upright, which meant my crutch fell to the side to hit the wall with a bang.

"Aha!" The blur of color whacked my chest with a pillow, doing absolutely nothing beyond helping me dry off.

"Annie?"

I froze, focusing on the redheaded beauty who stood before me, standing at a mere five foot four and barely a hundred pounds of fury, brandishing a goddamn throw pillow as a weapon.

Her wide blue eyes left my face to take a trip down my body. It could have been a physical touch for all it was doing to me. I felt myself shift and harden, belatedly realizing I was fucking naked in front of my best friend's little sister. And apparently getting an erection over how her shirt clung to her breasts.

"Blaze?" she gasped, eyes locked on the one part of me that really shouldn't be participating in this reunion.

CHAPTER FOUR

*A*nnie

I WASN'T one to go charging into other people's bathrooms, but Ben hadn't answered my multiple texts and calls which made me worry. When I used the spare key to get in his house, I'd heard the water running but nothing else. For all I knew, Ben had slipped, hit his head, and was bleeding out on the floor all alone. My brother wasn't going to die on my watch, goddammit.

What I did not expect, however, was a grown-up Blaze, naked with water sluicing down the nicest body I'd ever seen. Muscled shoulders wider than the doorway, tapering down into a trim waist and a trail of hair that led—

"What are you doing here?" I gaped, finally able to wrestle my gaze away from the world's most perfect dick. It was long, even before it jumped and grew under my gaze. Girthy too, which was a nice add-on to the length. Definitely above average. Not that I'd seen a whole lot of human dicks. Just a few in college and they'd definitely been average if Blaze's was the yard-stick we were using for comparison.

Young Annie would have swooned and fell to the floor in a puddle of blushing giggles if this had happened years ago. Between the ages of nine and twelve I'd had the biggest crush on my brother's best friend. Walking in on Blaze naked would have triggered a crush so deep I never would have gotten over it. But alas, that hadn't happened, and when Blaze got his first girlfriend his freshman year of high school, that bubble had burst. After a pathetic amount of secret tears and pep talks, I moved my attentions elsewhere.

Instead of answering me, Blaze snatched the pillow from my hands and pressed it over the aforementioned impressive dick, much to my dismay. Although everything else still visible was lovely to look at too. The man had stacks of muscles piled on top of one another, as if he had more than the six hundred muscles a normal human being possessed.

"I live—" Blaze shifted mid-sentence and bit off his words in a grimace.

My gaze finally took in more than just his impressive body and noticed the crutches leaning against the wall. Then I looked back to see his one leg had long red lines running up the thigh with yellow bruising mixed in. A hot burst of sympathy tamped down all the lust that had taken over my brain at the dick sighting.

"Oh my God!"

I lurched forward, intent on helping by maybe holding up his shoulders, or just letting him put his weight on me, I don't know. But it didn't work out the way I intended. The second I got close, he lurched back and let out a mighty groan. I screeched to a halt, not wanting to hurt him further, but didn't account for the water that had pooled by his feet. My sneakers went for a ride, and as is natural, I grabbed for something to keep me on my feet. Namely, Blaze.

Next thing I knew, I was on the floor, the breath knocked out of me. Blaze was lying on top of me, his heavy weight sending a dark, delicious thrill through me. Maybe it was just the oxygen loss making my head feel like it was floating away from my body. The damn pillow was pressed between us, which was a shame. This was as close as I'd ever get to that nice of a dick. Brainiac girls like me didn't date specimens like Blaze. That was just a fact of life.

"This is just like *The Proposal*," I said absentmindedly, allowing the giggle making its way out of my mouth to release in the awkward silence between us.

Blaze's dark brown eyes went positively feral. His hair was a wet mess, but it was the dark scruff along his cheeks and chin that made me pause. I'd never seen Blaze with a beard, but he pulled it off. Really, really well. My nipples hardened and I wasn't sure if he felt them through my thin camisole or if he'd just had enough of being on top of me, but he hopped to his feet. It was slow and awkward, and praise Jesus, he had to let go of the pillow to make it to standing, giving me another blessed vision of that dangling dick. I'd seen horses in vet school hung with less than that.

Blaze snatched the pillow off my stomach and covered himself again. He grunted as he looked down at me, then extended his hand in my direction. I would have rather grabbed his dick, but I didn't think that was an option based on the way he was grinding his teeth. I slid my palm against his, surprised when his hand enveloped mine completely. He tugged and suddenly I was standing just a little too close to him. It was like the air was thinner in a three-foot radius around him. I backed up to the doorway and folded my arms across my chest, hoping to hide my nipples. I should have brought two pillows.

"What are you doing here, Annie?" he asked, his voice tumbling over rocks while he spoke. I'd never heard someone say my name like that and I almost thought of offering to pay him if he'd say it again. He'd probably kick me out though, even with an injured leg. Blaze had always had dark and stormy eyes, but now they were positively thundering.

"I w-was hoping to talk to Ben. Thought he might have

slipped." I forced a laugh while Blaze glared at me. "Turns out, I was the one to slip."

Was that even my voice? I sounded like I'd smoked a pack of cigarettes this morning. I cleared my throat.

"You were going to save him with a pillow?" Blaze asked, not one ounce of humor on his face.

The fog of looking at a naked Blaze was finally clearing and I was getting a little pissed off. Why was he so damn grumpy? This was my brother's house. I visited all the time.

I put my hands on my hips. "And you were going to slay the intruder with a crutch and a bad leg?"

His jaw muscle twitched. "Better than a fucking pillow."

I couldn't deny that the pillow had been a stupid thing to grab, so I deflected. "Here, let's get you back in the shower before you mess up your leg any further." I'd heard rumors he was back in town after a work injury, but I didn't realize it was this bad. Poor guy needed some help.

Blaze batted me away as I approached again. "You should probably go."

I reached for him again. "I'll help you get in the shower and then I'll go." And because I could never seem to keep my mouth shut when I should, I added, "I can't help you with that though," pointing to the pillow which hid that impressive dick.

Blaze backed up with a limp and a death grip on that pillow. "It's just been awhile. Ignore it."

Okay, sure. As if that could erase the sight of his cock growing right before my eyes. I reached for him again, but Blaze grabbed one of my wrists, stopping me. "Annie."

"What? Why won't you let me help you?"

He leaned in close to my face and I stilled. Damn. The attractive teen I'd known had grown into an intimidatingly handsome man.

"You. Should. Go." He said it so quietly and forcefully I found myself nodding in agreement.

"Okay." I stepped back and he released my wrist. I turned in the doorway at the last second. "Just be careful, okay?"

"Go, Annie!" he shouted.

"I'm going!" I shouted back, closing the door and then sagging against it. I took the first full breath I'd had in the last ten minutes, giving valuable oxygen to my brain.

"Holy shit," I whispered to myself.

I heard the glass shower door clang shut, making me flinch. I pushed off the door and stumbled into the living room, not registering the meager furnishings in my brother's place. I'd been here so many times I could navigate the space blindfolded.

I nearly tripped over my bag where I'd left it in the living room when I grabbed the infamous pillow I'd never be able to look at again. Remembering why I was here in the first place, I grabbed the bag and lugged it down the hall to the guest room, purposely humming so I wouldn't hear the shower running as I passed the bathroom. My brain was already replaying all the dick sightings and that was not going to help me have a conversation with my brother. I needed to wear Ben down and get him to agree to me moving in temporarily, not have Blaze's dick imprint on my brain.

Stepping into the guest room that Ben hadn't allowed me to touch with paint or even a pretty bedspread when he bought the place, I could swear I smelled Blaze. The bedsheets were pulled back and wrinkled, as if someone had slept there. A warning bell clanged in the back of my head, dread lining my gut. Was Blaze sleeping here?

Anger flared and I forgot about him being injured. There was a hierarchy in life and sisters came before best friends. If anybody was going to be using Ben's guest bedroom, it should be me, dammit. I couldn't go back to Grandma Donna's, I just couldn't. I'd woken up in the middle of the night to mumbled talk about where to rub the Bengay. And then I'd heard yelps a few minutes later as Juan Carlos remembered he didn't wash his hands and now his balls were on fire.

A girl didn't need that kind of trauma.

I dug through my bag and changed into jean shorts and a T-shirt seeing as how my pajamas were soaking wet after Blaze lay on me. A heat wave pulsed through my body just thinking about it.

"Focus, Annie," I muttered to myself.

I left my bag in the guest room and went to wait in the living room. When Blaze hobbled out into the living room in a pair of sweatpants and an old Auburn Hills Police Department T-shirt, I had a whole argument lined up as to why he needed to leave. He sat on the chair furthest from me, putting the crutches down on the floor and lifting his bad leg with both hands to get it settled at a good angle. His feet were bare, which should have been a turnoff. I mean, feet were gross, especially men's. But Blaze had nice feet. Like the kind that could be in a flip-flop commercial. Well formed, nails clipped, and barely a dusting of hair. Maybe he got regular pedicures out in Los Angeles. I'd heard men did that there. But enough about feet, I had a bone to pick with Blaze Hellman.

"I didn't know you were here," I blurted out, needing to say something to fill the silence. I wasn't good with silence. Why be quiet in a room with someone when you could talk and chat and share? "And where the hell is Ben?"

CHAPTER FIVE

laze

IF EVER THERE was a time I found myself angry at my own body, it wasn't when my femur cracked, or my shoulder dislocated, or even when my extensive injuries meant I would never go back to being a stuntman in Hollywood. No, the anger flared hot and bright because I'd popped a boner in front of Annie. Freaking Annie. What the fuck was wrong with me?

I reached out and turned the knob in the shower to straight cold, my skin flinching as tiny icicles rained down. Even then, the damn erection wouldn't go down. It was like Superman, impervious to the kryptonite of cold showers. I just kept replaying the sight of her standing there in the doorway with shorts that hugged her hips and a shirt that left almost nothing to the imagination. And I had a really fucking good imagination.

Gripping the base of my cock, I squeezed as hard as I could stand, figuring if I choked off the blood flow, maybe it would go down. I couldn't leave this bathroom until it did. I closed my eyes and rested my head against the smooth white tiles of the shower wall. Goose bumps lined my skin but all I could feel was her body underneath me. How every curve she'd grown since I left Hell had been plastered against me.

"Ah fuck," I muttered. My brain went right for the sight of her when I scrambled off of her body. That stupid shirt had gotten soaked and I could see the dusty pink outline of her nipples. How the fuck was I ever going to get that sight out of my brain? I reared back and let my forehead bang against the tile a few times.

I must have rattled something loose because it hit me all at once.

Ben.

He would absolutely kill me for thinking of his sister like this. And for seeing her in whatever outfit that was. Did girls actually go around in shorts that didn't cover their ass? Or shirts that were so thin and tight they might as well not be wearing one? I mean, I knew they did. I lived in southern California where clothes seemed optional at most places of business. Hell, I'd always appreciated that kind of attire. But on Annie? My best friend's little sister? The girl who'd been so much like my own little sister I'd pulled pranks on her just like I did my own brothers?

Ben would have a very valid argument that I should never be thinking of her in that way. As if she was the most gorgeous woman I'd ever laid eyes on. As if nothing mattered except getting my hands back on that creamy skin of hers. So I thought of Ben walking in the door, his fist smashing into my face. The hurt expression behind those coke-bottle glasses.

And just like that, the erection went down.

I shut the water off and grabbed my towel, glaring at the throw pillow that lay on the floor. Of all the stupid weapons for a young woman to grab to defend herself. I'd have to have a conversation with her about self-defense.

You know. Once both of us had forgotten about this little incident.

With considerable effort given my leg was now throbbing, I dried off, tied the towel around my waist, and hobbled out of the bathroom on my crutches. Thankfully the hallway was clear and I made it to the laundry room without incident. I closed the door and quickly changed into clean clothes from the dryer. With Ben's angry face top of mind, I went into the living room, bracing myself to see Annie again if she hadn't left altogether.

I turned the corner and there she was, sitting on the couch, arms folded across her chest, a frown puckering her face. Thank God she'd found some decent clothes. Not that the cutoff jean shorts she was currently wearing weren't showing enough of her muscular legs to have me counting off the ways Ben would hurt me if I didn't get my mind out of the gutter. I took my time getting settled on the chair furthest away from her so I could put Annie back in the box I'd always kept her in. The one clearly labeled "like a sister."

"I didn't know you were here. And where the hell is Ben?"

The words gushed from Annie's mouth like they always did. The girl was insanely smart, just like Ben. And she'd definitely gotten the red hair gene, but other than those two things, the brother and sister were completely different. Where Ben was quiet and hard to figure out, Annie told you exactly what she was thinking before you even asked. If there was silence, she'd find a way to fill it up. At least some things hadn't changed over the last few years.

I sucked in a deep breath and looked over at her, telling my eyeballs if they even thought about drifting south to take in her baseball tee that should have been boring but was actually sexy as hell, or those legs that looked like she ran a half marathon every day, I'd literally gouge them out with a rusty spoon.

"Ben had to leave again this morning. Something about an app crashing."

Annie just stared at me with those wide, blue eyes, which gave me time to take her in without my erection standing between us. The freckles across her nose had lightened but were still there. She'd lost the roundness in her cheeks somewhere over the years, letting defined cheekbones and the swoop of long dark eyelashes transform her into a stunning woman. Her hair was a dark auburn red, highlighting her creamy white skin.

She appeared the same height she'd been in middle school though, which I could imagine pissed her off. She'd started drinking the protein shakes Ben and I drank in high school. We thought she was just copying us as she frequently did, but she'd gone off about wanting to top out at five foot ten. Obviously the protein hadn't had the same effect that it did on Ben and me.

She clapped her hands suddenly and I blinked back to the present. "Okay, well, that leaves us with some decisions to make."

I frowned, not following. "Huh?"

Her mouth tipped up on the side. "I see you haven't gained the use of more words since you've been gone."

I narrowed my eyes at her and she chuckled, the sound stirring something in me that had me shifting uncomfortably in the chair. She moved too, pulling her legs under her and putting the other pillow on her lap. The one that matched the pillow I'd used to cover myself in the bathroom. I swallowed hard and focused on Ben's fist coming toward my face.

"I'll spell it out for you. I'm looking to stay here for awhile. And it looks to me like you're staying here too. Is that right?"

I latched on to the only thing that mattered. "You want to stay here? Like, overnight?"

Annie worried her bottom lip with her teeth, drawing my attention there. She released it and spoke. I didn't catch a damn thing she said.

"Blaze?" she asked, peering at me like I'd lost my mind.

Which I had. Why was I staring at Annie's mouth? I shook my head and cleared my throat. It was safer to look over at the huge television mounted on the opposite wall. "Sorry, what?"

She huffed, but kept going. "I was saying that hearing about Juan Carlos's balls just isn't something I can do any longer. No one should have to live with that, you know? I need a place to stay and my brother's house seems like the obvious choice. Just until I get my clinic open and can afford an apartment of my own though, don't worry."

My gaze swung back to her. I could still see her, but only through a haze of red. "I'm sorry, what? Whose balls? Do you need me to set him straight?"

Was she dating some asshole named Juan Carlos? Had he hurt her? I was already scooting forward on the chair, grabbing my crutches. I wasn't sure how I'd fare in a fight right now, but I was willing to try.

"No. Wait, where are you going?" Annie leaped to her feet and stood in front of me.

Which put those thighs right in my field of vision. Was she trying to kill me?

"Juan Carlos is Grandma Donna's new boyfriend."

I stared up at her, processing that information. Then I was grimacing.

"Yeah, so you see why I have to move out." Annie moved away and flopped back down on the couch. "So let's make a deal. You can—"

"I'll move out," I cut her off.

I hadn't meant to offer it. I rather detested the idea of going back to Mom's house, but I couldn't let Annie be miserable either. I'd lived away from home for awhile now and she deserved the same opportunity. Besides, Ben was her brother.

Annie twisted her hands in her lap, frowning almost as much as I was. "Where will you go?"

I shrugged and tried to act like it didn't matter. "Back to my mom's."

"Weren't you living there when you first got back to Hell? I was getting my hair trimmed at Curl Up & Dye a few days ago when Poppy came in for a perm. Did you know women still did perms? Anyway, she said you were finally seen leaving Nikki's and she was grateful for it because she was starting to wonder if you'd up and died from your injuries. Cricket told her to hush her mouth and I said your schedule was none of her business."

"Annie." I cut her off when she took her first breath. How she could string so many words together on just one lungful of air was truly an incredible feat.

"Yeah?"

"I don't mind moving back home. Just need to wash the sheets for you." I scooted forward and got to my feet with the help of my crutches, only wincing for half a second when I put too much weight on my bad leg. I needed to get that brace back on before I did more damage. But first, I needed to get away from Annie and everything her presence seemed to bring to mind.

Annie jumped to her feet, the pillow spilling to the floor in her hurry. "No! I can't do it. It's against my nature to put someone else out for my own gain."

She stood right in front of me and looked up through lashes she must have enhanced with makeup. No woman had lashes that long and dark without help, did they?

"How about this? You take the guest room and I'll take the master until Ben gets back. We can both stay here."

My brain nearly exploded with the possibility. "Both? Stay here?"

She was nodding, that auburn hair dancing around. I wanted to run my fingers through it and see if it was as soft as it looked.

Dammit.

No. I did not want to do that. I needed to get away from her.

"Yeah. Ben's liable to be gone for a week with the way he's been working. We can both stay here until he's back and then we can figure things out."

Annie smiled at me as if she'd solved all my problems.

Except the biggest problem stood right in front of me in cutoff jeans and a body that once a man noticed, he couldn't un-notice. And I'd fucking noticed, all right.

Then again, moving back in with Mom wasn't something I

was looking forward to. I was getting a headache just thinking about her fussing over me constantly. She'd licked her fingers and tried to straighten my hair before I got out of the car to go to physical therapy, for God's sake. A twenty-six-year-old man couldn't let that continue and still claim to have a pair of balls.

"Okay."

I said it and instantly regretted it. Especially when Annie's face brightened into a blinding smile that felt a little like staring directly at the sun. Then she wrapped her arms around me and burrowed into my chest, laying her cheek against me for just a moment. I swallowed hard and found a new appreciation for my crutches. My hands were busy and I couldn't hug her back, which saved me from wondering where to put my hands. Where on Annie's body would they not get off on touching her silky skin? Then she was backing off, clearly oblivious to the turmoil I was feeling inside.

"All right, then. All settled." She turned around and put the pillow back on the sofa, giving me a front-row seat to the kind of ass women in Hollywood got cosmetic surgery and personal trainers for.

I dropped my head and prayed for strength. Before she could turn around and see what she was doing to the front of my sweatpants, I hobbled back to the hallway, intent on getting back into my room where I could lock the door and pretend I wasn't sharing a house with Annie McLachlin, my best friend's sister.

"Oh, I have to head to my clinic. Want me to make you some lunch before I go?" Annie called out.

"I'm good," I said back, the words nearly strangled in my throat.

The last thing I needed was help from Annie. She'd already done enough. And she didn't even know it.

CHAPTER SIX

$\mathcal{A}$nnie

"WELL, you can't just not eat, Blaze." I ran after the infuriating man, tapping him on his beefy shoulder. When my fingertip hit rock-hard muscle, I almost wanted to keep it there and explore the topography. The scowl he tossed over his shoulder made me snatch it back.

"I can do it myself, Annie."

I crossed my arms over my chest and narrowed my eyes. "Can you though?" When he just kept scowling, I flung my arms out to the side. "Oh for crap's sake, just let me make you a sandwich. It's not a big deal. I'm making one for me anyway and I'm kind of a culinary genius with sandwiches. You know, I'd almost forgotten how stubborn you are."

He turned slowly and awkwardly in the hallway with his crutches. When the full force of those dark eyes hit me, I kind of wished I'd just taken his refusal for lunch and gone with it. There was an intensity to Blaze that hadn't been there when we were kids. Sure, he'd always been quiet and moody, but never

lethal in his frowns. Now though, it was like he was wearing a
suit of steel armor, expecting the situation to turn bloody at any
time. I just wanted to make him a sandwich.

"If I agree, will you let me eat without talking?"

That...was not the answer I was expecting. "Sure?"

His mouth hitched up on one side and I almost wanted to
pat myself on the back for making it appear. "Not sure you can,
huh?"

I stuck my tongue out at him like old times, just proving that
a girl can age, but sometimes she doesn't grow up. Turning, I
went back out into the living room and then into the kitchen,
pulling sandwich fixings out of the refrigerator. I could hear the
squeak and clatter of Blaze's crutches following me. Thank goodness my brother still splurged on grocery deliveries. If he didn't,
he'd only have a single box of crackers past their expiration date.

Turkey, lettuce, tomato, and mayonnaise for me. Pastrami
and mustard for Blaze. I paused as I spread the mustard on the
whole wheat bread. Maybe he didn't like pastrami anymore.
Maybe Los Angeles had given him a newfound love of vegetables
and tofu and other things that shouldn't be food. I turned my
head to ask him as he settled at the tiny bar that separated the
kitchen from the living room.

"Do you—"

"Shht!"

I gave Blaze a withering look, but all he did was raise his
eyebrows innocently. Shaking my head, I got back to making our
sandwiches. If he didn't like it, that was his problem. Should
have let me talk.

I slid his plate to him and slapped a napkin next to it. He
dipped his head in what I assumed was his form of non-verbal
thank you. I rolled my eyes at how similar he and Ben were and
then sat in the other barstool to dig into my own sandwich.

After swallowing the first bite, I opened my mouth to say
something, but Blaze made some weird clucking noise, looking
like he was thoroughly enjoying my inability to keep quiet. Irrita-

tion spiked and I resorted to the only weapon I learned a long time ago that a little sister has: payback.

I took a huge bite of sandwich and dramatically groaned around it, rolling my eyes back in my head. I kept chewing, staring at the far wall where Ben had put up a paint-by-number Grandma Donna had given him as a house warming gift. She was many things, but a good gift giver was not one of them. I could feel Blaze's stare drilling into the side of my head. I let out another quick moan and licked the mayo off my finger in what may have been a bit of overkill.

"Annie," Blaze ground out.

"Ah! No talking, Blaze," I chastised him with wide, innocent eyes.

His narrowed right before he plopped almost his whole sandwich on the plate and leaned back on the barstool. "Fine. You can talk."

"Oh, why thank you, Mr. Hellman. I appreciate the permission."

He stared at me with a blank expression. I stared right back, sandwich forgotten. His bushy eyebrows were dark slashes over his eyes, adding to the severity of his face. Even his cheekbones were harsh bumps that ran parallel to his granite-hard jawline. It was like the bone structure of his face was made for frowning.

"So...what have you been up to since I saw you last?" Blaze asked slowly, as if the normal conversational question had been painful for him.

I put my sandwich down and thought about it. It was actually hard to think with his dark gaze trained on me like that. "Uh, well, I got my master's degree, became a certified veterinarian, and leased a place on Main Street."

"So...not much?" His lips were tugging upward and I found myself smiling back.

"I'm no millionaire app maker, but..."

The smile fully formed on Blaze's face and I amended my

previous thought. Blaze's face was made for that mischievous grin.

"Ben's accomplishments do tend to make you feel a bit lacking…"

"Tell me about it. I had to grow up with him." I picked up my sandwich and took another bite.

"So did I," Blaze said quietly.

My eyebrows pinched together. Those two had been thick as thieves, as Grandma Donna used to say. Why would Blaze be sad about growing up with my brother?

"I thought—"

"Tell me about your clinic," Blaze said at the same time.

I swallowed and found myself launching into my favorite subject, telling him all about the exam room setup, the decorating left to do, and when I planned to open to the public. He ate his sandwich and nodded along, looking like he was actually interested. I knew I was talking too much, as was my habit when I was nervous—or at any time, let's be real—but he was finally eating and that felt like an accomplishment. I thought maybe he needed a distraction from his injuries.

Dabbing at my mouth with the napkin, I swallowed the last of my sandwich. "Want to come down to the clinic with me? Check it out?"

His gaze dropped to the brown granite countertop. "Nah, I'm going to hang here."

Disappointment swooped through me, which made zero sense. I didn't actually want to hang out with Blaze, nor did I want to babysit someone at the clinic while I was working feverishly to put it together. But the helper in me felt like Blaze needed a heaping-size dose of help.

"I actually have an issue with the layout of the back room. Could really help to have a second opinion."

My layout was perfect, but he didn't need to know that. I worried the napkin around the edges, waiting for the answer I was hoping for. Unless Blaze had changed—and that was, unfortunately, a high probability given the years that had passed—he would bend under the weight of obligation. He'd never let me down before, even with all the teasing and grunts he seemed to reserve just for me when we were kids.

Blaze plopped his napkin down on the empty plate. "Fine."

He sounded anything but fine. I also knew that was as good of an answer as I'd get. I hopped off the barstool and took both our plates to the sink. "Great! We just have to put some shoes on and then we can go."

I looked down at his bare feet, just now realizing how his bad leg was stuck out to the side, unable to bend enough to hook his foot over the rung of the barstool. "Do you need—"

"For fuck's sake, Annie, I got it."

I held my hands up. "Okay, okay. I was just asking. Being polite and all..."

Blaze shot me a look like he was imagining choking me to death. I gave him a wide berth as I exited the kitchen to find my shoes. Before he could hobble back, I'd moved my bag from the guest room to the master bedroom. By the time he got shoes on by himself, I'd stripped the bed and thrown the sheets in the washer. I heard a few grunts and even a groan of pain from the guest room, but I kept my lips zipped with considerable effort.

I zoomed past his door, only giving him a side-eye glance to make sure he wasn't passed out in a puddle of sweat. If I could get him in a chatty mood, I'd have to find out what had happened to him. When he was naked, I'd been a little too preoccupied staring at his dick to take in the extent of his injuries. Maybe getting out of the house would put him in a brighter mood. Then again, this was Blaze. Brighter moods weren't really his thing.

I waited until I heard the creak and click of his crutches coming down the hallway before grabbing my purse and jingling my keys by the front door, as if I hadn't been waiting for a good five minutes for him to be ready.

He growled, but he let me open the door for him while he

navigated leaving the house with crutches, a brace probably made by NASA scientists given its bulk and crisscrossing straps, and zero patience for any of it. I locked up and hustled down the stairs to unlock the passenger side door of my car.

Blaze stopped, his mouth dropping open.

I opened the door, not at all bothered by the squeal that could have been fixed with some WD-40 had I had the time or inclination to see to it. I gestured for Blaze to get in, but he remained frozen. When I huffed my irritation, his head popped up to frown at me.

"This is still your car? I thought Ben had you get rid of it?"

I put a hand on my hip. They always did this. He and Ben thought they had some kind of say in my life, butting in to make decisions that weren't theirs to make. Maybe it had been okay when I was a little kid, but last I checked, I was a card-carrying grown-ass woman.

"Blaze? Get in the damn car."

He rolled his lips inward before giving a rough shake of his head. "That's a hard no."

I changed tactics, shrugging my shoulders. "Okay. If you're scared, just say so."

"I'm not scared, I just don't think riding in that tank is what's best for me right now."

I shut the passenger door and walked past him to get around the hood. I patted him on the chest. "Scared. I get it."

Waves of frustration permeated the air between us. When my back was to him, I let myself grin. In three, two, one...

The creak and click of his crutches sounded behind me right on time. The passenger side door opened, and even though it would have been easier if he'd just gotten in when I was there to help him, Blaze somehow got himself into the car, his end of his crutches stowed between his legs and the other end leaning against the window.

I sank into the driver's cracked leather seat and cranked the engine. When it didn't start the first try, I ignored Blaze's huff that said "I told you so" and gave the accelerator a quick press before trying again. This time, the engine turned over and roared to life. I shot Blaze a satisfied smirk, which he purposely ignored.

The trees flicked by as I drove us toward downtown in silence. When I accelerated through the back half of the only roundabout in town, the damn car backfired. I was used to it, but poor Blaze nearly hit his head on the roof of the car, he startled so badly.

"What the fuck?"

I shrugged and tried to keep my face from heating. "It's part of her charm."

Blaze ran a hand over his chest like he was recovering from a near heart attack. "I need to have a chat with Ben," he mumbled.

"Maybe when you call him about my car, you can tell him you're living with me."

Blaze's gaze snapped to me, just like I knew it would.

That shut him up at least.

CHAPTER SEVEN

laze

BROWN HAIR in a bun up ahead. Just outside the barber shop.

"Shit!" I muttered, loud enough that Annie heard me over the rumble of her ridiculous car. The thing was actually pretty rad in a *Dukes of Hazzard* kind of way, but it was just so weird to see Annie still driving it. She seemed more like a brand-new convertible kind of woman, not a '70s muscle car kind. Then again, I'd been away from Hell for awhile and maybe I didn't know Annie as well as I thought.

"What? It didn't even backfire!" Annie sounded defensive.

I scrubbed a hand over my eyes and blinked hard, focusing on the woman up ahead. She turned to say something to the friend by her side as she was walking away and I realized it wasn't Dani by the shape of her mouth.

"Nothing," I muttered, biting back further curse words. Maybe I needed to stop taking the pain meds the doctor had given me. They were making me hallucinate on a perfectly good weekday afternoon.

"Who are you glaring at?" Annie chirped, her head swiveling in a circle from my face, to the road, the sidewalk, and back again.

"Nothing, Annie. Just...park this beast, would you?" I couldn't have her getting in my head and realizing I was hallucinating. Or obsessing over someone who I despised. I was totally over Dani, I just wasn't used to being back in town with the possibility of running into her.

"Okay, okay, grumpy."

Annie masterfully whipped the car into a parking space right on Main Street. I may have grabbed the handle above my head, but that was mostly just to give her shit. She could drive this car better than half the stunt doubles in Hollywood.

"Well, here she is," Annie said proudly, pointing through the windshield at a small space in front of us that lacked signage. There was a shiny glass door leading into the clinic, weathered brick lining the outside of the shop. If I remembered correctly, this used to be a candy shop when we were little.

"The old candy place?"

Annie turned to me with a knowing smile. "Still smells like toffee."

I remembered that had been her favorite. "You think parking might be tight?"

Annie tilted her head back and forth. "I'll have two designated spaces. This one and that one." She hitched her thumb over her shoulder. "I'm a one-woman show, so I can't really have too many furry patients in the clinic at one time anyway. Plus the rush is mostly first thing in the morning as people slam Coffee. After that it lightens up."

"Sounds like you've thought this through quite a bit."

Annie stared up at the clinic with a look of pride that made me jealous. "Yeah. It's my dream."

Before I could spiral down into my wallow where all my own dreams had been shattered, I pushed open the car door and kept myself busy with trying to climb out. This thing was so low to the ground I might as well have ridden to town in a goddamn go-cart.

"You want some—"

"I got it," I cut her off.

And I did. It was ugly, but I managed to get to my feet, crutches in hand. Annie closed my door for me, giving me a look that said she thought I was an idiot. And I definitely was. Despite thinking I hadn't noticed, Annie had engaged in psychological tactics that read me like a manual with pictures. She got me to agree on us living together, made me lunch when I wasn't hungry, and then here I was at her clinic showing my face around town when that was the last thing I wanted to do. If I didn't watch it, she'd ask me for my firstborn and I'd promise her that too.

"Okay, so there's still a lot of decorating to do, but I have the bones of the operation done." Annie held open the front door, waiting patiently as I clicked and clacked my way through.

The hardwood floors were impeccable. The walls were a dove gray that would be easy to keep clean. The feel was open and airy, but still homey even without the decoration she talked about.

"I need chairs and a side table for up front. Plants. A picture or two. But check out the exam rooms." Annie led the way behind the front counter and down a short hallway. A door to the right showed a table that folded down from the wall and a sink-and-cabinet set that would probably hold all the equipment she needed. A door to the left held the same thing. It was the room in the back that intrigued me.

"Oh my God, Charlie finished my stall!" Annie clapped her hands and ran to the metal rings that fashioned a stall in the middle of the room. "Okay, so where should I put this bad boy? Against the wall? In the middle? By the rollup garage bay?"

Depressing thoughts tried to pull me down with them. The ones that compared where I was at in life to Annie. Or to my best friend, the millionaire. The comparison showed me sorely lacking, but before I could spiral down, Annie tossed that wide grin at me, her enthusiasm barreling through to pull me out. I latched on and focused on her questions.

"I assume that's for the bigger animals? They'll come through the rollup, right? So closer to the rollup is probably best." I'd had to work with some animals on a few movie sets and they were temperamental at best. I couldn't imagine trying to move a sick one.

Annie snapped her fingers and darted across the room to shove some boxes out of the way. "You're so right."

I was halfway across the room when I realized I wouldn't be able to help her. Not with crutches, a bum leg, and a shoulder that could barely hold a coffee cup.

"How about you hold on. I'll text my brothers and get a few of them over here to help you move the stall."

Annie quit shoving the box that looked heavier than her car and blew a strand of hair out of her face. "Yeah, that might be a good idea."

"Oh yoohoo!" called a female voice from the front of the clinic. "Annie? You here?"

Annie rolled her eyes and mouthed, *Get ready.*

"I'm back here!" she shouted over her shoulder.

Footsteps came down the hall, pausing just inside the back exam room. Poppy and Penelope. Fucking hell. This was exactly why I wanted to stay holed up in my room.

Poppy's eyes practically glowed when she saw me. "Why, hello, Blaze. Haven't seen you in a long time; thought I heard you've started up physical therapy over in Blueball. How's the leg?"

I looked down at my leg in the heavy brace and then back at Poppy, making sure my voice came out unfriendly. "Feels broken."

She opened her mouth but nothing came out. Mom would kill me later when she heard all about this conversation, but I wasn't up for small-town niceness. One good thing about LA was people didn't give a shit about you, which meant they didn't bother asking invasive questions. Poppy turned to Annie with a bright smile.

"Could you come help me pick out flowers at Petals and Thorn? My granddaughter's engagement party is this weekend and you have much younger taste than me."

"Oh, sure!" Annie looked around the room at the mess. "I'll be right back, Blaze."

"Actually, we need to talk about your parking job, missy," Penelope interjected, ever the meter maid, even when off-duty.

Annie folded her arms across her chest, glaring at the woman. "What about it?"

"That's a reserved spot."

"Yes, I know," Annie said with more ice in her tone than I thought she had in her. "It's reserved for my vet clinic. The one we're standing in right now. The one I own?"

Penelope sniffed. "I need to see the permit."

"Oh for fu—"

"Penelope, dear. Perhaps we can just drop it for today?" Poppy interjected, looking like she wanted to keep the peace, which was weird for her. Normally she liked stirring up the crazy.

The three women walked off down the hallway and out of the clinic, bantering back and forth. I let out a huge breath and wondered for the millionth time what I was doing here. Annie said she needed help with her clinic, and based on the number of boxes everywhere, she did. This place wasn't even close to being ready for an opening and she'd told me she wanted the opening in just two weeks.

The place was impressive, honestly. I shouldn't be surprised. She was always super smart like Ben. But what she didn't have that Ben did was the ability to focus. Or to tell people to go to hell so she could get her own work done.

I looked around the room, a mental to-do list forming that was getting longer by the second. No use just standing here like an idiot. I hobbled over to the first box on the floor and pulled out my pocketknife to cut the tape. The thing was full of nail clippers, a weird grinder-looking contraption, ear syringes, and an assortment of speculums that made my asshole clench. It took some doing, but I got the box down the hallway to the first exam room. I put two of everything in the cabinets and then moved to the second exam room.

Annie came sprinting in as I finished unloading the first box. She was out of breath and still somehow the most beautiful woman I'd seen in ages.

"Sorry about that. I was just on my way back when I saw Coffee is having a fundraiser. Can I get you a coffee? Goes to a good cause."

I frowned. "What's the cause?"

Annie bit her lip. "Um...I have no idea."

This woman was exasperating. "Yeah, black coffee. Here." I dug in my pocket for cash.

"Oh, it's on me. The least I can do with you helping out around here." She looked pointedly at the empty box. Right before dashing away again.

I shook my head and headed for the back room for another box of supplies to put away. If Annie would just focus on her clinic instead of everything else going on around her, she could have this place ready to open in days. When my leg needed a break, I sat on the counter up front and pulled out my phone.

There was one benefit to being back in my hometown. My brothers. The ones I'd ignored for the last few years as I licked my wounds and tried to make something of myself.

Me: Any of you available to help me move something?

Daxon: Depends what it is.

Callan: Of course. I'm off at six tonight.

Ethan: Wow, Daxon.

Daxon: What?? He's my brother but I draw the line at dead bodies.

Me: It's not a fucking dead body, asshole.

Daxon: Hey, it's a fair question. You've been in a mood since you've been back. Heads might have rolled.

Callan: Not helping, dude.

Ace: I'm on a shift right now, but if it slows down, I can swing by with my crew.

Ethan: I can come by right now actually. Where are you?

Me: At Annie's new vet clinic on Main.

Daxon: I can come right now too.

Ethan: You just want to flirt with Annie.

My growl echoed off the empty walls of the clinic.

Me: No one's flirting with anyone. Get your asses over here.

I got off the counter and got busy putting more supplies away. Annie eventually came back, our coffees almost cold after she'd been asked to help someone with their dog while at Coffee. She bent over to help me pull an ultrasound unit out of its box, her shorts riding so high on her thighs I had to look away and think of Ben's face to keep myself in check.

Maybe inviting my brothers over here wasn't such a bright idea.

CHAPTER EIGHT

*A*nnie

I FELT like I'd accomplished more than was humanly possible in one afternoon and yet I'd barely been inside my clinic today. My stomach was growling by the time Blaze and I finished unloading the last box of supplies. I spun in a circle, taking in the progress that had been made. All because of Blaze.

"Holy shit, it looks like a real vet clinic!"

Blaze nudged the last box closer to the doorway. He'd been smashing them and putting them in the dumpster in the alleyway behind the clinic. I told him he was doing too much, what with his injuries, but he'd waved me away and that had been that. Trying to help Blaze was like trying to make a cat take a bath.

I moved without thinking, the physical exertion of the afternoon burning away the uncomfortableness between us that had arisen because of this morning's *The Proposal* moment. At least for me it had. I threw my arms around Blaze's neck and gave him a hug. I realized the error of my actions—not when I got a whiff of soap and something uniquely Blaze that made my insides turn to liquid, but when a male voice catcalled from the hallway.

I let go of Blaze so fast he almost went down, shuffling backward awkwardly with the crutches to stay on his feet. My face went hot and I felt like Grandma Donna had caught me with my hand in the cookie jar.

"Don't stop on our account, Annie with the pretty fan—"

"That's enough!" Blaze cut off Daxon, giving him a dark look.

"Daxon and Ethan! What are you doing here?" I smoothed down my shirt and hoped I didn't have dirt smudged on my face. There was a whole lot of handsome jammed into this tiny exam room.

Ethan pulled me into a hug that felt entirely different than hugging Blaze. I'd always liked Ethan, of course. The triplets had been a year ahead of me in school, infamous for their good looks and impossible charm. Callan had been nice to me, but in an acquaintance way that felt a little detached. Daxon had been too busy with all the girls beating down his door to give me a second glance. Ethan, though, had always taken the time to be good to me.

"Limps-a-lot over here asked us to stop by and help you move something," Daxon added helpfully, coming over to thump Blaze on the back.

"Oh! The stall!"

It was weird to see Blaze with his brothers all grown up. Daxon was slicker than owl shit, his good looks so perfect he looked like he could be on the cover of a magazine. He'd been a clothing model in high school, a fact that made him practically royalty around here. In contrast, Blaze was handsome in a more wild manner. His hair was longer. His scruffy beard was unruly. Even his expression made you think twice before talking to him. There was just something rougher around the edges about Blaze, that while it didn't make him any less handsome, it made him less approachable. And that roughness hadn't been there when we were kids.

"Heard you're opening a vet clinic, Annie." Ethan put his arm around my shoulder and steered me out of the room. I heard the click and squeak of Blaze behind us. "Gonna be a boss babe, huh?"

I nodded, shooting Ethan a saucy smile. "Yes. The whole time I was getting my master's degree I was thinking about being a 'boss babe' one day."

"Seems like just yesterday you were following Blaze and Ben around, begging for them to slow down so you could catch up," Daxon piped up from behind us.

Ethan laughed. "Yeah, I remember that. We used to call you our little sister."

"Okay, here's the stall I need you to move." Blaze swung past us into the back room in a hurry, cutting off our trip down memory lane. He moved so quickly on those crutches I dodged out from under Ethan's arm and went to grab for Blaze. He looked down at my hand on his stacked bicep, the tension suddenly thick between us.

I whipped my hand off him like I'd been burned. "Sorry, I just think you're moving a little too fast."

Blaze glowered at me, while Ethan snickered.

"Well, she *is* a veterinarian. She'd know best," Daxon said dryly. "Blaze is kind of a bear."

"Bit of a porcupine, if you ask me," Ethan added, unhelpfully.

"A sloth on those crutches."

"Stubborn as a mule."

"Enough!" Blaze barked.

I rolled my lips in and pleaded with myself not to laugh. I hadn't been around the Hellman brothers in so long I'd almost forgotten how much they teased each other.

"We need the stall over by the rollup. If you're done being jackasses." Blaze's voice held a hint of laughter under the grumble.

Ethan held up his hand, index finger held high. "Just one more. Annie, are you a beaver, because...dam!"

"Okay." Blaze hobbled over to stand in front of me, blocking his brothers' view of me.

Daxon clasped his hands under his chin. "Ahh. Do you love Annie like no otter?"

The laughter I'd been holding in couldn't be contained any longer. I bent over laughing, my forehead resting on Blaze's back. I felt him stiffen but then my forehead began to bounce. I stared cross-eyed at his shirt in amazement. Blaze was laughing. Quietly, but still.

"Shut the fox up," I heard Blaze mutter so quietly I almost missed it.

Another peal of laughter had me sagging against him. I finally pulled myself away and wiped under my eyes, darting around him to address his brothers.

"Enough with the animal jokes. Move my stall already, would you?"

The boys all grumbled, but moved as one unit to take up position around the metal bars. I opened my mouth to warn Blaze about helping in his condition, but he cut me a look that had me staying quiet. Thankfully, he didn't do much but direct the other two as they lifted the stall bars and put them into place. Something that would have taken me all day and a considerable amount of elbow grease was done in two minutes.

I darted around the bars, checking it out from every angle. "Thank you, guys. This is perfect."

Ethan lifted his arm with a grin and I expected a hug. What I got instead was Ethan reversing the trajectory of his arm and patting his hair instead while darting glances at Blaze. These boys were weird. Always joking around. I was glad to see Blaze interacting with them though. I knew they'd missed him when he was away. And as much as Blaze would deny it, I think he missed them too. If that sparkle in his eye that had lit up when they arrived was anything to go by, maybe his brothers could be instrumental in healing whatever had left him with a sour look on life.

My stomach let out a growl that was heard by everyone in the room. Sheepishly, I patted my stomach. "Been working hard today."

Blaze tossed his head in the general direction of the front of the clinic. "Come on. Let's get dinner."

"Sweet, where are we—"

Ethan elbowed Daxon. "Don't you remember? We have that...thing."

Daxon frowned, looking from Ethan to Blaze. "Oh, yeah. That dinner thing. Totally forgot."

We all walked to the front of the clinic while I tried to ask Ethan and Daxon about their dinner plans and Blaze kept interrupting me. This was just like when we were kids, me playing monkey in the middle, except I was an adult now and I didn't appreciate them keeping me out of the loop. But whatever, I was hungry and all I cared about was getting some good food in my stomach.

Ethan and Daxon both gave me a quick hug before walking off to their cars. Blaze frowned at the back of their heads until he turned to look at me.

"Forty-Diner sound good?"

"To go?"

Blaze shrugged. "Probably for the best."

We fell into a slow rhythm next to each other walking on the sidewalk on Main Street. The sun was just beginning to set in the west, dipping behind the tall tips of the pine trees.

"I'd almost forgotten how funny your brothers are."

Blaze grunted. His crutches clacked along the sidewalk a few more paces. "I almost forgot too."

And that right there almost cracked my heart in two. Those five boys had been thick as thieves when we were kids. They'd banded together after their father left them and traveled as a pack. You didn't mess with one brother without getting all four of the others showing up to put you in your place. They were a true brotherhood.

So why had Blaze cut himself off from his brothers?

CHAPTER NINE

laze

"SERIOUSLY?" Annie was looking at me like I committed a sin. "You got a grilled chicken salad with no dressing?"

I settled the to-go bag at my feet, along with my crutches. She slammed her door and fired up her car, getting it to start on the first try this time.

I shrugged, trying valiantly not to show that the smell of her fries and cheeseburger was making me salivate. "Not all of us like to eat junk food."

She shot me a look and backed out of the parking space. "Um, yeah, I think everyone does actually like junk food."

I bit back a smile. Teasing Annie had become my new favorite hobby. Along with forgetting how annoying and wonderful my brothers were, I'd forgotten how much I enjoyed Annie's spirit. She was always energetic, even as a little kid. The woman practically ran everywhere, a habit I thought she would have grown out of. And then there was the way she'd give someone the shirt off her own back if they displayed even the slightest bit of needing it. My brain took off on that tangent, imagining Annie without her shirt on, which was not where my brain should have gone.

"Listen, I can't work out like I used to, so the only way to keep my physique in check is to watch what I eat. And believe me, my mother was not feeding me healthy food the whole time I was staying with her." Plus I'd been wallowing and hadn't cared enough to watch what I ate. Today had been a turning point for some reason. I hadn't necessarily left the wallow, but I turned my back on it at least.

Annie laughed as she drove. "Loved ones have a way of thinking love can be distributed based on calories. The more calories, the more love. Or in Grandma Donna's case, the more butter, the more love."

"Pull over!" My gaze had snagged on a tiny brown blob off the side of the road. We'd passed downtown, the houses giving way to pine trees and shrubs. I'd seen my fair share of wild animals having grown up in Auburn Hill, but this struck me as odd.

Annie gasped and pulled to the side of the road without a single hesitation. "What?"

"Out there." I pointed, watching the brown blob move. "It's an animal."

"Coyote?"

I narrowed my eyes. "No. The tail's all wrong."

"Bear cub?"

"Nah, too lean." I grabbed the door handle and Annie put her hand on my shoulder.

"Wait! Are you going out there? We should probably call animal control. It might be rabid."

I took my eye off the animal long enough to look back at Annie. "I think it's a dog."

Her eyes went wide and then she was a rush of motion, charging out of the car and coming around to my side to help me out. I cursed my crutches for making me slow. She turned on the flashlight on her cell phone and kept it aimed right in front of our feet. The ground was uneven and thick with weeds. Thankfully there was a full moon, so we were mostly able to see where we were going. When we got within twenty feet of the animal, we came to a stop. It was a dog all right. A puppy of some sort. It was trembling and hunkered down, obviously scared.

I lowered myself down to the ground slowly, my bad leg stuck out in front and my crutches lying next to me.

"Can you get your cheeseburger?" I whispered to Annie, sudden inspiration hitting.

She darted away without a word. In the meantime, I wanted to see if the puppy would come to me.

"Hey, little fella. Or girl, I guess." I crooned in a low, calm voice. "I won't hurt you. You look a little scared."

The puppy lifted his head and sniffed the air.

"I know what it's like to be scared. They say it's easier if you have people around you to make you less scared. That's why I'm back in town. Maybe I could help you be less scared?"

He crawled forward a few feet and then stopped, still sniffing the air.

I heard Annie coming back, her approach quiet and slow. I quit yammering like an idiot. When she was next to me, she sat on the ground, her knee touching my thigh.

"Here," she whispered.

I took the Styrofoam container from her and opened it. The smell of juicy cooked meat hit my nose. The puppy froze and then jumped to its feet. I could practically see him straining forward for another whiff.

"Here, puppy. We have some dinner for you. We won't hurt you."

With the clumsy gait of a puppy, he came bounding over, stopping just inches from my outstretched hand. He lowered his head and sniffed my fingers, his big dark eyes trained on my face. I smiled at him and he made a decision in that moment. He crawled right in my lap and laid his head down on my leg.

Annie let out a soft yelp next to me, sounding like she might be crying. Her hand came over to grasp my knee. I broke off a chunk of meat and fed it to the little guy. He ate it all almost without chewing.

"I'll have to buy you a new cheeseburger," I whispered to Annie as I fed the puppy some more.

"I don't care. Just make sure he gets enough to eat."

We sat in silence, feeding the puppy almost the entire beef patty before he laid his head back down on my leg. Purpose surged through me. I was on crutches and trying to recover, but I could help this little guy.

"We should take him home. Do you mind?" I asked Annie, petting his head and seeing his eyes fluttering.

Annie looked up at me, her eyes shining with tears. "Do I mind? I'm a veterinarian. I love animals." Then she frowned. "But we need to see if he's chipped. He might belong to someone and they're looking for him right now."

"Now or in the morning?" I asked, knowing which one I hoped she answered.

Annie looked back down at the puppy, seeing the way his eyes had closed, like he trusted us so much and his belly was so full, he was willing to sleep on a stranger.

"Morning," she answered softly.

It took a lot of help from Annie to get up off the ground with a puppy in my arms, but she got it done. She did have to argue with me to hold him while I hobbled back to the car though. The second I was in the passenger seat, she handed him back to me. I could have sworn the little guy let out a sigh as soon as he was back in my lap. I hadn't had a chance to have a dog in LA. Apartment living wasn't conducive to owning a pet who needed space to roam and a backyard to pee all over.

Annie got us home and helped both of us into Ben's house. I slid right off the couch to sit on the floor. The puppy, having had enough of a nap, turned in circles, darting across the floor before falling on his face and racing back to me. Annie spread our food out on the coffee table, digging into her fries.

"I'd just like to point out that my junk food just saved the day." She shot me a triumphant smile. "Can't entice an animal with a chicken breast salad."

I bit back a grin. The puppy crawled over my legs, falling all over the place as he went. "I bow to your superior nutrition knowledge."

Annie snorted and shared a fry with me. As she leaned over, she left her Styrofoam container unattended in her lap. The puppy pounced, burying itself facedown in the pile of fries.

Annie shrieked and I lunged over to try to pull him away. Instead, he darted left, intent on leaving the scene of the crime with at least the fries in his mouth. Unfortunately, I grabbed quickly, missing him and finding myself with a handful of Annie's boob. She shrieked again and I snatched my hand back.

"Fuck, I'm so sorry," I muttered, feeling my face turn red.

The puppy sat on the other side of the room, munching on his fries, oblivious to the havoc he wreaked. Annie started giggling. Then her giggles turned into whoops of laughter and I found myself smiling along. How could today get any more awkward anyway? She'd seen me naked and then I grabbed her boob. Ben would be horrified.

Annie sat up straight, wiping her eyes. "Dang. I've laughed more today than all of last month. You're all frowny and serious, but damn, you make me laugh, Blaze."

It wasn't a compliment per se, but something glowed inside me as if it was. As a stunt double, I was used to operating behind the scenes. I did my job well and the audience wouldn't even know that it was me doing the stunt and not the famous actor. I didn't need the spotlight, in fact, I ran from it. But praise from Annie's lips held a weight I hadn't known I needed.

I cleared my throat, not at all sure what to say to that. "What kind of monster lets a puppy loose on the side of the road?"

Annie turned her attention to the puppy who'd just finished

the last stolen fry and lay down on his side as if he was too full to romp around.

"Well, we don't know yet if that's the case. If he's not chipped and there are no lost puppy signs around the county, then we can curse the bastard who'd do something like that."

"Hmm." I had a feeling our little puppy didn't know what it was like to be around loving people. And if I was honest with myself, I really hoped he wasn't chipped.

"Knock, knock! Open up, my Annie boo Bannie!" came a muffled voice from the front porch.

Annie froze, then shouted back, "Grandma Donna?"

I winced at all the shouting. "Annie boo Bannie?"

Annie slapped my leg. "Do not say one word."

I held my hands up. "I wouldn't dream of it."

Annie narrowed her eyes at me, but jumped up and ran to the front door. The puppy rolled to his feet and came over to sit on my lap. When the voices came nearer, he began to shake. I put my hands on his back and whispered to him about being perfectly safe.

"You leave me to go live in sin with a man?" Grandma Donna stood halfway between the front door and the living room, her hands on her hips as she took me in. "Although, I gotta say, he's got a puppy on his lap and isn't that just the sweetest thing you've seen in ages?"

Annie ushered her grandma to the couch and sat down with her. "Yes, yes. Super sweet. What are you doing here?"

Her grandma huffed and folded her arms across her ample bosom, bumping the small reading glasses that hung down from a string around her neck. She'd aged since I'd seen her last, but then again, she'd always seemed old to me when I came over to play with Ben. Kids always thought anyone over forty was ancient.

"I came to see how my granddaughter is adjusting to living on her own only to find she's living with a man!"

Annie rolled her eyes, but I could see her foot tapping out a rhythm on the floor from my vantage point. Interesting. Annie was nervous.

"I'm not living with a man."

Her grandma looked at me. "Is that not a man?"

"Most definitely is, I assure you," I answered dryly.

"See?" her grandma huffed. Then she turned to me with a smile. "How you doing, Blaze? Heard you took a tumble, but the crotchety old gossips who live on my street said it was from a street race down Beverly Hills Boulevard in a stolen car. I can't help but think that's not accurate."

I ran a hand over my chin and the puppy jumped up to lick me. "That's not quite accurate, no."

Grandma Donna sat back on the couch. "Knew it. Those old biddies are more trouble than they're worth."

She was referring to Poppy, Yedda, and Penelope, who all lived on her street. She'd been feuding with those ladies for as long as I'd been alive. Nice to know some things never changed.

Grandma Donna pinned Annie with a look that meant business. "Explain to me what's going on here."

"I'm living here at Ben's, just like I told you. Come to find out, Blaze happens to be living here too."

Grandma Donna's eyes narrowed. "And where is Ben?"

"He had an urgent business trip. Something about his app," I added.

Her finger waggled from Annie to me and back to Annie. "So you two are living together?"

"No!" Annie said.

"Yes," I confirmed at the same time.

Grandma Donna's lips pursed while she thought it through. Then she turned to me and I felt a bit like I might start shaking with the puppy. "You best keep your pants zipped, Hellman."

"Yes, ma'am." I glanced down at the crutches on the floor. "As you can see, I'm nursing a broken leg and a dislocated shoulder, so I can assure you that anything like what you're thinking is out of the question. I'm here to rehab."

Annie's face was brighter than a tomato right now, and if her grandma wasn't right there, I'd tease her relentlessly at how uncomfortable she looked.

"He doesn't think of me that way, Grandma," she said on a groan, burying her face in her hands.

Oh, if only she knew.

I glanced up at Grandma Donna and she was looking right at me like she could read my damn mind. I carefully kept my face blank until she swung her gaze back to Annie and stood. A trickle of sweat dripped down the back of my neck.

"Well, I won't keep y'all. I have my own man to get back to. I'll see myself out."

"Tell Juan Carlos I said hi," Annie muttered, looking quite conflicted between not liking her grandma's boyfriend and wanting to be kind.

At the entrance to the living room, Grandma Donna turned. "My Juan Carlos had a fractured hip when we first met and we still managed to...you know." She gyrated her hips in a manner that had my gaze darting down to the floor. Wow. I definitely did not need to see that. Ever.

Annie groaned. The puppy let out a whine.

"I got my eye on you two."

And with that warning, she was gone.

Awkward silence filled the room until the puppy let out a yip. Annie's head finally came up from the cushions of the couch where she'd buried herself. Her auburn hair was a mess around her face. I could barely see her freckles through the red staining her cheeks.

"Well, that was entertaining," I said dryly.

Annie groaned and flopped face-first back on the couch.

CHAPTER TEN

$\mathcal{A}$nnie

"Okay, well, that was...something..." I trailed off, staring over Blaze's head, unable to look him in the eye.

Leave it to Grandma Donna to make things awkward between us. She'd known about my crush on him when we were kids, but she also knew he never looked at me that way. So why did she have to open her big mouth and imply he'd be hitting on me now that we were both living at Ben's? Now I couldn't even look at him and I really wanted to.

Nothing was sexier than a hot, grumpy guy and a puppy.

Blaze pulled the puppy into his lap and I couldn't help but sneak a peek. Yep. Cuteness overload.

"I'm going to just gloss over that visit from your grandma. Sound good?" Blaze's voice held barely contained laughter.

"Yes, please." I chanced a glance upward and found him smiling at me. Like, an actual, full-out smile. And holy shit, with the puppy right below that smiling face I felt a distinct clench in my ovaries. It had been years since I saw that kind of smile on

Blaze's face. He used to let them fly as often as his teasing, but I noticed that he'd changed in the years between. The seriousness had taken over.

I shot off the couch and picked up the remains of our dinner off the floor, purposely ignoring Blaze's existence. I rushed into the kitchen with the trash as a way to escape before my body did something stupid and developed a crush on Blaze all over again. That would be a disaster. I had too much to do with getting the clinic going to waste time pining over a guy who would never look at me as anything other than his annoying little sister.

"I think I might head to bed. Get an early start tomorrow," I said loudly enough Blaze could hear me from the kitchen.

He grunted, which in Blaze language probably meant he heard me.

"Are you going to have the puppy sleep with you?" This was stupid, shouting from the kitchen to have a conversation, but it was just easier this way.

I checked the dishwasher, seeing there were two plates and a single knife in there. Not enough to bother running it tonight. I squeezed my eyes shut and berated myself for letting my brain drift to visions of Blaze and the puppy snuggled up in his bed. Grandma Donna had put some dangerous ideas in my head.

"Stupid, stupid," I muttered, shoving in the drawer I'd left open earlier.

"What's that?" came Blaze's voice from the doorway.

"Oh!" I jumped a foot in the air, clutching my shirt. "Jesus, Blaze.'

He looked confused. "Sorry. Didn't mean to scare you but I figured if you were going to keep asking me questions, I'd just come in here."

The puppy rounded the corner much too fast and fell face-first as he slid. He shot up and ran over to sit on my feet. I took the excuse to not look at Blaze and bent down to pet the puppy.

"I thought you needed help getting off the floor."

"I'm not that helpless." Blaze paused while I hoped he'd just turn around and leave the room. I needed to get my head straight before looking at him again.

"Actually, could you drop me off at physical therapy on your way into town tomorrow?"

His tone of voice had me looking up. His hand was rubbing the back of his neck. For a guy who looked like he'd been born sure of himself, he looked pretty damn uncertain.

"Of course," I heard myself say. I pretty much jumped at the chance to help people and this might be the first time Blaze had ever asked me for help. I stood, pulling the little guy into my arms. He reached up to lick my cheek and my heart melted.

"I hope he's not chipped," I whispered, as if saying it out loud was a sin. As a veterinarian, we always hoped people chipped their pets in case they got lost. But this guy was so cute, I hoped Blaze could keep him.

Blaze hitched one side of his mouth up. "Yeah, me too. You think he's a full-breed labrador?"

I looked down at the puppy and gave him a cursory exam. "I'd say yes based on looks, but tomorrow when we check if he's got a chip, we can run a DNA test with a little of his blood."

Blaze was studying the puppy like he could figure it out just by concentrating hard enough.

My heart dropped. "You aren't one of those people who only thinks a dog has value as a purebred, right?"

Blaze's head snapped up and he met my gaze with horror. "No. Not at all. I was just thinking about training him. Labs are great working dogs. We'd just gotten our first K9 when I was with the police department. Always thought I'd transfer into that unit if I got the chance."

I cocked my head. This was information about Blaze I hadn't known before. I had already left for college when he left the police force. We'd fallen out of touch by then and I was pretty hazy about why he'd left the force. "Why didn't you?"

Blaze's eyes glazed over, looking like he wasn't still here in the kitchen with me. "Just wasn't meant to be."

He turned and started hobbling away on his crutches without another word. I looked down at the puppy who looked longingly at the empty doorway. I shrugged and the puppy reached up to lick me again. I shut the light off and went after Blaze. I caught up to him just outside his bedroom.

"Can you put him on my bed for me?" he asked, his voice lacking all emotion. He didn't even turn to look at me.

I frowned, but squeezed past him to go into his bedroom and put the puppy down. I swallowed hard and tried not to eye the bed where he'd be sleeping in just a few minutes. Blaze was my brother's best friend. He was so off-limits I might as well develop a crush on one of Janie's goats from her yoga classes.

"Okay, well, good night, then." I slipped past him again, standing awkwardly in the hallway as Blaze entered his bedroom. The puppy spun in manic circles on his bed, making an absolute mess of his sheets and blanket.

Blaze never answered, so I shut his door and went to my own bedroom, mind spinning. Something had happened to Blaze, I was sure of it. He'd always been quiet and more reserved than his other brothers, but he'd never been harsh. Or rude. Or downright ogre-like. And even though it was none of my business, I was going to get to the bottom of what happened.

Blaze needed help, clearly.

And I'd be the girl to give it to him.

My alarm went off the next morning, pulling me from a dream that had me squirming in bed and wishing for just a few more minutes so I could finish it. I was going to kill Grandma Donna for putting ideas in my head. Or maybe seeing what Blaze was packing under those sweats he always wore had triggered something in my subconscious.

I shoved the hair out of my face and put my palms on my hot cheeks. Definitely a morning for a cold shower. I flung off the covers and found my favorite pair of scrubs. The ones with the flamingos all over them. The big pink birds had sunglasses and flip-flops on. It was so ridiculous I loved them. I tiptoed by Blaze's door and went into the bathroom, cursing my brother for not buying a house with more than one bathroom. He had cash to spare and went cheap on the house. Only Ben.

After a lukewarm shower and some time spent putting some spackle—as Grandma Donna called makeup—over my freckles, I pulled on my scrubs and left the bathroom. I let out a yelp and stepped back so fast, I hit my head on the doorframe.

Blaze was standing there in his bedroom doorway without a shirt and the puppy in his arms. "Sorry again for scaring you."

Oh, heaven have mercy. The man had a sexy morning voice. The kind that makes you want to leap back in his bed and snuggle with him all morning. I must have taken too long to answer because Blaze bent down and put the puppy on the floor.

"Check this out." He stood back up and the puppy danced between our feet, not sure who to shower his love upon.

"Watch me," Blaze barked.

My spine went straight and I fucking obeyed, watching Blaze like my life depended on it. A few seconds later, I realized he meant the puppy, who was on his little haunches, staring up at Blaze like he hung the moon. I understood the feeling.

"Down."

The puppy lay down, his little tongue coming out to hang out of his mouth.

"Oh my God. He's so good!"

Blaze's smile was lopsided as he looked at me. "I know, right? We worked on a few commands last night and he instantly picked them up."

I clapped, then sat on the floor. Incredibly, the puppy looked up at Blaze, who simply said okay, before the dog came rushing over to sit on my lap. He was a little bundle of energy and I was already in love with him.

"You're such a good boy, aren't you?" I gave him belly rubs while he lapped up the attention. "You know all your commands already, don't you? You're just so cute I want to squeeze you."

I looked up at Blaze, who was adjusting the front of his sweatpants. I looked away again, not needing to see that. Not when it brought all kinds of things to mind, namely, the exact size, shape, and color of Blaze's dick. Jeez, it was warm in here.

"Um, I was wondering if you thought of a name for this little guy?" Great. Now all my conversations were going to have to be while I stared at the wall or the puppy. Looking directly at Blaze was getting harder and harder.

"No, not yet," came Blaze's rough voice. "If he's not chipped, maybe then."

I nodded, climbing to my feet. "Probably for the best. Naming him will make you fall in love with him." I hooked a thumb over my shoulder. "I'm going to make some food for the day. You want anything?"

"Nah, I'm good."

"Might want to grab a shirt before we go," I grumbled, needing him to cover up all the muscles that were staring at me. I could have sworn I heard his smirk, it was that potent.

After going into his room for a shirt, Blaze's crutches followed me down the hallway, the tumble of the puppy colliding with the walls interspersed with the squeaks. I could practically feel Blaze's gaze on my back, making walking normally difficult.

As soon as I reached the kitchen, I got busy making sandwiches. Blaze got out some lunch meat and fed it to the puppy, muttering about needing to get dog food. I put some strawberries in a plastic bag and handed them to Blaze, along with his sandwich.

He almost didn't take them. "I don't need anything."

I pushed the bundle into his hands. "Just take it, would you? I can't help helping people. It's my love language."

My head snapped up and I locked eyes with Blaze. "N-not that I love you or anything, but you know what I mean. I just enjoy helping people. It's what I do."

Blaze lifted one eyebrow. "I'm aware."

I frowned at him. "What's that supposed to mean?"

He shrugged. "Just noticed you spend more time helping other people than helping yourself."

I scoffed. "No, I don't. Besides, even if I did, what's wrong with that?"

And thus began the argument that lasted the whole way into my car with the puppy and across town to physical therapy. By the time I dropped Blaze off and kept the puppy with me, I was well and truly over whatever had taken over my brain the last twenty-four hours. Blaze was way too argumentative and grumpy for me to entertain a crush.

Even if he did look like an injured professional athlete in those sweatpants and T-shirt that barely contained his muscles. As soon as he was safely inside the physical therapy building, I turned to the puppy. He had his front legs up on the arm rest, nose pressed to the window, whining for Blaze.

"Listen, mister. I know how you feel, but you're barking up the wrong tree. Don't get your heart set on that boy." I shook my head and turned the car in the direction of my clinic.

"Don't get your heart set on that boy, Annie," I repeated to myself.

CHAPTER ELEVEN

laze

"ONE MORE TIME and then you can head home to ice that leg."

My physical therapist, Ronnie, was a masochist. Had to be to torture a fellow human like this. Sweat lined every inch of my skin. I'd passed ten on the one-to-ten pain scale a few seconds after walking in here. Deciding yesterday to quit taking the pain pills had obviously been a massive mistake.

At least all the physical pain had taken my thoughts away from the look on Annie's face when I'd shut down on her last night. I hadn't even told my brothers everything about what had happened back when I quit the police force. Some things were better left in the past, shoved under the rug and forgotten about.

I pushed off the bench and gritted my teeth as I came to standing with the parallel bars on either side of me in case my leg gave out. Every muscle fiber in my bad leg screamed with the effort. Nausea bubbled up in my stomach. A bead of sweat ran down the side of my jaw and I didn't even bother wiping it away. Who cared if I dripped sweat all over the equipment? Served

Ronnie right to have to clean up after me. If he didn't torture me like this, I wouldn't sweat all over his clinic.

"Excellent progress, Blaze." The guy sounded so happy I wanted to punch him in the face. If I didn't think it would cause my leg more pain, I would have. "Go home and ice it. And then try to walk around the house without the crutches. Let's see how that goes."

My hands shook as I reached out for my crutches, pulling them under my arms and hobbling out of the parallel bars. My entire right side ached like I'd been hit by a bus going full speed. If I didn't get away from here, I might say something I'd regret later. I gave Ronnie a head nod—the best I could do at the moment—and headed outside. The glass door nearly clipped me in the face because I was moving so slowly. Fucking hell. You'd think they'd make an easier door to manage at a physical therapy clinic. I made it to the little bench outside the clinic and collapsed in a sweaty heap of frustration.

Two months ago I'd been leaping from tall buildings. Crawling through movie sets filled with mud and even a choreographed sword fight across boulders in a rushing river. There wasn't much I couldn't do. Now I couldn't fucking stand up from a chair without crying like a toddler.

My phone rang from my back pocket and I dug it out, expecting to send it to voicemail. But it was Ben.

"Hey," I managed, still too pissed off to be cordial, even to my own best friend.

His deep chuckle had me calming down. "You sound like you've had the same morning I have."

I huffed through my nose. "'Fraid so. What's wrong in your world?"

"Stupid app. I swear. They want unicorns and werebears in outer space. Oh, but it's not Christmassy enough. Space werebears aren't fucking festive, okay?"

That got me smiling as I looked across the street to the National Cat Protection Society run by one of the old ladies

Grandma Donna had a beef with. Yedda had owned that place for as long as I could remember.

"I don't know, man. Werebears can shapeshift, right? He could become Santa. Or the reindeer."

There was silence on the other end. "Well, shit. I guess you're right. You might have just solved my issue. Now do you know anything about why the app keeps crashing when the unicorns shoot their rainbow farts?"

I shook my head. "What the fuck?"

Ben laughed. "Never mind. What's got you so pissed off today?"

"Physical therapy."

Old man Lenny came out from the back of the cat place, stopping to kick a weed that had sprung up in the crack of the sidewalk. Ace's fiancée told me he came to her yoga class regularly, but I didn't think any of that zen meditation stuff Addy was always going on about was helping him. He looked angry.

"Wish I was there to buy you a beer. I could use one myself right now." Ben sighed. "And I need to call Annie. I was supposed to talk to her two nights ago and I never got a chance. Some issue with Grandma or something."

I sat straight up, forgetting all about Lenny or physical therapy or werebears. No way in hell was I broaching the subject of Annie. Not when I had the inclination to blurt out that I'd been naked in front of her or that I'd grabbed her boob by accident.

And fucking liked it.

"Uh hey, can I ask a huge favor?"

"Bigger than moving in with me?"

I rolled my head around my neck. "Listen, shithead. If you don't want me in your house, just say so."

Ben chuckled again. "Of course I want you there, but I have to give you shit about it. So what's the favor?"

"There's this puppy."

"Did you do something boneheaded like take him home with you?"

I winced. "How'd you guess?"

"You forget I've known you your whole life. You and Annie are the only people I know, besides Yedda, I guess, who would take home animals off the side of the road." Ben sighed. "I assume that's where you found this puppy?"

"It's like you and your grandma are mind readers," I grumbled.

Ben laughed. "I'm so glad you moved back to Hell, I don't care if you adopt twenty dogs. Just make sure they're well trained so they don't pee on my couch. I bought that sucker new, I'll have you know."

I barked out a laugh. "Wow. Bought a piece of furniture new? That's unlike you, Ben." The fucker could buy a thousand brand-new couches if he wanted to.

"Just saving my pennies, bro. Actually, remember that squirrel you trained when we were, like, ten? He actually ate out of the palm of your hand. Never seen anything like that."

I grinned. "I have a way with animals."

"Too bad it's not with women."

That stung. I knew he meant it as a joke, but the truth still hurt a little. I wasn't good with women. That's why when I'd moved to Los Angeles, I made it clear to every woman I met that I was only in it for the sex. Harsh, yeah, but it had been the truth and I always wanted to lead with honesty to prevent messy entanglements.

"Says the single guy," I shot back, earning me a groan and a laugh.

"Whatever. Just keep the puppy out of my bedroom, okay?"

My brain instantly shot to Annie in her teeny-tiny pajamas, occupying Ben's room. "Don't worry about that."

When we hung up, I texted my brothers to see if I could get a ride home. I didn't want to bother Annie when I knew she had so much to do, and quite frankly, I needed a little time away from her. While I waited for a response, I contemplated my conversation with Ben.

I'd lied to him.

Okay, he hadn't straight-out asked me about Annie, but I didn't tell him she'd moved in either. That was a lie of omission. Guilt weighed on my shoulders. I'd have to talk to Annie about it first. Maybe we could come up with a way to position it that wouldn't have her brother wanting to rip my head off. My phone pinged, saving me from envisioning his fist coming toward my face.

Ethan: Yeah, I can grab you. No work today. Stupid parts aren't in for the gas water heater I need to install at Mrs. Trudowski's place.

Me: Thanks, man.

Daxon: When can you drive your truck again? Because this ride thing is getting old.

Me: Shut the fuck up. You haven't given me a ride since I've been back.

Daxon: Hmm, I guess I'm just tired of you asking for a ride.

Me: I could move back to LA if it bothers you that much.

Ace: Boys. Don't make me come over there with the Love Shirt.

I squeezed my eyes shut and prayed for patience. Mom had taken one of Dad's old undershirts after he left us and wrote on it with a big black marker. The Brotherly Love Shirt. Every time two of us got in a spat, she stuffed us both into the shirt. We had to cooperate with each other like conjoined twins for however long Mom left us in the shirt. It was humiliating and highly effective. I still had nightmares about that shirt.

Callan: I'd pay to see the two of them in that thing again.

Me: Can I just get a ride before I die of sunstroke out here?

I shut my phone off and shoved it in my pocket. Maybe Daxon was right. Asking my brothers for a ride was getting old. I'd have to suck it up and work on my walking today without the crutches even if the pain made me want to pass out. I wanted to be independent again. As soon as fucking possible.

Ethan's work truck eventually pulled up in front of the physical therapy clinic, his big smile shooting out the open windows a sight for sore eyes. Maybe some of his happiness would rub off on me on the ride home. I grabbed my crutches, stood with my good leg, and hobbled over. He didn't open the door for me, which I appreciated. A man wanted to do some things on his own, a concept Annie did not understand. Although I totally ate that sandwich she made me before therapy started. Not that I'd tell her she was a lifesaver or anything. Or that her sandwiches were better than Mom's.

Once I was settled, Ethan clapped me on the shoulder. "Man, it's good to have you back. Daxon is giving you shit instead of me for once."

I grunted.

Ethan wasn't deterred by my lack of conversation. He was a bit like Annie, happy to fill the silence with the sound of his own voice. Hell, I wondered why the two of them had never dated since they were so similar. The thought of Ethan with Annie made the nausea come back full force.

"So when are you hoping to be back to work?" Ethan was asking. I'd missed the first part of whatever he'd said.

I looked out the window at the new businesses that had gone in on Brinestone Way. This wasn't a topic I'd wanted to discuss just yet, but leave it to my nosy brothers to jump right in. Might as well get it over with now.

"I'm not going back."

The truck lurched to the right before Ethan straightened it out again and shot me a look. "What do you mean?"

Irritation bloomed. Maybe from the pain pulsing from my leg. Or maybe as a cover for the humiliation I felt returning home an unemployed, broken man. Or maybe it was just that Ethan's question had shined a spotlight on the shit pile I'd been wallowing in for nearly two months.

"I mean I lost my job. They need a stunt double right now to finish filming, not months from now when I've rehabbed. And the doctor says he doesn't recommend going back. My leg won't ever be as strong as it was which means no studio will hire me. They're already contesting the insurance money owed to me in court right now."

Ethan yanked the wheel and came to an abrupt stop on the side of the road, dust pluming behind us. "Those fuckers didn't pay you when it was their set that put you in the hospital?"

I sighed, feeling slightly better at seeing his anger on my behalf. "I've got my lawyer on it, but you know how these things go. The studio has deep pockets. Add in lawyer fees and I don't expect to see a single penny."

Ethan sat there fuming. I let him stew on that. Lord knew I'd spent enough time stewing on it too the last two months. When he finally huffed out a sigh and got us back on the road, I figured he'd come to accept the situation for what it was, just like I had.

"So what's the plan for after you're rehabbed? Be a cop again?"

I reared my head back. "Fuck no."

Visions of Dani's eyes going stone cold, threatening me about our relationship made me shudder. No way in hell was I going back to being a cop. Especially knowing Dani was still with the force. I'd made mistakes there, for sure, but none as idiotic as falling for my boss. At eighteen, I'd had stars in my eyes, thinking I'd found the perfect woman for me. I'd been thinking of forever and Dani had been thinking of ways to use me for her own personal gain.

"You can come help me, if you need work."

I blinked and took in the truck I was riding in. The bounce in the seat. The smell of fresh-cut wood coming from the back. While I loved my brother for offering me a job, I needed to find something that was just my own. I clapped him on the back of the shoulder and gave it a squeeze. He let the subject drop.

"Hey, do you mind stopping by Annie's new clinic?"

"Sure." Ethan shot me a grin that said he figured I had something on my mind where Annie was concerned. He wasn't exactly wrong, but that wasn't why I wanted to stop by. I wanted to see if that puppy was chipped. If he wasn't, I was adopting him today.

There wasn't any parking when we got there, so Ethan had to park a block over. I left my crutches in the car, somehow getting up on the sidewalk with the help of one of those parking meters to grab hold of.

"Stubborn mule, for sure," Ethan muttered, staying right by my side. He may have been going slow to be nice, or maybe because he thought I might fall and need his assistance, but either way, I appreciated it.

The sweat was flowing again by the time I made it to Annie's place. She let out a squeal and came barreling out the door. The puppy trotted after her, dancing on my feet, before lying down and rolling over. If I could have squatted down to pet him, I would have. As it was, I was just trying not to pass out.

"What are you doing without your crutches?" Annie fluttered around me, shock and concern clear on her face.

It should have been annoying. All her attention and jabbering on, but being able to surprise her made something glow a little brighter in my chest. Maybe it was my pride trying to pick itself up off the floor.

"Wanted to see if the little guy was chipped."

Annie finally came to a stop in front of me, a knowing look on her face. "Nope. And no lost dog posts anywhere I can find."

I felt the grin split my face. This felt right. "Then he's mine."

"You betcha. Want me to chip him right now?"

I shook my head. "No, not yet. I have something in mind first."

Annie and Ethan looked at me in confusion. I wasn't divulging the plan that was hatching in my head. It was a long shot and probably wouldn't work out, but what did I have to lose right now? I couldn't do much in the way of a career at the moment, but I could do this.

Ethan left to bring around the truck, saying it was for getting the puppy in safely, but I knew it was because he didn't want to see me walk all the way back without my crutches. Annie kissed the little guy on the head before handing him to me. In a weird way, it felt like the puppy was our furbaby and we were the proud parents, making me feel all kinds of weird things. Nice things. Things that felt like something I thought I'd never have.

"See you at home?"

Annie laughed. "See ya, roomie."

CHAPTER TWELVE

*A*nnie

TIME HAD GOTTEN AWAY from me today. The puppy had been my shadow as I set up the chairs that had been delivered to the vet clinic. The little guy had been my first test patient, trying to lick my face as I scanned him for a chip. I'd let out a relieved sigh when nothing was detected. I would have felt horrible delivering the news to Blaze that this little wiggling mass of puppy love belonged to someone else.

On top of that good news, it seemed like Blaze and I were on a good track to forgetting the weird tension between us. He still wouldn't let me help him very much, but at least I hadn't been picturing him naked when he came to pick up the puppy. I'd have to tell Addy the meditation methods she'd taught me were really coming in handy.

The sun had already set by the time I made it back to Ben's place, my car letting out one final backfire to announce my arrival. There was a dark SUV parked out at the curb. Either we had company or Blaze had gotten his car back.

I tugged at my shirt, suddenly self-conscious. I was a hot mess and I knew it. My hair was sticking to my sweaty face. There was a smear of paint on the back of my scrubs. I'd started putting pictures up on the wall at the clinic. Then I decided I didn't like them and had to take them down, rearrange them, patch the wall where I'd left holes, and paint over it once the patch dried. Of course, being me, I backed up into the wet paint while trying to eye the new placement of the pictures. I didn't even know the paint smear was there until Cricket came over with an afternoon coffee that saved the day, and pointed out my blunder.

Unlocking the front door, I smelled food cooking and nearly drooled down my chin. That coffee had been hours ago and my one sandwich for lunch hadn't accounted for all the running around I did today.

"Honey, I'm home!" I hollered, finding myself hilarious.

A grunt from the kitchen said Blaze didn't find me as funny. The puppy came running around the corner of the kitchen and face-planted on the hardwood floor before righting himself and racing over to me. I squatted down and gave him all the belly rubs.

"Hello, my sweet boy! How was your afternoon with Mr. Grumpy Head?"

"Hey, I heard that."

I looked up to find Blaze in the doorway, a kitchen towel slung over his shoulder. The crutches were nowhere to be found and he'd shaved down his beard to just a five o'clock shadow. The usual scowl was in place, but there wasn't much fire behind it. I opened my mouth to ask what he was cooking, but got interrupted.

The puppy suddenly jumped up and barked right in my face. Then he ran off into the kitchen like his hind legs were on fire. Blaze and I looked at each other and then went after him, Blaze limping quickly next to me.

"What is it, boy?" Blaze asked. The puppy was barking his head off over by the stove.

"Oh, shit, the oven!" I ran ahead and pulled open the oven door. Smoke flowed out, making me cough.

"Watch out!" Blaze barreled by me, oven mitt in hand to pull out a cookie sheet of something.

I went to the window over the sink and opened it to let the smoke out. The puppy quit barking, seeing that the humans had arrived on the scene.

"You trying to burn my brother's house down?" I said, teasingly.

Blaze brought the sheet over to the sink to see if the food he'd been cooking was edible. Little black lumps sat on the sheet.

He gave me a deadpan look. "How'd you know?"

"Think any of it's salvageable?"

Blaze peered into the cookie sheet. "How do you feel about eating charcoal?"

I tilted my head back and forth. "I hear it's good for teeth whitening."

The corner of Blaze's mouth tilted up. "I saw a frozen pizza in the freezer I probably can't burn."

He put the cookie sheet in the sink, dumped a healthy amount of dish soap in it, and turned on the faucet.

"How about you let me make the pizza."

Blaze scratched where his full beard used to be. "I was trying to do something nice. I remembered your favorite food when we were kids was tater tots."

I clapped him on the shoulder like I thought a guy friend would do when what I really wanted to do was throw my arms around him and give him a hug for being so sweet. Blaze gave me a confused look.

"They say it's the thought that counts. How about you get the pizza out and I'll work the oven?"

He and I worked together to get the pizza going, chatting

about the puppy and where we thought he'd come from. Blaze was actually answering me in full sentences instead of grunts and one-word answers.

"I took some blood to run that DNA test too, so we should hear back in a week or two." I set the timer on the stove and leaned back against the counter. "Did you think of a name for him yet?"

Blaze looked down at the puppy sitting there patiently waiting for food to drop. "I had a few names in mind, but now I'm thinking Tate."

"Tate?" I looked at the dog in question to see if the name fit him.

"Yeah. Short for tater tot."

I whipped my head up to see Blaze smiling at me. Why did his smile always do something funny to my stomach? "He kind of looks like one."

"And he smelled them on fire. You know, they train dogs to detect embers. He might have a good sniffer on him."

"I think you just found his name." He and I stood there smiling at each other, two proud parents.

The oven timer went off, startling me. We got the pizza out, cut it, and had a seat at the kitchen table to eat it. Blaze handed me a napkin while Tate lay at his feet. Being a smart woman, I waited until Blaze had eaten a few slices before talking. Despite the silence, this felt nice. Almost comfortable.

Though I was still conscious of the heat coming from his good leg under the table. If I moved my knee just an inch, we'd be touching. How did a man radiate heat like that?

I got nervous and opened my mouth.

"So how did PT go today?"

Blaze grunted. Shoot. Should have waited until he had a few more slices of pizza before asking that one. He took another big bite, chewed, and then wiped his mouth with his napkin before putting it down next to his plate.

"He's the devil in a polo shirt."

I couldn't help but laugh because I knew what he meant. Ronnie had worked on Grandma Donna after her knee replacement two years ago. I'd come home from college to help her the first week out of surgery and I'd been shocked at the things he expected her to do so soon after surgery.

"Ronnie is all smiles and encouragement while you bust your ass. Makes you want to punch him in the face."

"Yes!" Blaze scooted back from the table, gesturing to his leg. "He had me standing from chair height today, walking without crutches, and then he told me to spend more of my day out of my brace. He's insane."

"So I see you're walking without crutches, but have you taken the brace off today?"

Blaze looked down at Tate, suddenly interested in petting him at the table.

"Blaze?"

He sighed and looked back up at me. "Not yet."

I gave him a smile of encouragement. "No time like the present."

He gave me that deadpan look again, but there was no disdain behind it like there used to be when he teased me. "Has anyone told you your chipperness is annoying?"

"Chipperness isn't even a word. And yes, you've told me plenty of times." I clapped my hands and swiveled to his bad leg where it was resting at an angle away from the table. "Chop, chop. Let's go."

"You know, maybe I should wait—"

"Oh for heaven's sake, Blaze, just take the fucking brace off." I knelt down by his leg and began to figure out how the straps worked.

"Annie boo Bannie. That mouth," he chastised me, a smile tugging on his lips.

I glanced up at him. "Only Grandma Donna calls me that."

"That doesn't go that way."

I flicked his shin, careful not to flick him on the femur where the actual injury was. "Well, if you'd help instead of tease me, we could get this thing off faster, you know."

He bent down, helping with the straps around his calf, but then I couldn't get his sweatpant leg above his knee. The damn brace was too bulky.

"Take your pants off," I ordered, seeing no other way to get the brace off.

"Wow, Annie. A little more finesse would be nice," Blaze answered smoothly, his voice so deep and rich my muscles almost gave out. I put a hand down on the floor so I wouldn't fall back-ward on my ass.

"Seriously, Blaze?"

He bit back a smile, holding my gaze while he reached for his waistband. I saw a strip of tan, muscled belly before I looked away. I swallowed hard and reminded myself that Blaze was off-limits. He saw me as a little sister and nothing more.

"You can look now," Blaze said dryly.

I looked back, careful to keep my gaze on his leg and not the picture of Blaze Hellman sitting in a chair in his navy-blue boxers with my face just inches from his lap. I yanked a piece of Velcro on his brace and he let out a yelp.

"Jeez, Annie. Gentle." He reached down and helped me with the other two straps, our hands batting each other out of the way.

"Aha! I knew it!" came a loud voice through the little strip of window on the front door. "Caught you on your knees, young lady!"

I froze with one of my hands in Blaze's, my head nearly in his lap. My face flamed bright red, seeing the situation through my grandmother's eyes. Blaze looked at me, his eyes practically dancing with humor and something else I could only describe as straight Blaze charisma. I'd seen the way his eyes would light up around girls when we were in high school. He'd never looked at me that way, but I'd somehow made a study out of Blaze. As if he set the mold for the opposite sex. And that smolder was definitely bouncing around in those deep brown depths. It sent more heat to my face than Grandma Donna and her ridiculous claims.

I rolled my eyes and cleared my throat, my gaze darting away from Blaze. "Just come in, Grandma!"

"Can't. Locked," she shouted back through the front door, her eye and the side of her nose still pressed to the glass.

"Excuse me," I mumbled, pushing up to standing.

Blaze let out a grunt that sounded less like his normal ones and more like a man in pain. That's when I realized I'd pushed myself up with my hands on his bad leg.

"Oh shit, I'm sorry," I said quickly, patting his leg, as if that would erase the pain I'd just caused. Of course, in my frenzy of an apology, my patting may have been a bit off course. I tapped against something that did not feel like Blaze's leg.

Blaze grabbed my wrist and we both froze. Dear God, I'd just groped Blaze while my grandma was watching.

"Guess that makes up for the boob grab?" I asked weakly, pulling my hand away and sprinting to the door to let Grandma Donna in.

She nearly fell inside when I swung the door open, having pressed herself up to the glass with all her weight. I caught her and set her on her feet, glasses swinging like a weapon.

"Jeez, Madonna, I was just helping Blaze get his brace off like Ronnie told him to. You want to have to explain to Ronnie why Blaze isn't making progress?" I used the nickname I'd given her when I was little and couldn't pronounce Grandma Donna. I only used the nickname now when I was less than pleased with her.

Grandma visibly shivered. "God no, that man has a little bit of the devil in him. He's probably a spin instructor in his spare time."

Blaze placed his brace in the chair I'd vacated and put all his weight on the table to push to his feet.

"Oh, don't get up on my account!" Grandma Donna rushed

past me to flutter around Blaze. "You poor thing. I remember what it was like to be laid up after my surgery. Shoot, I should have brought one of my pies. They're healing, I tell you. That bitch Poppy tried to tell me my apple pie bottom wasn't flaky enough last Thanksgiving at the church picnic, but I set her straight. Grandma Donna doesn't have no soggy bottoms, let me tell you."

"Okay, Grandma," I interrupted before she could embarrass me further. Did she wake up each morning and ask herself "how humiliated can I make my granddaughter today"? "What did you come by for?"

She looked between the two of us, taking in Blaze in his boxers and me with the face that felt hotter than the surface of the sun. "You sure you two weren't—"

"No!" we both said at the same time.

"Well, hell. I was hoping you two pulled your heads out of your asses and got on the pleasure train before it left the station without you."

"Grandma," I said sharply, not letting my brain even go there. There would be no train, no pleasure station, and no taking a ride on anything. "What did you come over for?"

Grandma sighed so heavily her lips flapped. "Fine. Don't say I didn't try." Then she beamed over at me as if she hadn't just accused us of carrying on in some form of sexual activity that I was not comfortable discussing with my grandmother, for crap's sake.

"I ran into Nikki Hellman today—"

"Oh shit," Blaze muttered.

Grandma kept right on going. "—and we hatched a plan I think you'll like." She put her hands up in the air like she was picturing something amazing. "We want to throw you a grand opening party for your vet clinic. What do you think?"

My jaw dropped open. I wasn't exactly sure what to think. I hadn't even set an exact day I expected to be open. Sure, it would be soon—ish—but planning a party meant this was actually happening. And accepting help from Grandma and Mrs. Hellman felt kind of weird. I liked to be the one doing the helping, not the other way around.

"I think it's a great idea," Blaze said confidently, as if this had anything to do with him.

"Great!" Grandma Donna turned to Blaze. "Because you're going to help us plan it!"

CHAPTER THIRTEEN

laze

ANNIE'S GRANDMA WAS A HOOT.

I liked how she got Annie's cheeks burning. Hell, even her neck was red at this point. And she wasn't exactly wrong. When Annie had been kneeling there in front of me, I'd gotten some ideas. Some really raunchy ideas. Some ideas that had no business in my head.

"We're going to need someone to help us with the heavy lifting. That's where you come in," Grandma Donna dipped her head in my direction before bending down to pet Tate, who was jumping up on her legs. I needed to train him not to do that.

"I don't know," Annie hedged. "Blaze is still rehabbing and I don't know exactly when I'll be ready to open. Probably best to skip a big party."

Grandma Donna opened her mouth but I beat her to it. "Absolutely not. Your clinic needs a grand opening so everyone in town knows you're open for business."

"Exactly!" Grandma Donna squealed, standing up. "I'll meet

with Nikki tomorrow and let you know what we come up with."
She swung her gaze to me. "Blaze. Put some pants on, young
man."

And then she swept out the door, leaving Annie and me in
awkward silence. Tate let out a whine. Annie squatted down to
pick him up. He placed kisses all over her face and I found
myself jealous of a dog.

"Finish your pizza," Annie said, heading to the kitchen for
more. She came back with another slice on her plate and Tate
hot on her heels. I moved my brace to the floor so she could
have a seat.

"Sit, Tate." The little bundle of energy skidded to a halt and
sat down, staring up at me with so much love and trust I felt
something shift. I really enjoyed training him and I thought
there was more I could do, given a bit more time.

"You think training dogs could be a career?" The question
was out there before I realized it wasn't just a question I asked in
my head.

Annie put her slice of pizza back on her plate and swallowed.
"Heck, yes. Are you kidding me? Dog trainers are in high
demand. So many people adopt a little puppy because they're
cute and then freak out the first time they pee on the rug. They
come into vets asking for training help all the time. The clinic I
had a rotation at during college was constantly referring out to
reputable trainers."

I stared at Tate, seeing something form in my mind. A
dream, maybe. Something to reach for. Something to get me out
of the wallowing I'd been doing. For good.

"I was thinking more along the lines of training work dogs." I
lifted my head and looked at Annie. She'd sweated off her
makeup today, revealing the freckles across her nose and cheekbones. Even her mascara was smudged beneath her eyes, but
those eyes sparkled as she thought about my suggestion. She was
so different from the perfectly put-together women I'd met in

Hollywood, yet no one could possibly be more beautiful than her.

"Oh my God, yes, Blaze!"

I could think of other situations where I wanted her to say things like that.

Fuck. I needed to focus on the conversation, not on things that would get my face bashed in.

"You really think so?" I asked, feeling self-conscious about verbalizing something I hadn't even worked out in my head yet. That was unlike me. Normally I'd toss around an idea for weeks or even months before telling anyone about it.

Annie was nodding, pizza forgotten. "Yes! I believe there might be certifications and things, but training work dogs would be incredible. You did say you wanted to work with the K9s before you quit the force, right?"

I had to clench my jaw to not go down that mental path. Thinking of everything that had made me quit the force was enough to spiral me down into the wallow and I had no intention of letting it suck me back in.

"I'll look into what training I need, but in the meantime, I can see how things go with Tate."

Annie patted my hand where it rested on the table. She looked as excited as I felt. "I can talk to the vet I interned with tomorrow. He'd know of some trainers you could talk to. Get a feel for whether it's the right fit for you."

Annie kept me entertained while we finished eating and cleaned up the kitchen. She told me all about the crazy pets and their owners that she'd dealt with at the clinic during college. By the time she excused herself to go take a shower and head to bed, I found myself smiling, thoroughly enjoying my evening in a way I wasn't used to. My favorite type of night previously had involved absolute silence and a good book, not a woman who talked a mile a minute. I'd always lived alone for just that reason. Finding myself enjoying rooming with Annie was a surprise.

I let Tate out to pee in the backyard, thinking if my leg held up, I might just try to mow the grass tomorrow. The blades were so tall at the moment, Tate nearly got lost. He came barreling back in the house, jumping around my feet as I got everything locked up.

I shot him a grin and picked him up to rub behind his ears. "Get ready, boy. Tomorrow the training picks up. You're going to be my star student."

Tate let out a bark and then licked my face. Well, shit. There I went grinning again.

Once I was in my room, I pointed to his bed. He went right over, turning in a circle a few times before lying down. I could hear the shower going across the hall. My brain skidded sideways before I could rein it back in.

"Don't, Blaze. Just don't." I pulled my T-shirt off and had my hands on the waistband of my boxers when I changed my mind. I couldn't sleep naked now. Not when Annie was only a few feet away. Even with a wall between us, I had to keep a cloth barrier between us. Just felt safer that way.

I put my brace back on and lifted my leg into bed. My hands served as a pillow behind my head as I gazed up at the ceiling. My leg ached, but it felt like a good hurt. The kind that comes from working hard and making progress.

The shower turned off and I faintly heard Annie singing. I cringed. The girl still couldn't sing. I'd had to sit through enough of her choir concerts from elementary school to remember she couldn't carry a tune if it jumped in her arms and held on tight. Something about the off-key notes struck me as amazing. Like she was giving me an inside look at her real life.

This wasn't like most of the dates I'd gone on in LA. The women there had shown up with a thick layer of makeup and a dress that emphasized their curves. Sex had just been a way to get off, and even without a stitch of clothing on, I never got to see the real woman underneath the facade. They were gone before the morning light showed their real skin tone, or messy hair, or morning breath. Living with Annie showed me who she really was.

Turned out I really liked who she was.

Through the paper-thin walls I heard her footsteps pad down the hall. I heard the door close and the creek of the floor as she walked around Ben's room. I wondered if she was naked and wet, trying to pull on pajamas that were nothing more than scraps of material. I found myself listening for the squeak of the springs as she eased herself into bed. I shut my eyes and gripped the sheets.

Do not picture her in bed, I told myself.

I felt myself harden and hated myself for it. I tried picturing my sutures when I first woke up from surgery. I even tried remembering the face Dani had made when she broke up with me in the most stunning fashion possible. And even though both of those scenarios were usually enough to have me close to nauseous, my dick still got hard. I reached down and gripped the base through my boxers, squeezing the blood flow off.

Rubbing one out would really help me get to sleep.

Then again, if I could hear the damn squeak of Annie's bed, she'd certainly hear me getting off. I could stick a pillow over my face, but even then I couldn't guarantee I wouldn't grunt at the end. I'd tried sneaking into my girlfriend's bedroom my senior year of high school. We almost got away with it too, except for the very end when I'd made a noise and didn't even know it. Her father had stormed up the stairs and I'd had to flee through the window with my dick still hanging out of my pants. I'd learned a hard lesson that day: I made noise when I orgasmed.

Thinking about orgasm noises wasn't helping me with this little problem. I threw back the covers and swung my legs over the side. Tate lifted his head, probably wondering what my problem was. I stood up as quietly as I could and crept out of my room. If I couldn't sleep, I could at least get some water in the kitchen. That room was further away from Annie. Maybe I could get my head screwed on straight with a little distance.

I stood by the kitchen window, staring out at the wood fence line I could barely make out in the dark and trying to focus on my possible career path instead of Annie in those skimpy pajamas she liked to wear. I mostly had everything under control when I finished the glass of water. I turned to leave and bumped right into Annie.

"Oh!" she squealed.

I threw my hands out and grabbed her arms to hold her steady. There wasn't a single light on in the house and yet I could see her just fine up close. She wore those pajamas again, the shorts as skimpy as a bathing suit bottom. The top was even worse. Just thin white cotton with tiny straps and a pathetic attempt at covering her nipples.

I swallowed hard and realized my dick was back to being rock hard. And she could probably feel it, given that her body was pressed close to mine.

"Sorry—" we both said at the same time.

I let her arms go and tried to shuffle back a step. Her tongue darted out to lick her lips and I almost groaned out loud. Her hair was down and still damp, the bright red strands flickering around her bare arms. I could just make out the flowery scent of her shampoo.

"I, uh, couldn't sleep," she whispered, her gaze darting down to take in my entire body.

Fuck. That wasn't helping.

"Me either." The words scraped my throat as they left my mouth.

She took a step closer, closing the distance I'd tried to put between us. What the hell was she doing? She would have to have been blind not to see the way my boxers were tented. Her hair brushed my bare chest and I shivered. My hands were already clenched into fists at my side.

I would not touch her. Under any condition.

She tilted her head back, as if offering her lips up on a silver platter. She didn't look appalled like I thought she would. She looked...excited. All the blood left my brain, traveling south. I forgot about all the reasons I shouldn't. All the reasons I'd regret if anything happened between us.

"You should probably go," I whispered in warning. And I meant it. If she didn't leave in the next three seconds, I was going to pick her up and spread her open on this countertop so I could find every single freckle she possessed. Right before I slammed my aching cock inside of her.

Annie lifted up on her tiptoes and whispered, her lips tickling my ear, "I live here, remember?"

That was all it took. Every reason, hell, the main reason for not touching her, was front and center in my mind. Ben.

My best friend's sister was not for me. No matter how badly I wanted to taste her lips or grab her hips to watch her skin flush pink. She was forbidden fruit.

I'd fucked up too many times to let myself be tempted now. Not when my one and only friendship was on the line.

With immense regret, I stepped back. And then again.

My gaze never left her face as I grabbed my dick and strangled it into submission. She stood there like a siren, her nipples beaded into tight buds I wanted to get my mouth on. Instead, without a single word, I turned and hobbled past her, not stopping until I reached my room and shut the door behind me. I rested my head back against the wood and let myself feel the physical ache from turning her down.

Fuck me, I almost crossed a serious line with Annie tonight.

Tate looked over. I could have sworn he made a face at me. If dogs could talk, he would have simply said one word. The same one that was tumbling through my brain.

Dumbass.

CHAPTER FOURTEEN

$\mathcal{A}$nnie

I SLEPT LIKE SHIT.

Which was becoming a habit lately. It was either Juan Carlos bellowing about his balls, or Blaze showing me his. Okay, fine, he never showed me his balls per se, but I had seen them. And last night, I'd felt the moment his cock grew hard. I'd watched it transform right in front of my eyes, tenting his boxers and awakening something in me that I'd been pushing down and ignoring with all my might. But it was no use.

I wanted on that damn pleasure train.

With Blaze.

The moment alone with him at midnight had shown me that his dick was like my very own Pinocchio. Blaze had told me to leave, but his dick said otherwise.

I wiped my forehead, feeling like a transformation had happened overnight. I'd gone from harboring a supersecret crush on my brother's best friend to realizing he actually wanted me back. If it wasn't for the layer of nervous sweat coating my skin,

I'd feel like an absolute bombshell of a woman. Maybe, just maybe, I could coax Blaze to cross that line with me.

It was that thought that got me out of bed before sunrise and at the clinic before Blaze woke up. I got busy setting up all the last-minute things for the clinic, my brain elsewhere. When I found myself cleaning the same exam room table for the third time, I threw down the disinfectant bottle and headed for Coffee. This called for emergency coffee, even if it cost more than my current budget allowed for.

The usual morning line was already dwindling by the time I took my position. My gaze went out the window as my brain spun, reliving that moment with Blaze in the kitchen. Shelby Thorn was on a ladder outside her flower shop, hanging ribbons from her shop's sign. I blinked, remembering the Grunion Run Parade was this weekend. I forgot about that. I also forgot how Shelby said she was slammed with work considering the parade committee had hired her to do all the flowers for the pageant afterward. Yes, Auburn Hill dressed up teen girls at a parade about fish. We were weird like that.

"What can I get you?"

I spun back around and saw that it was my turn to order. Dante, the barista behind the counter, gave me a patient smile. He'd been working here for as long as I could remember.

"Hey, Dante. Sorry for spacing. Can I get two of the nitro coffees, please?"

He rang up my order and I moved over to wait for my coffees. I'd ordered one for Shelby too. Poor thing was working so hard to spread the word about her new flower shop. Even though she was new in town, she was quickly becoming a good friend, maybe because I recognized that entrepreneurial spirit in her. Female business owners had to stick together.

"Did you see Blaze leaving physical therapy yesterday? Even in a leg brace, that man is hot."

The excited whisper hit my ears and I froze. I slowly turned, trying to look nonchalant as I shamelessly eavesdropped. Two women whom I'd gone to school with were waiting for their coffees just a few feet from me. They'd been one year older than me.

The leggy brunette with the outfit of an Instagram model answered her friend. "I was thinking he might be at the parade this weekend. Might be a good opportunity to run into him."

The blonde with boobs spilling out of her top—and boy was I jealous of her gorgeous curves—answered. "Accidentally, of course." Then she laughed with her friend. "I don't think that man has ever cracked a smile, but I don't care. He can frown at me all he wants while he gives me multiple orgasms."

My jaw dropped. I wasn't a redhead for nothing. Anger and jealousy bubbled up my spine like a tidal wave of red-hot lava listening to these two women who didn't even know Blaze. They talked about him as if he was an expensive handbag to be seen with for the weekend. I took a step forward to say something, but froze when they continued.

"I heard he dated Danette way back when. She's never talked about it except to imply that she trained him." The brunette rolled her eyes. "Obviously she didn't do a very good job since he moved away. I'm just glad he's back. Out of all the Hellman brothers, he's the mysterious one. The one you just want to crack, you know?"

"You know how much I love a good mystery," the blonde simpered.

Their names were called and they walked away with their coffees, taking their stupid conversation with them. The happy little dream bubble I'd been in this morning burst. It had felt like it was just Blaze and me living together and no other outside forces involved. But that was insane. This was Hell after all. Gossip and shenanigans were daily occurrences here. If I wanted to get Blaze's attention, I needed to make my move now before the vultures started circling.

But let's be honest. I couldn't compare to those two ladies. They had style, confidence, and buxom good looks. I had freckles, skinny legs, and a penchant for talking too much on occasion. The only thing I had going for me was that I was beginning to understand Blaze.

He wasn't just a mystery to be solved. He was a human being who'd been seriously injured on the job and had to rehabilitate himself while also creating a new career path. Not an easy task. And despite his silence on the subject, I knew something had happened to make him leave Hell in the first place. Whatever it was had changed him. And I wanted to know why. Not to solve the mystery of Blaze, but to help him overcome whatever psychological damage it had done.

He wasn't a puzzle to solve. He was a human.

A very hot one.

I got my two coffees, delivered one to Shelby who profusely thanked me from atop her ladder, and then headed back to my clinic to get to work. If Grandma Donna and Nikki were going to throw a grand opening party, I needed to get my shit together. And I needed the time to sort out my feelings.

Two hours later I had the instruction manual spread out on the floor of the back exam room, cursing at the X-ray machine that wasn't communicating with the remote. I'd already given myself enough radiation exposure from trial and error today to ensure I'd pick up a radio station from across the country.

"Why are you not working?" I whined at the remote. It didn't answer me, unfortunately.

"I'm on a break, jeez."

My head snapped up. Addy, Meadow, and Cricket stood in the doorway with cheesy grins on their faces.

"Ladies!" I threw down the remote and jumped to my feet to give my best friends a group hug. "What are you guys doing here?"

I backed up and waved them inside the expansive back exam room. Addy headed for the stall bars Blaze and his brothers had moved for me. Meadow zeroed in on the X-ray machine. Cricket had a seat on the floor and lay there spread eagle. The four of us had bonded the last two years, finding adult friendship that we hadn't had when we were in high school.

"I can't do one more perm on an old lady or I'm going to scream," Cricket groaned. "When I opened up my own salon, I envisioned bridal updos, balayage, colors the world has never seen before, even an undercut or two, but all I've done is perms and sets!"

I chuckled. "Are you just now realizing the cool kids move away from Hell once they grow up?"

Cricket groaned again. "I go to bed smelling like ammonia. I think it's embedded in my pores."

The X-ray machine whirred to life. I looked over to see Meadow's bare foot up on the plate while she hit buttons on the remote. The damn thing clicked and her foot materialized on the screen above her head.

"Hey! How'd you do that?" I'd been dealing with that remote for an hour with zero results. "Also, you should be wearing the lead apron."

Meadow shrugged. "Just hit a couple buttons and bam. There's my foot in all its bony glory. Also, I go through the metal detector every day for work. I'm probably radioactive at this point. What's a little more?"

Meadow worked at the prison on the outskirts of town. She saw things most humans didn't and still managed to be a normal woman. Well, as normal as Meadow could be.

I looked over at Addy to finally get an answer as to what they were doing here, but she had both legs up on the stall bars in the splits.

"Oh shit, that looks painful." I grimaced.

Meadow came up next to me. "She's such a showoff."

"You know I heard you can break your hooha doing that shit," Cricket said from the floor.

Addy looked over her shoulder at us, a serene smile on her face. "Having a strong and flexible pelvic floor is actually one way to have better orgasms."

Meadow hustled over to the bars. "Move over, bitch."

We all laughed, especially when Meadow couldn't even get both legs up on the bars, let alone try for the splits. We finally all joined Cricket on the floor.

"Not that I'm not grateful, but what's with the visit?"

Meadow, the speaker of the group, laid it out for me. "Grandma Donna has asked us all to help with your grand opening. We didn't feel comfortable agreeing until we knew this was what you wanted. We know she can get a little carried away."

I loved my friends, and especially now, when they showed they understood me better than anyone. "I appreciate that, believe me. I know how insane she can get at times, but yes, I'm fine with the grand opening. I wasn't at first, but Blaze convinced me to do it."

"Blaze, huh?" Addy pounced and I realized my mistake.

I hadn't told them I'd moved into Ben's place. Or that Blaze was living there also. I probably should have, considering Addy was engaged to Ace, Blaze's older brother. And Cricket was best friends with Callan, Blaze's younger brother.

"So, I kind of forgot to tell you..." I began.

"Spill it, woman," Meadow snapped.

So I did. I told them every last detail, and by the time I was done, Cricket's mouth was hanging open, Addy was shimmying her shoulders in some weird dance that would probably cause a rain shower by this afternoon, and Meadow was looking at me like I just announced I moved in with Magic Mike.

"So...you *like* him, like him?" Meadow asked, a devious grin forming.

"No," I answered, my face blazing bright red.

Cricket nearly peed her pants with her tinkling laughter. "Your face says something else, sweetheart."

I rolled my eyes. "Fine. I kind of do. But it wasn't until last night that I realized maybe he could be feeling the same way. Now I'm not sure what to do about it."

"Do about it?" Meadow practically shouted. "You grab that

man and plant one on him. Make him realize how much he wants you. Make your move, mama!"

I looked down at my sneakers. "I kind of tried last night and he told me I should leave."

Meadow snorted. Addy reached across the circle and put her hand on my arm. "I'm about to marry his older brother, but even I can't say I truly understand Blaze. He's complicated, mostly because he's quiet and always in his head. I do know those boys are good people. He's probably not wanting to cross a line with you due to his friendship with Ben. So you'll have to do the heavy lifting here to get things started."

"You need a plan," Cricket added helpfully.

"A seduction plan!" Meadow hollered.

"Did I hear seduction?" Another female voice sounded from the doorway. I really needed to start locking the front door to the clinic.

All heads spun to see Lucy Sutter standing in the doorway of the exam room. She had a huge bag slung over her shoulder. It looked like one of those giant purses moms wear to haul all their kid's crap in.

"Lucy!" Meadow hopped to her feet to hug her. Lucy was married to Bain, who happened to be Meadow's boss at the prison. "How are you?"

"I'm great. Just coming by to see when this clinic will be open." She looked over at me. "My girls want to get a bearded dragon and I refuse to get one until we have a local vet."

I stood too. "I should be open in two weeks. We'll have a grand opening party, which you're invited to, of course."

She beamed at me. "Excellent. Now, who needs help with a seduction plan? I'm a bit of a matchmaker, you know." Lucy elbowed Meadow.

Meadow's smile froze. "Yeah, you definitely got involved with Judd and me." We all remembered how Lucy kept pushing the two of them together. Of course, it had all worked out. All you had to do was watch Meadow's face when someone said Judd's name. She melted like an ice cream cone in the middle of summer.

"It's Annie," Cricket said. I shot her a glare. "What? You need a plan."

"I don't know the man in this scenario..." Lucy trailed off hopefully but I kept my lips zipped. "But the right clothes, a little bit of ambiance, and a solid line is always a good start. Play up your natural assets and then be confident. You can screw up so much, but confidence will cover all that."

"That's actually not bad advice," Addy said. "Although, I'd add that going topless always helps. A nice pair of laser beams will stun him long enough for you to go in for the kill."

"Wow, Addy, that's surprisingly violent advice coming from you." Although I remembered that being topless was how she and Ace connected and now look at the rock on her ring finger.

"I could help so much more if I knew who we were talking about here." Lucy looked from face to face. When none of us gave up Blaze's name, she pouted. "Fine. But call me if you need reinforcements. This kind of thing is my jam."

"Okay, well, thank you." I patted her on the back and walked out of the room, hoping they'd all follow me. I loved my friends, but I needed to get back to work if that grand opening was going to come together.

And I needed to formulate a seduction plan in my head before I went home. It probably wouldn't work, knowing Blaze's level of stubborn, but then again, maybe I needed to look less at his harsh facial expressions and more at his dick, his own personal lie detector test.

CHAPTER FIFTEEN

laze

SMALL MIRACLES, like Annie being gone from the house when I woke up the next morning and Tate picking up yet another command after only thirty minutes of work on it, had made today a damn good day. I'd made myself walk down the street without my crutches. A few neighbors had waved to me as I went, but I didn't know who the hell they were. It was weird being back in Hell. I'd almost forgotten how friendly people could be outside of the city.

But as the afternoon ticked away, nerves began to kick up at how things would be between Annie and me when she got home. I'd barely slept last night, only to have a nightmare about the entire town of Hell walking in on me when I had my hand down Annie's skimpy pajama shorts. My watch had gotten stuck on the drawstring and I couldn't get it out. I didn't even wear a fucking watch and now I certainly never would.

I was attempting to make a chicken stir-fry for dinner when I heard Annie's ridiculous car backfire its way into the driveway.

My plan to act natural, like my cock hadn't tried to grow out of my boxers and find the heat between her thighs last night in the kitchen, was already failing. My ears were tuned to every noise, picking up the keys jangling as she got out of the car. The car door slamming. Her tennis shoes jogging up the stairs of the porch. I turned down the heat on the stove. I wasn't doing a repeat of the burned tater tots.

The door opened and then closed. I heard Annie's bag hit the ground and then the pad of her feet as she walked past the kitchen to her room. That was odd. Where was the cheesy "honey, I'm home" that made a smile slide onto my face?

"Annie?" I called out, giving dinner a stir.

"Yeah?"

"Everything okay?" I cringed. Dumbass. Of course she's not okay. Your dick was feeling her up last night when she was just trying to get a glass of water. She had every right to be pissed at me.

But this was Annie and I'd always protected her. I teased her to the point of almost crying, but I always looked out for her. A kid stole her *Squid Girl* eraser one year and I'd had a talk with him the next day. He'd not only given it back but bought her a set of all the characters in eraser form. I didn't even know what the hell a *Squid Girl* was, but it made Annie cry, so I set him straight.

Unfortunately, I was the bully this time. I'd made Annie so uncomfortable she wasn't chatting a mile a minute like usual. I slammed the wooden spoon down on the counter and squeezed my eyes shut. Silence came from the direction of the bedrooms. Fuck. She couldn't even answer me. I needed to go apologize.

I turned the burner off and limped my way across the kitchen, only to run right into Annie as she came around the corner.

"Oof!" She bounced off me, but I grabbed her just like last night. Her smile was a little wobbly around the edges, but she didn't look pissed at me.

"We have to stop meeting this way," I grumbled, still feeling like an asshole and wondering how to apologize for last night when I was pretty sure just the scent of her shampoo wafting up between us was enough to get my dick to start the very same bullshit that got me in trouble to start with.

I let go of her arms and shuffled back a step. Then I noticed what she was wearing. Even shorter shorts clung to her shapely thighs and don't get me started on the top. It was sheer black lace, her nipples perfectly outlined, straining to get through as if it was arctic in here instead of a normal seventy degrees.

"Fuck, Annie..." I groaned, dropping my head. How the hell was I supposed to survive this kind of torture?

She swept around me, heading into the kitchen as if she wasn't practically naked. "Let's make dinner. I'm starving!"

"Me too," I grumbled under my breath, turning around and instantly regretting it. The backside of her shorts made her nipples seem tame by comparison. The woman didn't have the largest breasts, a fact I caught her lamenting in the mirror one day after she hit puberty. I teased her relentlessly about being flat chested, even when she wasn't really. She just had athletic boobs. Enough to jiggle when she walked without a bra on—which she did a hell of a lot—and that seemed enough to make a man wild with lust if the tent pole in my pants was any indication.

But her ass? Fucking hell, it was perfect. Pert round glute muscles with just enough womanly curves to make my hands itch to grab hold and never let go. And those shorts didn't even cover the bottom curve where her ass hit the top of her thighs. I wanted to trace my finger along the crease and watch her shiver. Then again, if I did that, she'd probably slap me. And rightly so.

"I'm so glad you started dinner. I could eat a whole cow." Annie was chatting away and all I could do was stare at her ass like the fucking jerk I'd somehow become. "Let's class it up with place settings, shall we?"

And then she bent over, opened the lower cabinet door, and

rooted around for fucking place mats. With her ass in the air like an invitation.

I squeezed my eyes shut and spun around to get the hell out of there and instead ran right into the fucking doorframe. Pain lit up my face and shoulder.

"Fuck."

"Blaze? Are you okay? Oh my God, let's get you some ice." Annie's hands steered me over to the chair at the little table, pushing me down until I sat. Tate scrambled around, finally settling down at my feet, probably thinking it was dinnertime, and if he was a really good boy, he'd get some table scraps.

I kept my eyes closed, not because of the pain, but to block out the sight of Annie practically in her birthday suit. I also prayed for the patience of a monk. I was going to need that chaste vibe to get through the night without doing something I'd regret later.

"Here." Annie plopped down on my good leg and I lurched forward in shock. My eyes flew open to see her just a few inches away, an ice pack headed for my face. I didn't know what to do with my hands, so I let them dangle at my side. Her nipples were literally just inches away, taunting me to touch them.

"Annie." Words were hard to squeeze past my throat.

She pulled the ice pack from my throbbing eye and traced her finger across my cheek. Her blue eyes held so much concern I felt like an ass for where my brain had gone. "Did you get your cheek too?"

I swallowed hard, grasping for any mundane thought that might get my dick to settle down. How could she not feel that? I was harder than the fucking crane I'd fallen off of on the movie set and she was sitting right on it. I was going to hell for this. Shit, I was already in hell, feeling her lush curves pressed against me and not able to do anything about it.

"Blaze?" Annie whispered.

My eyes flew open and she licked her lips, somehow even closer.

Fuck. Me.

I lifted my hand to push her back and somehow found myself settling my palm against the dip of her waist. She sucked in a deep breath, her eyes melting right in front of me. My other hand joined the first, my pinky finger celebrating the top curve of her ass. I dropped my head to her shoulder and let out a groan.

If she didn't push me away, I was about to do things that couldn't be undone. Why wasn't she pushing me away?

"You should probably go." The words tasted like a dirty lie, but I said them anyway.

I heard the ice pack hit the table and then her hands were in my hair. She gripped my hair hard and yanked my head up. Pain bloomed across my scalp but it was nothing compared to the burn that had started up inside my body, knowing I wanted Annie more than I wanted to live to see another day.

Her eyes had lost that hazy look. In fact, they looked down-right pissed. Good. It was about time she was pissed at me. I steeled myself for her to let me have it. For her to jump off my lap in disgust. For Ben to come home and kick my ass for even thinking about his little sister that way.

Her perfect lips parted. "I don't think I should."

And then she laid her lips on mine and stunned the reply right out of my mouth. She didn't waste time and the woman knew how to kiss. Her teeth nipped at my lower lip and then she was back to slanting her lips across mine. My hands gripped her waist tighter, and holy fucking shit, my cock grew painfully tight under her squirming ass. Her tongue swiped at my lip and I opened my mouth to plunge my tongue inside hers without even thinking about what I was doing. I was running on instinct and hormones, a deadly combination when my brain turned off.

Hands combed through my hair, fingernails scraping across my scalp. Goose bumps formed along my skin. My hands began to roam, one up to her straining nipple to provide it relief in the form of my fingertips, and the other down to her ass, confirming that squeezing it was exactly as wonderful as I imagined.

She made a little noise in the back of her throat and lust surged forward so strong I gripped her hips and repositioned her without breaking away from her mouth. She knew what I wanted and helped pull one of her legs to the other side of the chair as it groaned from our weight. Now straddling me, warm heat between her thighs ground down on my erection. Her arms wound around my neck and held us together so tightly it felt like she thought I'd run away. As if I'd wish to be anywhere else except plastered to this woman.

The kiss went on and on, neither of us coming up for air. I lost track of time altogether. I wasn't even Blaze Hellman, kissing his best friend's little sister. I was just a man, lost in the best kiss of his life, trying to get closer to a woman who turned him inside out with just a blue-eyed glance. A woman who was kissing him back with the same level of enthusiasm he felt for her.

My hand slid down from Annie's waist to under the waistband of her shorts. Her skin was so silky smooth I hoped my callouses wouldn't hurt her. Annie's hips undulated just right, providing friction to the tip of my cock wedged between us. My hand left her ass to slide over her hip and down the front of her shorts. My fingers found the source of the heat, parting her and sliding down into silky wetness. Some primitive part of me grunted and beat my chest for having this effect on her.

Annie gasped, her mouth leaving mine as she reared back. My eyes flew open and I saw the lost look on her face. Her cheeks were bright red, her eyes so unfocused I wasn't sure if she even saw me any longer. Even her hair was a mess, though I couldn't remember having my hands in it. Her lips were wet and swollen, a little pink from my beard.

And there was my hand. Down Annie's shorts.

Just like my dream.

CHAPTER SIXTEEN

nnie

IF HEAVEN COULD BE FOUND in Hell, it was here on Blaze's lap, his lips all over my skin, his rough hands stroking every inch of me. He was hard as steel, the feel of his cock under me turning my body into a single pulsating nerve ending. I was so close to orgasming from dry humping him. I just needed a few more seconds.

And then his fingers found my clit and all that pleasure ramped up into something so explosive the top of my head was in danger of imploding. I'd made out with guys before, and certainly had sex, but those occasions were like blending up oatmeal and calling it ice cream. There was absolutely no comparison.

Then hell came crashing back in. He froze and I whimpered, rotating my hips against his fingers. Just. Need. A. Little. More.

His fingers suddenly disappeared and I had to blink my eyes a few times to pull him into focus. The look on his face instantly shut down the pleasure train barreling down on me. He looked horrified.

Blaze stood up, nearly dumping me on the floor. At the last second, he grabbed my arms and pulled. My feet found the floor and no sooner did I grasp for the table to hold me upright than he was out the door. At the doorway to the living room he spun back around. His hand lifted and he pointed at me angrily, his mouth opening and then closing again.

He grit his teeth, looking impossibly sexy. His cock tented the entire front of his jeans. His hair was mussed from running my hands through it. Even his shirt was askew on his massive upper body.

But his face. Fuck. His face had shut down entirely.

He spun and stormed out of the room without a word. A few seconds later I heard his bedroom door slam. My body sagged against the table, and even Tate whined from underneath it, sensing that something both wonderful and terrible had happened.

My fingers skated across my lips, feeling them as if for the first time. I swallowed hard and tried to tamp down the leftover want that pulsed through my body. I'd never experienced a kiss like that. So wild and out of control, lacking finesse but so much better for what it represented: two people so into each other the kiss was as natural as the dirt in the hole I was about to go bury myself in.

I squeezed my eyes shut and felt humiliation squeeze all the excitement out of my limbs. I shot my shot and got shot down. Simple as that. And now living here with Blaze was going to be a lesson in torture and unrequited longing.

"Shit," I muttered under my breath, falling into the chair and trying to get my brain to focus on next steps. Did I act like nothing happened? Bury my true desires under a blanket of humiliation? Try again?

Tate put his front paws on the edge of the chair and stared

up at me with his deep brown eyes. I pet his head and wondered what the hell just happened.

"Sometimes I wish I was a dog. I'd just get fixed and lick my own butt when I needed a little excitement in my day."

Tate licked my hand and I bent to pick him up. I could use some snuggles from someone who held no judgement. The problem was, kissing Blaze was nothing like I expected when I planned this little seduction scene. It was better. The best kiss I'd ever had. He threw himself into it like he'd die if he didn't taste me.

And then he threw cold water in my face by leaving.

I took Tate into the kitchen and saw that we'd ruined dinner again. I put Tate down and rescued what was left of the stir-fry in the pan, putting some on a plate for Blaze. I wasn't sure if I hated him because he'd basically ruined me for any other man on the planet, but I couldn't let a fellow human go hungry because of me.

I covered the plate and tiptoed to his room. I put his dinner on the floor and rushed into my own room to change into long flannel pajamas. When I was settled in bed and Tate was curled up next to me, I texted Blaze.

Me: I left dinner outside your door.

Several minutes passed and I died a slow death waiting for a response. Was he ignoring me? Or did he just not have his phone with him? I tried again.

Me: I have a shipment of meds coming early tomorrow morning, so I can't take you to PT...sorry.

Several minutes passed and I was about to put my phone down and stare at the ceiling all night instead of sleep, when an answering text came in.

Blaze: Okay

I glared at my phone, wishing it a long and painful death. Okay? Okay?? All that sexy times in the kitchen and then I get an "okay"?

Not okay, mister!

I slammed my phone down on the bedside table, not even caring at this point if he could hear me. He deserved to have his sleep disturbed by my wrath. "Okay" was the shittiest word in the dictionary. Be annoyed. Be ecstatic. Hell, be bitter and bitchy. But never be okay. Okay was the vanilla of thirty-one flavors. The sand in the crotch of your swimsuit after a great day at the beach. The deep sea documentary when the new season of Bridgerton was waiting to be binged.

Tate whined and I tried to take my steaming down a notch. Sprouting a gray hair or losing a month of my lifespan over Blaze and his bullshit "okay" answer was not acceptable.

"Come here, buddy." I pulled Tate in closer, laying my cheek on his soft little head. "At least you won't push me away."

And there I lay for the next few hours until sleep finally took me away into a sleepless zone where a certain Hellman brother wasn't stirring me into a sexual frenzy and then leaving me high and dry. Or wet, as it were.

The sun hadn't even come through the holes in the blind slats when I threw the covers back. I found my most comfortable pair of scrubs and rushed through the process of getting ready. When I crept through the house, the plate of dinner I'd left Blaze was still outside his door. I was hungrier than a bee in a tulip field, but I'd have to wait and get something at Coffee. No way was I spending one more second in this house with Blaze and his dark cloud of confusion.

My anger had settled overnight, leaving me with a sad realization that Blaze didn't have the courage to take what he wanted. He wanted me, of that I was certain. But whatever bullshit he had in his head was holding him back, and I was not in the mood to shovel bullshit.

Maybe later.

If he asked nicely.

I whistled as I unlocked the front door of the clinic, refusing to let Blaze and his pile of shit rain on my parade. I had ten days left to get my clinic in order before the grand opening party. And what I texted him was true. I had an early morning shipment coming in. All the meds I'd need to start up my clinic. This shipment had weighed down my credit card more than all the textbooks in college, so you bet your ass I was going to be here to make sure every last pill and salve I paid for was delivered.

I was knee deep in stocking all the little bottles and tubes of medicine behind the check-in counter when a voice called out from the front door.

"Yoohoo!"

I stood, rubbing my low back and stomping my feet to get feeling back in them. Yedda stood in my doorway, a yellow tabby with the cutest grumpy face I'd ever seen in her arms.

"Hey, Yedda, how are you?"

"Well, I'm fine, Annie, dear, but Sunshine isn't feeling so good." Yedda came all the way in, her neon-orange track suit lighting the way. "I know you're not open quite yet, but I didn't want to drive all the way to Blueball today. Not with my hip acting up. Can you look at her?"

I dusted off my hands. "Yedda, how does it feel to be my first customer?"

She grinned so wide I saw where her dentures ended. "Feels quite natural, actually. You've been part of Auburn Hill for so long it always felt odd to take my beloveds to another town. I'm glad you're opening your clinic, dear."

I took Sunshine out of her arms, amused when the cat intensified her frown. She must have gotten her name in the same way that large men were called Tiny. "What seems to be wrong with this little ray of sunshine today?"

"See her eyes? They're so goopy. I already cleaned them out once today and have the scratches to prove it." Yedda pulled up the sleeves of her jacket to show a couple red lines that must have stung.

I winced. "Let's see what I can do." I brought them back to the first exam room and took a look at Sunshine's eyes, dodging the swipes of her claws. It was a pretty easy diagnosis of an eye infection. I managed to get drops in her eyes and handed Yedda a bottle with five pills to hide in her food, one each day.

"This should fix her right up. Come back next week if she's still having issues."

Yedda held Sunshine close to her chest while the cat gave me death glares. The thing kind of reminded me of Blaze, to be honest. The thought of which made my heart hurt. I could help Blaze, just like I'd helped Sunshine, if he'd just quit swiping at me and let me in.

"What do I owe you?" Yedda asked, suddenly looking quite frail.

"Nothing at all! You're my celebratory first customer, remember? Just tell your friends about me." I walked with her to the front of the clinic.

Yedda patted my cheek with a liver-spotted hand. "You're a good egg, Annie McLachlin."

A thought occurred to me. "Hey, Yedda?"

"Yes, dear?"

"Why do you like cats so much?" I'd grown up knowing she was the crazy cat lady, but I'd never understood why.

Yedda's face went dreamy, the kind of face people make when they talk about the one subject that lights their soul on fire. "I adopted a cat the year before I got married. Did you know I was married?" She carried on before I could answer. "Well, he left, the no-good, rotten cheat. And that cat was with me for another fifteen years. Other men came and went but that cat was my ride or die. If a cat can bring that much love over that long of time, they deserve to be treated better than a spouse, don't you think?"

Yedda shot me a wink and sailed out of the clinic, nearly catching Sunshine's tail in the door when the door swung shut and she was still shuffling out.

I sat there staring out at the occasional car that drove by on Main Street, thinking that if things didn't improve in my own love life, I might have to consider adopting a cat. Snuggling with Tate last night had been therapeutic. Although the fact that I was coming to understand Yedda's inner workings was making me a bit nervous. It was just a quick slide into "crazy cat lady" territory.

I blinked out of my musings and checked the time. Blaze would be at physical therapy right now. I pressed a hand to my stomach to stop the automatic buzz that took flight there every time I thought of that maddening man.

If I rushed home right now, I could have almost an hour of time at home without Blaze. I could grab that vibrating toy I'd bought at the Hardware Store when Addy and I visited a few months ago. Give it a spin to ease some of the ache Blaze had caused and then not finished. Maybe a quick release would cut down on the sexual buzzing and let me be around Blaze without losing focus.

Without giving myself time to talk myself out of it, I grabbed my purse, locked the clinic, and made my way home. If Blaze couldn't give me the orgasm I needed, I would have to take things into my own hands. And for the next thirty minutes or so, I had the house to myself. No worries about anyone else hearing me. I could moan, even chant Blaze's name and there was no one around to make me feel embarrassed. I was going to set that vibrator on high, baby.

CHAPTER SEVENTEEN

laze

I HAD to splash water on my face to wake up the next morning. I'd spent most of the night alternating between straining to hear Annie in her bedroom and flagellating myself mentally for kissing her.

And fuck. That kiss.

I'd kissed plenty of women before. Beautiful women. Short women, tall women, women with all colors of hair and skin. I'd kissed women who I had feelings for and I'd kissed women who were just a drunk distraction without a name. But absolutely none of that had prepared me for the kiss with Annie.

For the first time in my life, I lost myself completely in the moment. It wasn't just the incredible pleasure that had coursed through my body as I inhaled her scent and taste. No, it was more than that. I'd actually craved to be with her. To throw off all desire to hole up by myself, as was my nature. When was the last time I preferred to be around someone instead of alone?

Everything about last night had left me off-balance. I'd

crossed a line in the bro code. Ben would kick my ass if he knew I kissed Annie. If he knew how I was thinking of her right this very second.

I stared at myself in the bathroom mirror, water dripping through what was left of my beard and into the sink. The brown eyes were the same. The beard that always needed trimming was familiar. The scars were all as I remembered. As much as I knew I should feel guilty for kissing Annie, there was not one ounce of remorse in me. I regretted nothing. And I would never apologize for it despite knowing I'd betrayed my best friend. Who the fuck was this man staring back at me?

My phone dinged and I glanced down, seeing that Ethan had texted me. He was here to pick me up and take me to physical therapy. I hobbled out of the bathroom and pulled a T-shirt over my head as I left the house. Ethan waved to me from the front seat of his beat-up truck. I'd quit asking the brother group chat for rides. I just went direct to Ethan. At least I had one available brother who didn't give me shit for asking for help.

I climbed in and put on my seat belt.

"Hey, bro. You happen to have any wood glue on you?"

Ethan gave me a funny look as he pulled out onto the street and headed for town. "Yeah, probably got some in the cross box." He tossed his head in the direction of the back of his truck. "Building a birdhouse in your free time?"

I screwed up my face. "Yeah, just what the town of Hell needs. A fucking birdhouse to feed the seagulls."

Ethan laughed. "Dude, did you hear what happened to Penelope yesterday?"

I shook my head. "You sound like Mom. All excited over the town gossip."

Ethan whacked me in the shoulder. "This shit is actually funny. She was in the middle of giving Amelia Jackson a parking ticket for her bumper being an inch over the line of the crosswalk on Main Street. I guess a seagull was hovering as they do, and one of Amelia's sisters tried to stop Penelope. She put the rest of her half-eaten hot dog on top of Penelope's head and the seagull swooped faster than Penelope could swipe it off. Damn thing bit so hard and fast Penelope's hair came clean off."

"Oh shit," I mumbled. That was funny, but also kind of mean. Penelope was just doing her job.

Ethan was laughing so hard, he barely got the words out around the gasps. "No, it wasn't her hair...it was...a...wig!"

I couldn't help a grin as I listened to Ethan wheeze-laugh. "Please tell me someone got a picture of the seagull flying off with a wig attached to its beak."

"Somebody not only got a picture, but I've already seen some memes."

"This town, man," I drawled, a weird sense of comfort rolling through me. This town was crazy, but it was home.

When we got to physical therapy, Ethan rooted around his work box and tossed me a bottle of wood glue. I evaded his questions, knowing there was no way in hell I could tell him that Annie and I had cracked one of the spindles on Ben's chair when she kissed the hell out of me last night. Which, of course, got me thinking about that kiss again.

Ronnie put me through my warmups, and when I paused in the middle of my first set of exercises, gaze trained out the window, lost in my own world, he let out a heavy sigh.

"Are you even here today?" He whacked me on the shoulder.

I blinked back to the present and rubbed my shoulder. What was with all the violence this morning? "Yeah, I'm here."

Ronnie gave me a look that guaranteed more squats than I ever wanted to do. "Dude, go home. You're ahead of schedule with your recovery anyway. And here, do these exercises at home and I won't tell your mama you slacked off today."

I gaped at him. "You'd tell my mama?"

Ronnie smirked. "You know it. Mamas in Hell are worse than siccing the devil on ya."

I shook my head, coming to my feet with one eye trained on

Ronnie at all times. "You're a scary motherfucker, you know that?"

He just grinned, confirming my belief. I hobbled out of the clinic and then realized I didn't have a ride. I had to call Ethan again who swore at me but said he'd be right there. That was the last straw. I was going to drive my SUV from now on. I'd just take the brace off to drive. I'd broken my femur, not my foot. Shouldn't be an issue. Ethan dropped me back off at Ben's and zoomed away.

Annie's car was in the driveway, making me pause. Why was she home? She'd been spending every waking hour at her clinic. Worry shot through me and I hustled up the porch steps, thinking something might be wrong. Despite the confusion that the kiss had added to our relationship, I would always be protective of Annie.

Tate greeted me, but didn't seem bothered, which I knew he would be if Annie was sick or hurt. That didn't seem to abate my panic though. She wasn't in the kitchen. Or in the living room. I went down the hallway to her bedroom, coming to a screeching halt at her doorway. Her door was wide open.

Fuck me running. I found Annie, all right.

She was lying on her bed, not a stitch of clothing on. One hand was on her own breast and the other was between her spread legs. Something bright pink vibrated in her hand. Her head was tossed back on her pillow, eyes screwed shut. She gasped, heat flooding up her neck and into her cheeks. I felt the inhale in my own body, everything in me tightening painfully. I was harder than a steel pipe before I took my next breath.

How could a man be expected to ignore that scene?

I'd tried to avoid her. I'd tried to tell myself she was off-limits. Hell, I'd tried to focus on how much she talked, highlighting everything that usually turned me off about a woman. Nothing worked.

Fuck this.

I was done resisting.

I stalked into the room, not a trace of a limp. I felt no pain. I didn't entertain a single thought of caution. I saw the woman I wanted sprawled out for my taking. A woman I knew wanted me back. And at least for today, we'd both get what we wanted.

Her eyes flew open and she gasped right as I reached her side. She tried to close her legs, but I was too fast. My hands held her open to my gaze. When I felt the muscles finally relax under my palms, I moved her hand, tossing her toy to the side. This pussy was mine now.

"Blaze." Annie sounded like she'd been running for miles.

I grabbed her tiny waist and pulled her to the side of the bed. Her gorgeous red hair streamed out on the mattress behind her. I dropped to my good knee, keeping my other leg out to the side and shouldered her legs wide open. She was wet already, a perfectly pink pussy waiting for my mouth. I swiped up the center of her, her taste blooming on my tongue and filling my senses. She yelled out my name, but other than an ear splitting "no," I wasn't stopping for shit.

I kissed her with every ounce of pent-up sexual desire that had been simmering between us since I moved in. There was nothing tame about the way she thrashed against the bed, her heels hitting me in the back. I attacked, letting the simmer turn into a boil. I kept my palm to her tight stomach, holding her in place for my mouth, my tongue, my chin. I gave her no rest, finding a rhythm of flicking and sucking that kept her chatting away above me. God, the woman could talk, even in the middle of sex. It made me smile against her flesh. I wanted to see if an orgasm shut her up.

I slid a single finger inside of her, my cock wishing it could be him, but I shut that thought down. This was about Annie. About giving her pleasure so overwhelming that I ruined her for other men. Yeah, I was that much of a bastard. If right now was all we ever got together, I'd make sure I was an imprint on her body.

Fuck, she tastes like heaven. Her slight body practically

vibrated around me. Her thighs clamped down around my head, her skin so smooth I wanted to rub my cheek across it and watch it bloom red. Instead, I added a second finger and sucked on her clit like it was the best thing I'd ever eaten.

And then the woman detonated. She screamed my name and shook like a leaf. Her hips bucked and I found myself fighting to stay facedown in her pussy. She was wild and out of control.

And yet somehow my plan backfired. Everything about this moment became imprinted on me.

"Blaze," she groaned, her body finally calming down, her screams more breathy groans.

I grinned still delivering light kisses against her thighs. Little love bites she'd see later tonight when she undressed. I guessed wrong. She wasn't quiet, even in the middle of an orgasm. I didn't know what I expected her to do next, but it wasn't to sit up and grab me by the hair. Annie leaned down into my face, her hair a tangled mess around her.

"I need more," she gasped.

I grinned harder. "I got more, baby."

She smiled so bright I lost the breath in my lungs. "Fucking give it to me, then."

I blinked and somehow I was on the bed, Annie beneath me and her legs wrapped around my waist as I kissed the hell out of her. Reality blacked out for long moments, the only thing tethering me to the present were her kisses and moans. We were both out of control, our hands tearing at my clothes until I was as naked as her. Teeth clashed in messy kisses that couldn't get us close enough to each other. I was teetering on the edge of slamming into her and blindly chasing my orgasm without a single ounce of finesse.

"Condom," I croaked.

Annie blinked and then moved faster than Tate when I dropped food in the kitchen. "Purse."

She rolled out from under me and jumped off the bed to grab

her purse off the floor. She pulled a packet out and dropped the purse again. "Let me do it."

She nudged my shoulder and I rolled to my back. She looked at me and licked her lips, looking like a kid in the candy store.

"Like what you see?" I said smugly.

Annie smacked my good leg. "You know I do." And then she was rolling the condom on my cock and I lost all other trains of thought. She straddled me and my cock jumped. "You good with me riding you? Spare your leg?"

I looked up at her, her gorgeous little tits beaded into tight buds, the skin at her hips already red from my hands, and her bottom lip being abused by her teeth as she gazed at me.

"Fuck, yeah. Do whatever you want to me, baby."

Annie didn't even hesitate. She lifted up, grabbed my cock, and pushed the head inside of her. Warmth surrounded me and I groaned. Fuck, if she didn't hurry up, I wouldn't be able to make this good for her. Annie's hands slapped down on my shoulders, her eyes round.

"You okay?" I asked, suddenly concerned. I was a lot bigger than her, and hell, I hadn't even asked about her past sexual history. Panic had my body freezing.

Annie swiveled her hips and another inch of me disappeared in her. "I'm fucking great," she drawled. "Just have to go slow to start."

The panic left me and the ego was back. "Why's that?"

Her gaze found mine again. "You know why."

I wiped my face and tried to look innocent even as she squeezed the hell out of my cock. "I'm afraid I don't. You better tell me."

Annie bit her lip again and sunk down further. We both let out a groan. "You're big, Blaze."

I tucked a lock of hair behind her ear and she turned quickly to nip at my thumb. Girl was a fucking wild cat in bed. A hot-tempered redhead who I wanted to tease almost as much as I wanted to fuck.

"Biggest you've ever been with?" Not that I wanted to even think of her with anyone else, but I needed to know.

Annie's eyes narrowed at me, but she sat up to take more of me. She was almost fully seated on my hips. Just another inch. "Maybe."

I sat up, pulling her into my chest, reveling in the feel of her naked body against me. "You want my huge cock to split you apart, baby?"

Her eyes lit up. "Oh shit. Give me all the dirty talk, Blaze."

Pleasure threatened to pull me under. "You like that? You want to hear how much I want to fuck your gorgeous pussy? How I want to push so far inside you that you scream my name?" Annie moved her hips, sliding me all the way inside. We both inhaled and I had the fleeting thought that I'd never felt better than I did in this exact second in time.

Annie let go of my shoulders and pushed me back until I was lying on the pillow behind me. "Keep talking and I'll keep riding."

I grinned and she grinned right back, keeping eye contact as she lifted off me and slammed back down. My hands found her hips and helped with the motion, finding a fast rhythm that had her hair flying and her hands scrabbling to perch on my chest. This position was like watching my own real live porno take place right in front of me.

My balls tightened painfully. Annie rode me like she'd been made for this. But it was my chest that got the biggest workout. It expanded with something far greater than lust for this woman.

"Has anyone ever told you how perfect you are?" I just said it, put it out there in the open. I was supposed to be talking dirty to her and I'd spilled my guts instead.

Annie's lips tilted up, just as her eyes glazed over and she sucked in a quick breath. Then her head tipped back and she moaned my name. Her pussy fluttered around me and I lost it, spilling into her without a choice. If Annie needed me, I was there.

CHAPTER EIGHTEEN

*A*nnie

BLAZE LIFTED HIS HEAD, gently pushing hair out of my face as I tried to blink back to consciousness against his chest. My cheek lay smashed against him as I sprawled on the bed because I didn't have the strength to reposition myself. I may have even drooled a little, but I was too spent to care. I'd be embarrassed tomorrow, when all the happy orgasm endorphins had faded away.

"Did I unalive you? I've never heard you so quiet." His chest bounced as he chuckled.

"Hmph?" Words were impossible.

His laughter eventually stilled, but his hand kept stroking through my hair. If I was one of Yedda's cats, I would have purred the house down. I didn't think I'd ever felt more content, more pleasured, more alive yet sleepy than I did at this exact moment.

When my muscles came back online and I was able to lift my head, I saw Blaze staring up at the ceiling. A sliver of unease ran through me. I could not have Blaze regretting what had been the best experience of my life.

"I can literally feel your brain vibrating right now." Blaze's gaze finally left the ceiling to peer down at me as I spoke. "Relax. Please. We're two consenting adults, okay?"

Blaze's jaw went hard and my hand automatically went up to smooth along his jawline. What was left of his beard tickled my hand. My other hand traced across his belly, watching the six-pack of muscles jump under my touch. A tiny trail of dark hair led lower, to the world's most perfect cock. A cock that was already hardening again under my gaze. Desperation flooded out the good feelings from before. One way to keep the good times rolling was to keep the sex going. I wrapped my fingers around his length and felt him grunt underneath me.

His hot length pulsed in my hand. I would have given it a solid tug to bring it fully back to life had it not been for the sound of the front door slamming. Every cell in my body froze. Blaze didn't even breathe. Then we were a blur of activity, Blaze grabbing the blanket at the foot of the bed and me rolling off the other side to land naked on the carpet between the bed and the window. My hip let out a shot of pain and my mouth let go of a squeal. I slapped two hands to my face to keep it together.

"Jesus, Joseph, and Mary!" Nikki Hellman's voice rang in the room. I could see her new kicks in the doorway from under the bed. "Are you still in bed at this hour? And what are you doing in Ben's room?"

Blaze cleared his throat and I had to roll my lips in to keep from bursting out in nervous laughter. "I, uh, wanted to test out his mattress."

"Naked?" Nikki sounded thoroughly disgusted and confused. "Well, I'm glad you have something covering you because—"

"Ooh, it's my lucky day!"

My jaw dropped open and little stars danced in front of my vision. Grandma Donna was here too. I saw her electric blue sandals walk across the room. In horror, I realized she was getting closer to Blaze. Naked Blaze. *My* Blaze.

But then the sandals stopped and her knees hit the carpet. Her face peered under the bed, glasses swinging and hitting the floor. "What are you doing down there, Annie? Did you lose your clothes too?"

I couldn't speak. Couldn't even swallow. What. The. Hell. Was. Happening?

Nikki burst out laughing. "Oh my!"

"Could we get some privacy, please?" Blaze bit out.

Grandma Donna's head lifted, thank the Lord for small miracles. It was kind of impossible to cover all the private bits here in this cramped space. "Fine. Take away all our fun."

"But we'll be in the living room when you find your clothes," Nikki added.

Grandma Donna made her way out of the room. "But no funny business!" she called over her shoulder.

"Too fucking late," Blaze grumbled.

I popped up, seeing the coast was clear. My face felt like it might have a fever. Maybe I was in shock. How could my best experience have gone to my worst in just a few short seconds?

Blaze threw back the blanket and climbed out of bed, taking care with his leg. If I was truly in shock, would I have paused to take in the magnificence of Blaze's naked ass? I mean, those rounded globes of muscle were a thing of beauty.

"Better get dressed. Those two won't leave until we talk about it."

I gaped at him. "We have to talk to them about having sex?"

Blaze pulled up his boxers and turned to face me. "Well, I doubt they're going to walk away from the week's best gossip unless we give them a compelling reason to keep quiet."

The blood left my face entirely. Oh shit. He was right. If Ben found out I'd slept with Blaze, he'd have an absolute conniption. He needed to hear it from us. See that we were serious about each other. Or maybe we weren't. I didn't exactly know because we hadn't had that conversation yet. Talk about bad timing.

I stood, a thrill poking through the horror in the way Blaze's gaze traced down my body before he turned his back to me with a furious glare. He could act like he didn't want me, but that ten inches of glorious cock I'd just ridden like a bucking bronco told me otherwise. I found my scrubs crumpled on the floor and pulled them on again. I needed to get this conversation over with. Then I could talk to Blaze and get things back on track before he had too much time to think things through. I knew how his brain worked. He'd find a way to suck out the happiness from what just happened and focus on the negative. I couldn't let him shut me down before we'd even gotten started. I'd gotten a taste of Blaze Hellman and I wanted an all-you-can-eat pass for more.

Blaze waited for me at the door of the bedroom, respectfully giving me his back. The whole thing felt like a scene out of my favorite Victorian romance novel, considering he'd just whispered deliciously devious things in my ear while he wrecked my body moments ago. Then again, I liked the way he always respected me. It's just that sometimes a girl wants to be a little dirty and disrespected in the bedroom, and now that I'd seen that side of him, I wanted more. A lot more.

"Let's get this over with." Blaze put his hand on my back, pushing me into the hallway. He grabbed my hand and pulled my thumbnail out from between my teeth. "Stop that."

I swatted his hand away and glanced over. "Did you want to put a shirt on first?"

"Nah. Maybe flexing the abs will keep your grandma from killing me."

He had a point. I'd never seen such bulky yet defined abs outside of an airbrushed advertisement for a gym with the word alpha in the title. Though I doubted Grandma Donna would kill him. She'd want to feel him up first.

"Well, there are the two lovebirds!" Nikki chirped as we entered the living room.

I sat down on the couch with Grandma Donna while Blaze leaned against the wall, his arms folded across his expansive chest. Nikki perched with her back straight in the recliner like some kind of queen, a little smile that spelled trouble on her face.

"More like bunnies with the way they were going at it," Grandma Donna added helpfully.

"Grandma!" I slapped my hand down on the couch.

"What? I'm happy to see you found the pleasure train." She shot me a wink that made me highly uncomfortable. I remembered the year she had the birds and bees talk with me. It had only created more confusion in my eight-year-old brain when she kept up the bird and bee metaphor throughout the whole explanation. I kept wondering if the bird would smother the bee because he was so much bigger. Or would the bee sting the bird if he got too aggressive? And why were birds and bees having sex? I'd never seen a bird-bee offspring. A biree? A beerd?

"Annie?"

"Huh?" I looked up to see all eyes on me. "Sorry, what?"

Blaze looked like he wanted to punch a hole through the drywall. The two ladies looked concerned to the point of making my cheeks heat, knowing I sat there looking like a girl who'd just gotten her world torn apart by a gorgeous man.

"Did Blaze take advantage of you?" Nikki asked gently.

"What? No!" I jumped to my feet and found myself next to Blaze. "Absolutely not. I'm not sure I want to have this conversation with y'all, but I have had sex before. If I didn't want to with Blaze, I would have said no and I know he would have stopped."

"Jesus, Mom," Blaze muttered. He wasn't even looking at me any longer either. He kept his gaze on the coffee table like he could incinerate it with just his laser stare.

"So Ben's okay with all this?" Nikki asked. I had to hand it to her, the woman did not back down from the hard questions.

"Ben doesn't know yet, so if you could both keep quiet about this, that would be great. In fact, I need to excuse myself to go call him right now." Blaze whipped around like he was actually going to leave me here with these two.

I grabbed his arm and he froze. "Wait! Don't you think I should be there for that conversation?"

"No."

I gaped at him. "No? Just...*no?*" I ran around to get in front of him and block his path to the bedrooms. "He's my brother!"

Oh, he was looking at me now, fire burning in those dark eyes. "He's my best friend."

"Congratulations. We know who Ben is," Nikki added dryly.

"Mom." Blaze looked ready to spit nails. He turned away from me. "I need you both to leave. Now."

Nikki stood, hands out in a gesture of peace. "Okay, son. Get your house in order and then come see me. We have things to discuss." She gave him a look that made me quake in my scrubs.

Grandma Donna followed Nikki out, tossing another wink over her shoulder as she went. "Oh, they're having a fight. You know the best way to make up?"

"Out!" Blaze called and the women didn't waste a second. The front door slammed and we were blessedly alone.

"Bye, thank you for coming!" I shouted, hoping they could hear me. A person should always offer pleasantries no matter what the situation.

The mood had veered drastically, the air thick with terse emotions that were mostly coming from Blaze. Ben was a big boy. He just needed to get over whatever archaic thinking that led him to believe I couldn't enjoy the anatomy Blaze had to offer.

But before I could open my mouth to say all that, Blaze swept by me, moving faster than a guy with a broken leg should. I caught up to him when he snatched the phone from his pants pocket in my bedroom. Ben's bedroom. Not that I was going to bring up that little fact right now.

"What are you doing?" I grabbed the phone from his hands and held it behind my back.

Blaze looked ready to ring my neck. "Stop being childish, Annie. I'm calling Ben."

"No, you're not." I took a step back, then another when Blaze stalked over like he intended to wrench the phone from behind my back. "You and I need to talk about *that*"—I pointed to the bed where the sheets were still rumpled—"before you talk to my brother about it. You owe me that much at least."

That caught him up short. Blaze glared at me with a war of emotions I couldn't pick apart. His jaw twitched as he stood there in silence. He must have come to some sort of decision because he stepped back and broke the staredown.

"Fine. I have to get in the shower first."

I frowned. Why must this man always walk away from me? He constantly retreated and I was sick of it. We just had mind-blowing sex! There was no reason for him to retreat any longer. "Why? Let's just talk."

Blaze stepped back in my space, the heat coming off his chest making me want to curl into him. Instinctively I knew that would not go over well right now. His face did not say snuggle time.

He dipped his head, the lines between his eyebrows deeper than I'd ever seen, which was saying something because he'd been born with a scowl on that face. "I can't have a conversation about how I fucked over my best friend while I still have the scent of you on my skin, Annie."

Oh.

Well, holy hell.

"Fine," I managed to mutter but he was already stalking away from me, snatching his clothes off the floor as he went. My door slammed and I lost sight of his fine form.

I stood there trying to catch my breath. The more my brain spun, the faster my heart rate went until I was just a few imaginary scenarios shy of having a full-blown panic attack. A cacophony of barking dogs interrupted my breakdown. Tate came running into the room, an excited yip from his own mouth.

"It's okay, boy. It's just my phone." I grabbed it off the bedside table and answered it without thinking, bending down to pet the puppy.

"Hello?"

"Annie. It's Ben."

The familiar deep voice had me squeezing my eyes shut. Talk about bad timing. My stomach swooped and Tate leaped up to plant a tongue swipe on my chin.

"Hey, brother. How is...wait. Where are you?" I had sudden visions of him heading home. As much as I loved my brother, that was the last thing Blaze and I needed today.

"I'm in Phoenix. Probably going to be here a bit longer, but I felt bad about leaving before we got a chance to talk. I'm just swamped with work."

I could hear explosions and possibly lasers in the background. You just never knew with Ben. For awhile there, when he was building his first game in high school, all I heard was farting noises coming from his room. I made the mistake of asking what he was doing out of concern for his digestive system. He was simply refining the sound the game made when a unicorn lifted its tail and shot out of its butt. I didn't ask questions after that.

"It's totally fine." I strained my ears to hear if Blaze was still in the shower. So far, the water was still running.

"I know you wanted a place to stay, but I already let Blaze take the guest room. Maybe when I get back we can go condo hunting for you? The clinic should be up and running soon, right? I can make the down payment and you can carry the monthly payments."

I sat down on the bed and blew out a breath. "That's super generous of you, Benji. I, um, I guess we can talk about that when you get back."

"Annie." His tone was that one he always took when he was

trying to talk logic to his little sister. The one that set my teeth on edge. Ben was a certifiable genius, but I was no slouch either. I didn't need things explained like I was still a little kid. "I have more money than I know what to do with. If I thought for one second you'd let me, I'd have already bought you a house outright. Just take the down payment."

"You know how I feel about handouts." I bit down on my thumbnail, chewing on what was left of it.

Ben sighed. "Well, you can't stay with me. Not with Blaze there. God, could you imagine?" He barked out a rueful laugh that had me feeling nauseous. "He's my best friend and I love him, but he's had a rough go in the female department. The last thing he needs is your natural happiness sending him spiraling off into depression. He needs to heal, physically and emotionally, and I won't have my sister involved in that."

"Yeah," I said weakly, not sure what I could possibly say to that insight into Blaze. I'd suspected as much, but I'd ignored my instincts the second I saw Blaze's gorgeous body.

"Let me just finish this project. Then, when I get home, we can work out the details of your living arrangements, okay? Can you hang on that much longer?"

The water in the bathroom turned off. Shit.

"Sure, Ben. Let me know when you think you're coming home." *Just in case I'm naked with your best friend.*

"Will do. Love you, Annette."

"Love you too, Benjamin the third."

His chuckle was the last thing I heard before he hung up.

I tossed the phone on the bed like it had bitten me. Shit, shit, shit. What were the odds that Nikki Hellman and Grandma Donna could keep their mouths shut about me and Blaze until Ben got home?

Or maybe keep our little secret forever?

CHAPTER NINETEEN

laze

THE WATER WAS ENTIRELY TOO hot, but I let it burn me. I deserved it and so much more for sleeping with Annie. Apparently, the time spent wallowing like a pig in mud hadn't been enough. I needed to fuck up my life in new ways to keep myself in this downward spiral of fuckery. It wasn't enough to lose my job, my career, my life in LA. No, I had to add losing my best friend to the mix. Because that was surely the only outcome to all of this.

I couldn't even blame it on the pain meds because I'd flushed those down the toilet last week. I'd let myself be led around by my dick, making decisions with the organ least likely to care about my long-term preservation. I'd fucked Annie and ultimately fucked myself.

The water started to turn cold, so I shut it off, yanking the towel off the wall and wrapping it around my waist. The mirror was fogged over and that was fine by me. I didn't want to see myself and have to examine what the hell I'd done. I was afraid if

I looked into my eyes long enough, I'd see the small thought in the back of my brain that I could not let myself entertain.

Part of me didn't regret a damn thing with Annie.

She was amazing in ways I could never have imagined. Her incessant talking made me smile inside, even as I frowned at her. She was happiness personified, always jumping in to help others when I would have told them to go to hell. For a few brief moments, when I sank into her heat and she surrounded my senses, I felt like her optimism had somehow transferred to me. Like when I was a kid and wished dropping my forehead to the textbook would let the information soak into my brain through osmosis, just touching Annie seemed to lighten my spirit.

And I fucking wanted more of it.

I stalked back into my bedroom, shoving my legs into sweats. The T-shirt stuck to my wet skin, but I didn't have time to care. I needed to talk this out with Annie. Not only for the sake of my friendship with Ben, but for the sake of my relationship with Annie.

She was sitting on the bed when I got to her bedroom, her gaze staring off into nothing. Her hair was still a sexy mess. I wanted to go over there and comb my fingers through it. Say something witty and wonderful that would make her lose the haunted look on her face. But I was me and eloquent words were not something that I was capable of.

"Annie," I said, my voice rough.

Her head popped up and she shot me a smile I knew was fake. "Hey."

"We should talk."

The edges of her smile wobbled and fell. Fuck. Why couldn't I be like Ethan or Daxon, a friendly quip on the tip of my tongue to set everyone at ease?

She patted the bed. Right where I'd dropped to my knees and tasted her for the first time. My groin tightened and I knew there was no way I could stay in this bedroom with her and focus on anything except how she felt under my hands. My teeth. My tongue.

"Let's take a drive."

Her face lit up. "You want to take a drive in my death trap of a car?"

The dark cloud pushing down on my chest lifted just a tiny bit. Maybe we could find our way through this.

Annie jumped up off the bed. "Oh! But I need your help with something first." She walked past me, her scent wafting over me. I needed a second to gather myself before following her down the hallway to the living room.

"What the hell happened here?"

Annie crossed over to the wall, where a curtain rod was precariously hanging from the wall. A line of nails was embedded at odd angles into the drywall, absolutely none of them doing anything to help hold up that rod. Annie picked up the nail gun and swung it around to point at me.

"I'm putting up the curtains Ben told me he bought for this window months ago!"

I pushed the nail gun away from my chest. "Watch where you point that thing."

She smirked, looking cute as hell with a power tool she had no idea how to use. "It has a safety, so it can't just shoot nails randomly."

I gestured to the wall. "Based on your work here, I don't want to take my chances." I took the nail gun from her hand and put it down. "Curtain rods need drywall screws, not nails."

Her face fell. "Oh."

I took a step closer to her, trying to soften my voice. "You decided that putting up a curtain rod right now was the highest priority?" We just had sex, got caught by our family, and now she wanted to put up curtains? Was there any wonder I didn't understand women? They made absolutely no sense.

Annie shrugged. "Wanted to do something nice for Ben."

I narrowed my eyes, not trusting her words at all. Something else was behind this sudden desire for curtains and I'd figure it out, one way or another.

"Why? He's your brother. He'll love you regardless of your decorating efforts."

Annie wouldn't meet my gaze any longer. Why was she so compelled to help everyone, no matter the cost?

I sighed. "I'll call Ethan. He can fix the drywall and have the curtains up in twenty minutes. You and I need to have that talk."

I took her hand and tugged her toward the front door, stopping so she could slide her feet into the shoes she'd left there. Her car backfired just out of the driveway, but I said nothing, ignoring her side eye and successfully keeping comments to myself. Insulting her car would not help the upcoming conversation. Hell, I didn't even know what I wanted to get out of the conversation, other than to make sure she and I were okay. I couldn't have her regretting what happened between us, or worse, letting it cause a rift.

Annie pulled off the side of the road, right at the top of the trail that led down the cliff to the ocean. I'd spend many a night down there on the sand, a bonfire blazing while we snuck beer as teenagers. Then I'd become the cop who had to break up such revelers, never arresting anyone, but making sure they got home safely.

The sand slowed me down, my leg letting out a wave of pain when it shifted on the way down the hill. Annie immediately stopped and put out her hand. My first instinct was to turn down her offer of help, but the fifty yards of sand in front of us had me changing my mind. Plus, it was Annie. She'd probably tackle me if I didn't agree to her offer of help.

Her fingers tangled through mine, the feel of her soft skin making me ache for a different situation. One in which I could openly explore this pull between us.

Annie stopped at the base of the trail, squinting out into the bright sunshine that hovered over the expanse of ocean. "I used to come here all the time with Grandma Donna when I was little. Maybe she liked how the sand and surf gave me something to play with, letting her off the hook for a few hours from my never-ending questions. But later, this place became a refuge for me."

I turned away from the beautiful scenery to look upon something far more beautiful. "I had a fort in my backyard. It was mostly just rotting wood and the trunk of an old tree, but to me, it was the place where I could just be."

Annie licked her lips, my gaze tracking her every movement. "That's something else we have in common. Trauma at a young age. I used to think that's why I liked you so much. Probably why you and Ben became best friends."

She turned to me, her blue eyes clear and serious. Her freckles were visible in the bold light of day. Annie had changed so much since we were kids, but those freckles reminded me of how she'd been in my life for as long as I could remember.

"And now?"

A ghost of a smile crossed her lips. "And now? I keep playing scenarios over and over in my head. Things that have not yet happened."

I instantly knew what she meant. It was the direction my brain went also. I'd even talked about it with a psychologist over the snack table before his scene in a movie we were both in. "Pre-grief."

Annie's eyes widened. "Yes! That's exactly it. I'm somehow protecting myself by thinking of the terrible things that could happen. Like being aware of them ahead of time will somehow make the shock and grief easier this time around."

She and I just stared at each other, a bond forming over shared grief. The kind that stays with you forever. How much had both of us been shaped by the events that happened so early in our lives? We were very different people and yet in that moment I felt like she was the only human on earth who truly understood me. Who saw the dark moments that stole over me and knew what they stemmed from.

A seagull squawked overhead and we both ducked, breaking the emotional staredown. "I'm sorry for not talking to you first before going to call Ben."

Annie nodded. "Thank you. I prefer to keep Ben out of it for now. If I were dating any other man, I wouldn't run to him and tell him the details, so why should you be any different? I'm not the little sister that needs protecting."

I tilted my head back and forth. "I see your point, but Ben is doing me a favor by letting me stay with him. Going after his sister seems like an offense he won't overlook." To put it mildly.

"Ben won't be home for another week or so. Can we please just see where things naturally take us? We can always tell him right when he gets home if we feel it necessary. I need to feel like I can stand on my own two feet without involving my big brother."

I gazed at her, knowing the right thing to do would be to tell Ben immediately and beg for his forgiveness. But I also cared about Annie and she was telling me she needed this time. And God help me, I would give it to her.

"Okay."

"Okay?" Annie squeezed my hand, sounding so hopeful and surprised, I felt a pang of guilt for being such an asshole that she didn't think me capable of flexibility in a delicate situation.

"I won't say anything to Ben, but where does that leave us?"

I watched Annie's cheeks turn pink, the sight making me bite back a groan. One time with her wasn't enough. Not even close to putting out the fire she caused with just one look from those playful blue eyes. Her thumb came up to her mouth and I batted it away before she could bite down. She gave me a look and I gave it right back to her.

"That leaves us living together." She looked up at me coyly. "Question is, would you like to stay in your bed or mine?"

I stepped so close she had to tilt her head back to hold my gaze. "Is that even a question?"

Before she could answer, I dipped my head and sealed my lips to hers. The wind blew a lock of her hair in her face, but a little thing like that wouldn't stop me. Nothing could stop me. I teased her lips open and tugged the hair out of our way. How many girls had I kissed on this exact beach? I couldn't remember names or faces, but I did know not a single one had blown my world apart like Annie. Her kiss made me feel like a superhero, like I could take on her family and somehow come out on top. As if all the shit that kept me in a dark place could be cleared with the help of a freckled, auburn-haired talker.

"Let's go home," I whispered.

Going up the hill was harder than going down. Pain made a bead of sweat drip down my neck. Annie tried to help me but she was too tiny to do much except tug on my arm. Her running commentary kept my brain from beating myself up about my slow recovery. I knew she was doing it on purpose, but hell, it fucking worked. I found myself with one last step to reach the top. My leg gave out at the last second and I stumbled onto the top of the ledge, my arms on Annie's shoulders. The poor girl almost went down with my sudden weight on her.

"Jesus, Blaze! Do you have to have so much muscle?" She laughed so hard as she staggered back to standing that it pulled a chuckle out of me too. "No wonder your crutches—"

"Well, isn't this cute," a voice that gave me nightmares interrupted.

Our heads whipped up in unison to take in a female cop standing next to Annie's car. Her dark hair was pulled back in a severe bun, her hands resting above her duty belt.

"Hey, Officer Danette. Everything okay?" Annie's chipper voice rang out in the awkward silence.

I pulled my hands off her shoulders and stood straight, wishing I was meeting Dani again under different circumstances. Or not at all.

Dani didn't take her gaze from mine, ignoring Annie completely. Annie's head finally shifted, glancing back and forth between us, sensing the massive tension.

"Dani," I grumbled.

"It's Danette," she said coldly.

Damn. The woman was as frigid as the last time I saw her. She'd cut me from her life without a single blink of her dark and disturbing eyes. Dani had the kind of beauty that made men stop in traffic to look at her. I'd known her well enough to know that beauty was born of a ruthlessness I wanted no part of.

"Awesome." I put a hand on Annie's back and pushed her to the car. "We were just leaving."

Dani spun, now including Annie in the conversation. "This isn't a parking space, you know."

Annie looked stunned. Everyone in Hell had been parking here at this lookout for decades and Dani knew it. Annie opened her mouth, but I cut her off. I didn't want Annie having to interact with this nasty woman.

I tried to control the pent-up venom in my voice, but was unsuccessful. "Good thing we're leaving. Take care."

I gestured to Annie and she climbed in her car, cranking over the engine the second we were both strapped in. Before pulling onto the road, she rolled her window down and flipped off Dani with a wink and a smile. I whipped my head around to see Dani glaring at us with murder in her eyes.

Annie whooped and took off down the road, leaving Dani in our literal dust cloud. "What a bitch!" she hollered, rolling up her window.

Annie opened her mouth again as the coastline disappeared in the rearview mirror, but I cut her off.

"Don't ask."

CHAPTER TWENTY

$\mathcal{A}$nnie

FOR A LONG MOMENT there on the beach, Blaze's eyes had held
such warmth and understanding, I could have curled up in them
and fallen asleep. Trauma was a beast no matter when you experienced it, but it was particularly troublesome when it happened
to a small child who didn't have mechanisms in place to handle
it. How much of my personality had been shaped by losing my
parents? How much of those pesky "not good enough" thoughts
had been born of loss?

Maybe I'd never have answers to those questions, but
standing there with Blaze holding my hand, showing me he
understood me, was a balm to my soul. It had felt like not one
person in my life understood me more than Blaze did in that
exact moment. I hadn't even felt the need to fill the silence with
the sound of my own voice. I didn't need words to know that I'd
finally been heard.

And then that bitch Danette had ruined the moment. I
didn't know their history, but based on what Ben had said and

the level of hate that had clouded the air on that cliff, some nasty shit had gone down. Blaze had gone silent on the ride home, not at all a surprise. I gave him space, making us dinner—if grilled cheese could be considered dinner—and then curling up next to him on the couch after. The television droned on, but I had a feeling neither of us was actually watching it.

"Time for bed?" I asked lightly, not wanting to assume he'd come with me. After the Danette encounter, I could literally feel him retreating with each moment that passed. Maybe not physically, but definitely emotionally.

He tugged me to my feet and followed me into my bedroom, stripping down to his boxers and pulling me into his hard body when we climbed in bed. He spooned me, his warmth making my eyes droopy before I wanted them to. I was dying to ask questions, using every tiny morsel of self-control I possessed to stay silent.

When I was just about to drift off into sleep, Blaze nuzzled my shoulder with his nose and tightened the arm around my waist.

"Thank you." He whispered it so softly I wasn't sure I heard him right. Or knew what he was thanking me for. Being there with him? Holding my questions?

Or maybe he just really loved my grilled cheese.

THE FOLLOWING week passed in the blink of an eye. Blaze and I created a rhythm living together, eating our meals at the tiny kitchen table, and sharing about our day. At night, he stayed with me, pulling me into his chest and holding me there. I was dying to reach behind me and feel the obvious desire I could feel pressing against me each night, but instinctively I knew he needed more than that right now. He needed to know I'd be there for him, without sex on the table. And being his friend, or secret girlfriend, or whatever we were doing, was not a hardship. I genuinely liked Blaze.

The grand opening party was this afternoon and I'd spent the day rushing around the clinic putting up last-minute decor while Blaze assisted on the higher-up stuff and trained Tate in between my freak-outs. Shelby came over with a huge bouquet for my check-in desk. I burst into tears while she hedged toward the door and Blaze laughed, the delightful sound of which was enough to dry my tears. He pulled me into his chest to allow me time to compose myself and reassured Shelby that this was normal behavior for me. I'd have to talk to her later and explain the tears were just a normal pressure release and I wouldn't make her uncomfortable ever again. It was a lie, but she was nice and I wanted to be her friend.

My phone rang as I was drying my face on Blaze's shirt. I showed him the screen and he froze, the soft smile on his face dropping.

"Hey, Benji!" I infused as much enthusiasm as I could into my voice. And it wasn't all that hard. I missed my brother. It was just that every day he stayed away, I could spend that time with Blaze.

"Annie. I'm so sorry I'm not there for your grand opening. Grandma Donna told me the place looks incredible."

I walked away from Blaze and looked around at the clinic all decorated for a party thanks to my friends and their excessive use of streamers and balloons. A warm sense of pride filled my chest. I did it. I'd gotten my clinic together in the town I'd grown up in, and as of this afternoon, I'd be open for business.

"It really does," I said softly. "But don't worry, I plan to be open for a long time, so you can come in anytime and check it out."

Ben chuckled. "Maybe I'll ditch this app stuff and come be your front desk person."

I frowned. "Are things not going well?"

His sigh made me worried. "It's not, but it's more the fact that this has grown into something bigger than I think I want. I liked it better when it was just me and my laptop, not a board of directors and investors and public reviews that like to skewer you over the tiniest details."

I stood there looking at the empty exam room, wondering when my brother had become unhappy with his job. From my perspective, he was living the dream, making games and making bank.

"Oh, Ben."

"Ah, don't worry about me. I'll figure it out. Today is about you, my little sister. You're a full-fledged veterinarian with her own practice! That's huge!"

I grinned ear to ear hearing the pride in his voice. I didn't have parents to tell me they loved me and were proud of my accomplishments, but I had my big brother.

"Thanks, Benji."

"Now get off the phone with the computer geek and wow everyone with your knowledge of all things animals. Talk their ears off."

I laughed. "You know I can do that, that's for sure. Love you."

"Love you too, sis."

I turned to find Blaze in the hallway watching me. His face didn't give a hint as to what was going on in that brain of his. He should take up poker. He'd be deadly.

"Do you miss him?" he asked quietly.

I nodded, walking over to him. "Sure do, but I'm not lonely. Surprisingly."

Blaze stepped closer, his limp so much better that only the few who knew him best would detect it. I was happy to count myself in that small circle.

"And why is that?" he asked, his voice dipping low. The kind of voice he gave me when we were curled up in bed together.

The voice that made my knees weak and my heart hope for all kinds of things.

His hand came up to push a lock of hair behind my ear, his fingers tracing along my jawline. My eyelids fluttered, forgetting where we were and what we were talking about.

"Huh?"

His mouth hitched up on the side. "Why aren't you lonely, Annie?"

That was easy. "Because of you. And Tate. And this clinic."

Satisfaction burned hot in his eyes. His dark glances always felt like he was eating me up, consuming me with a look. He dipped his head and brushed his lips against mine. I went up on tiptoes to reach for more when the tiny bell over the front door rang out. We jumped apart, Blaze's eyes still hooded as he looked at me. I felt the heat rise in my cheeks.

"Good day, Doctor McLachlin!" rang out Nikki's voice from the lobby.

Blaze gestured to the front and put his hand on my back. We walked down the hallway together and there were Nikki and Grandma Donna, big smiles on their faces. Grandma had on a new blouse, one with sloths all over it. Even her Crocs had plastic animal faces coming from the little round holes. This was Grandma Donna being festive. She gave me a big hug and looked around the place.

"It's stunning! I can't believe my little granddaughter is the new vet in town." She pressed her hands to her cheeks, eyes filling with tears. Which just made my eyes water, because crying was contagious, goshdarnit.

"Oh no," Blaze grumbled. His mom smacked him on the arm.

A tissue appeared under my nose and I nodded my thanks to Blaze. I think I cried at least once a day this last week as we approached the grand opening. It was nerves, fueled by hormones. Shark week always made me reach for the tissues. I even cried when Blaze spotted a box of tampons ripped open and strewn across the bathroom countertop and hadn't said a thing. He'd just collected them, found an empty wicker basket under the sink and put them in there with a flower from the garden of wildflowers out front. I mean, what male is that sweet? Of course I cried.

The door opened with a bang and Cricket and Addy made their entrance with gasps and greetings and hugs. The door just kept opening, people filing in and checking out the space. Food, set up by Nikki and Grandma Donna, was consumed, and when I had a second to breathe, I saw Blaze handing out drinks from behind the check-out desk. I didn't have a liquor license but because it was local kombrewcha—which was technically a health drink—everyone looked the other way. Well, hopefully Danette the Dickwaddle wouldn't show up. She'd for sure write me up just to piss off Blaze.

"Please tell me you're getting some of that." Meadow elbowed me so hard I might have to X-ray my own rib.

"Some of what?" I took a sip of my drink.

Meadow shot me a look that made me tremble in my scrubs. "You might as well have lasers shooting out of your eyeballs the way you look at Blaze. And holy hotness, I think I just orgasmed seeing the way he looks back at you."

Cricket snickered, nodding her head in agreement. Addy smiled softly. "Listen, I get it. Those Hellman boys are hot."

I shook my head, promising my cheeks extra pie tonight if they just didn't blush at this exact moment. "It's not like that. Blaze and I are just friends. Since living together, we've become better friends. He's a really great guy under all those scowls."

Meadow leaned in and whispered, "It's what's under those clothes that we're interested in."

The bell over the door rang out again, saving me from further discussion on that topic. "Oh, Annie! I need more help with my pussy!"

All heads turned to see Yedda in another brightly colored track suit, the familiar tabby cat in her arms, giving everyone an ill-tempered glare. Conversation died and more than a few snickers escaped at Yedda's word choice. I walked over and took the cat from her, rolling my lips in to keep from cracking up. I made it all the way to the check-in desk, where Blaze was currently standing, doing his own lip-biting habit to keep from laughing, when I lost it. I howled with laughter so loud the tabby jumped from my arms and darted across the lobby. People dodged out of the way and Tate thought a fun new game was afoot, yipping as he chased.

"Tate, heel!" Blaze commanded and the room froze again.

Tate ran right back to Blaze's side and sat like a good little boy. The tabby even froze, her front paw in the air. She gave Blaze impressive side-eye, even after I picked her up and took her back to an exam room for more eye drops.

When I came back out again, Blaze had a group of people huddled around him, asking him questions about his training of Tate. He looked a little green around the gills at the attention, but I gave him a smile and a thumbs-up. He'd signed up for an online class about dog training, taking the first steps to becoming a certified trainer. Maybe he could get clients already, giving him a new purpose that I knew he needed.

I spent the rest of the grand opening behind the desk, scheduling appointments and talking to Hell residents about their pets. If this pace kept up, I wouldn't have a day off until Christmas time.

"What can you feed a bear to make it less grumpy?"

I pulled my head up from the scheduling software and saw Ethan and Daxon. "Hello, boys!" I came around the counter to give them both a hug. Ethan kept his arm around my shoulders until Blaze sent him a deadly look.

"What are you two doing here?" Blaze didn't look excited to see them, but that was kind of the look he gave everyone.

"How else can we see our big bro except to find Annie?" Daxon asked, his eyes twinkling mischievously. "We know you won't be far away."

"She smells so much better than you two," Blaze answered quickly, putting his arm around me.

I wanted to curl into his side and breathe him in, as if snuggling in public was normal for us. Instead, I laughed and pushed him away, wishing desperately that I didn't have to pretend.

"If you don't have a pet for me to inspect or schedule, kindly move along to the food table."

Daxon lit up like the afternoon sun on the Fourth of July. "Oh, I have a pet you can inspect, Annie."

Blaze grabbed him by the back of his flannel shirt collar and dragged him away, grumbling something terrible in his ear based on the way Daxon's jaw dropped. Ethan just laughed and shot me a wink as he followed them. Not long after, when I spotted Blaze across the crowd, he was laughing with his brothers again. Sure, I was excited about my clinic being a success, but more than that, seeing Blaze with a smile on his face made my heart sing.

"I know that look."

I turned to see Lucy Sutter giving me a knowing smile that spelled trouble. "Not sure what you mean, Lucy. Just enjoying my grand opening."

Lucy didn't quiz me further, which only upped my nerves. She was always up to something, and dangling juicy gossip in front of her was asking for it. She simply stood up straight and clasped her hands in front of her.

"Actually, I came to ask if you and Blaze would help me put together an adoption event for the town. We have too many strays that come in every week. I want to find them all homes. Considering your business and Blaze's ability to train animals, you two would be the perfect fit. What do you say?"

"We say yes," came Blaze's deep voice behind me. His hand came to rest on my low back and all my resistance flew away.

CHAPTER TWENTY-ONE

laze

I WAITED a whole twenty-four hours after her grand opening before I couldn't handle it any longer. I'd pushed Annie away as much as I could the last week, nearly dying of sexual tension every night. I lay there in the dark, holding her close and staring at the wall, wondering what the hell I was doing with her. I knew I shouldn't be in her bed, and that not having sex with her wouldn't negate the fact I already did, yet I couldn't seem to find the strength to leave her side.

The way she defended me in front of Dani kept echoing through my brain. Or how she was running a new business and yet still found time to leave me a note when she left in the morning or to watch the new commands I taught Tate. She was quickly becoming my best friend, the one I called when anything new or weird happened. Ben had been my one and only friend for so long, it was disorienting to find myself trusting this slip of a girl I'd known my whole life.

Me: When do you think you'll be home tonight?

Annie: One more patient and then I'll head home. Grilled cheese or pancakes for dinner?

I chuckled as Tate whined up at me from where he sat on my feet. Annie was amazing at a lot of things, but cooking wasn't one of them. The woman had lived off sandwiches since living on her own in college, but I planned to fix that tonight. I stopped at the grocery store for a whole bag of ingredients I'd had to look up to understand. Recipes with more than twenty ingredients should be banned.

Me: Leave dinner to me. Plus I have a treat for you after...

Annie: Oh! Please tell me it's pie.

Well, shit.

Me: See you soon.

I heaved myself off the couch and leaned down to pet Tate.

"Hold down the fort, buddy. I have to go back to the store for pie. Then Annie and I will be home all night, okay?"

He licked my hand and trotted after me as I grabbed my keys. Being mobile enough to drive my own SUV was life giving. No brothers to beg a ride from and no heart attacks when Annie's sad excuse of a car backfired its way through town. I grabbed a peach pie at the grocery store and ignored the cashier's questions about showing up twice in one day. Small towns were too damn nosy for their own good.

Back home, I started chopping vegetables, firing up an old-school-rock playlist to get me through the tedious task. Tate hovered at my feet, waiting for food to drop, which happened more than I liked. Making shit from scratch was hard. But I wanted to do something nice for Annie. I wanted to take her on a date, albeit in secret here at the house.

"What is this?" Annie's excited squeal cut through the electric guitar solo. I spun to see her in the doorway to the kitchen, her jaw dropped. I turned down the volume of the music from my phone and gestured to the stovetop where the caponata was resting. Bread with butter and freshly crushed garlic was toasting in the oven.

"I made dinner."

Annie dropped her bag on the floor, picked up Tate who lavished her cheek with kisses, and came over to stand before me. She tilted her head back and the warmth shining through her blue eyes made me cup her cheek and kiss her. The simple brush of our lips turned heated the second we came together. Sweeping my tongue into her mouth I knew I wouldn't be able to take it slow any longer. I was done holding her at arm's length. I wanted Annie. Plain and simple.

A yip from Tate had us breaking apart with a smile. Annie's eyes had hazed over, a look that made me want to rush through dinner so I could see it again, this time without clothes and a dog between us.

"Have a seat, madam. Dinner will be served in just a moment."

Annie giggled and headed for the tiny table, talking to Tate the whole way in that high-pitched baby voice that made me smile and cringe at the same time. When she asked him how his day went with Mr. Grumpy Head, a weird lurch happened in my chest. Maybe it was hunger. I rubbed the spot and got busy plating our meal.

"Oh my God, Blaze," Annie moaned, tossing her head back and closing her eyes.

I shifted on my chair, rearranging the erection that had been plaguing me all week. "Annie," I warned.

Her eyes flew open as she chewed. "What?"

"You're killing me."

She looked lost for a second, before a blush stole over her cheeks. "Maybe I'm trying to kill you a little bit."

I put down my fork. The pasta was amazing, if I did say so myself, but I didn't want any more of it. "I also have an after-dinner movie planned."

"Oh?" Annie took another bite.

I wiped my mouth with the napkin and placed it on the table. "*The Proposal*."

Annie froze mid-chew. Her fork dropped to the plate and she lunged out of her chair to sit on my lap, her arms winding around my neck. "Seriously? We're watching *The Proposal?*"

I gave her a quick kiss and picked her up, thanking Ronnie for all the ridiculous squats he'd been making me do to strengthen my leg. Annie squealed with delight and the sound made that lurch in my chest happen again. Depositing her on the couch, I grabbed a throw blanket and settled in next to her. Once it started, I gave the head nod to Tate and he jumped up on the couch to snuggle in with us.

"I can't believe you rented a romantic comedy," Annie said dreamily when the credits rolled two hours later. Despite rolling my eyes at some of the scenes, I had to admit it was a cute movie. And that naked scene between the two main characters was remarkably like that day Annie had charged into the bathroom while I was showering.

"Figured you deserved dinner and a movie for putting up with me."

Annie twisted in my arms, sitting up to look at me. "I don't put up with you, Blaze. I kind of like you."

I pushed her hair behind her ear. "I kind of like you too."

I needed to kiss her. I turned to the puppy. "Tate. Down." He got to his feet and shot us a baleful look before jumping off the couch and snuggling into one of his puffy beds by the television.

Reaching for Annie, I pulled her across my lap. She straddled me, her cotton scrubs wrinkled from lying on the couch with me. She was so beautiful it made my ribs ache. She was sexy in her own right, but seeing her start her dream job and manage it like a boss was a whole other level of sexy. What this woman was doing with a loser like me was still a mystery. She could have any manner of man who held down a steady job, didn't need physical therapy to be able to walk, and smiled more than he frowned. Instead, she was here with me. And maybe it made me a bastard, but I was going to let myself take what I wanted.

Everything in me wanted Annie.

Naked.

Spread out before me, begging me to touch her, fill her, make her groan my name as she came on my cock.

"Annie," I breathed, feeling her soft curves press against me.

"Blaze," she said right back, her fingers combing through my hair. "I swear I'm going to train Tate to bite your toes as you sleep if you come to bed again only to spoon me all night."

I barked out a laugh as I gazed at her. "That's so cruel."

Her fingers tightened on my hair. "So is pressing that gorgeous body against me and not doing anything to ease the ache between my legs."

I stilled, giving her the promise she wanted while also making a million more silent promises to her. "Whatever you want, Annie."

She planted a kiss on my mouth that stopped the conversation. She didn't hesitate, just took what she wanted as her tongue touched mine. I found the hem of her scrubs and ripped the shirt over her head. Heat seared through my body. Dipping my head, I found her nipple through the lace of her bra, sucking on it like a man starved for weeks on end. Clothes flew off and I stood once again, holding Annie as the kiss continued through all the little interruptions.

I let Annie slide down my body, feeling exactly how much I wanted her. She grabbed my hand, as if to head to the bedroom, but I pulled her back and turned her. With my palm on her smooth back, I gave her a little push, nudging her down over the side of the couch. She went willingly, even giving a little shake of her hips as she offered herself to me. Her skin was so soft and white, little freckles dotting their way across her human terrain like a map. I had a wild thought to memorize every single one, knowing her body better than my own.

"I'm on the pill, Blaze."

Annie's voice brought me back, my fingers stilling between her legs where I'd found her wet for me. My eyes threatened to roll back in my head. I wanted to slide right into her heat. Take the invitation she was offering me. Fuck. I'd never wanted to feel a woman against my skin like I did now. But something stopped me.

I couldn't take that liberty when I could only offer her a date in secret. When her own brother didn't know we were together. When we hadn't even discussed if we were actually dating and not just fucking. As far as everything was concerned, we were just fucking. And fuck buddies did not forget to use a condom.

I placed a kiss on the flesh of her hip, easing away from her to grab my wallet on the coffee table. Rolling on the condom, I didn't waste time sliding inside of her. I couldn't address all the reasons why I chose to keep that barrier between us and I didn't want to give her time to back out either. Again, I was a bastard, taking what I wanted from Annie. She would be wise to send me packing.

Annie moaned, pressing her hips back and I forgot about everything except the feel of her under my hands. Her waist dipped in and I traced my fingers along her curves, grabbing hold of her hips and slamming into her a bit harder when she urged me on. I was so close to losing control, I bent over her and slowed things down. Gathering her red hair in my hand, I held it away from her face. She tilted her head and looked over her shoulder at me, that hazy smile making me wish for crazy things. Namely, a thousand more nights just like this.

The thought made me push away from her, my hand still caught in her hair. I gave it a tug and slammed into her. She moaned, her eyes fluttering closed. Ah, my girl liked it a little rougher. I pulled almost all the way out again and waited there. When Annie wiggled her hips impatiently, I pulled on her hair until she stopped. Then I slid all the way in again. The couch let out a squeak with each thrust. If I didn't take more care, I'd have to borrow Ethan's wood glue again.

"Blaze," she moaned.

"I know, baby, I know." Goose bumps lined my skin. I was both hot and shivering at the same time, needing to release myself into her, but holding back for her to join me. Fuck, it was good with Annie. So good.

I let go of her hair and reached around to find her clit. I played there as I slammed into her, faster and faster until she started screaming my name. I felt her tighten around me and I lost it, plunging into her without an ounce of finesse, then stilling as everything exploded into chaos. My feet slipped and I found myself lying on top of her and holding on for dear life. I was probably crushing her. I tried to stand up, realizing that I still hadn't gotten enough of her.

Maybe I'd never have enough.

Maybe I would spend the rest of my life wanting to bury myself deeper and deeper into this woman.

"We might have to buy a new couch," Annie said on a laugh, her face buried in the cushions.

I pulled out of her with a grunt and helped her stand. She wasn't steady on her feet—a fact that made my chest swell with pride—so I picked her up and walked us to the bedroom.

"Can I spoon you now without worrying about my toes?" I teased her.

But she didn't smile. She just turned in my arms to face me, a serious look on her face.

"It's time you tell me about Dani."

CHAPTER TWENTY-TWO

*A*nnie

BRINGING up someone's ex was pretty much the worst way to ruin the intimate moment, but I had to. I couldn't stay silent any longer, wondering what was going on in Blaze's head, and most importantly, his heart. He'd been holding back all week, holding me close, but not letting me in. While I may have been fine with that temporarily while he worked through some things, if we were to go on in this manner, I might lose my mind.

Blaze tensed up the second the words left my mouth, but he didn't let me go as we lay down on the bed, a fact I clung to as I braced for his rejection or deflection. Either was how he usually handled sensitive topics. His gaze slid to the wall behind me, his eyes sad and unfocused. I held my breath while he began to talk.

"She and I started dating soon after I joined the force. She was my superior, technically, though she never treated me that way. She was the most badass woman I'd ever met. Tough. Beautiful. And she always made me feel special, as if I was her favorite, which spoke right to my ego. We started dating in secret. I was young and stupid and naive. I thought I was in love with her."

My heart clenched, hearing him say those words about another woman. No wonder there was so much tension between them that day at the beach. I'd never loved a man before but I had to imagine seeing him years later after everything went to hell would be difficult.

"And then one day I found her taking drugs from the evidence room."

I froze but he kept right on talking.

"She denied it, of course, but I'd seen it with my own eyes. I let it go for a day, thinking it through and knowing I couldn't live with myself if I didn't put a stop to it. I confronted her, thinking I could talk some sense into her and get her to put it back." Blaze rolled his head back on the pillow and stared up at the ceiling.

My mind raced, realizing this story was about much more than love gone wrong. I wanted to hunt down Danette and punch her right in her perfect nose. Maybe grab that bun on the back of her head and give it a good hard yank. She was stealing?

"I confronted her. Annie, you should have seen her face. Everything beautiful about her turned ugly in an instant. She told me that if I reported her, she'd say I sexually harassed her. I couldn't believe what was coming out of her mouth. I probably kept harping about stealing being wrong, not realizing she was way past caring."

Blaze suddenly let me go, sitting up and resting his back against the headboard. He scrubbed his hands over his face and my heart bled for him. I scrambled upright and pulled his hands away, holding them tightly in mine.

"Hey, it's okay. You don't have to go on."

Blaze looked at me then, his dark eyes tortured. "I've never told anyone this."

If I thought all that was bad, I wasn't ready at all for the next thing to come out of his mouth.

"She, uh, had a video. Of us. On her phone." Blaze's hands tightened almost painfully. "I swear I didn't know she had it."

I blinked rapidly, trying to process. "A video. Like, a sex tape?"

Blaze didn't answer but the shame written across his face told me everything I needed to know. I felt sick to my stomach.

"She liked to, uh, role play. She pulled out her phone and showed me a video of her and me when I had her in cuffs." Blaze looked away and then back at me, his eyes glossy. "Without context...it looked bad, Annie."

I shook my head and couldn't seem to stop. "No. Blaze, couples make videos like that all the time. That wasn't your fault! She can't—"

"Annie." Blaze tugged on my arms, cutting me off. "It's over. It was a long time ago."

My jaw dropped. "But—but you left town. Is that why?" Ben had been devastated when he just left out of the blue. He called me that same night, pissed off and sad that his best friend had moved away without a single explanation.

"I was horrified. Humiliated. Disillusioned. All I could think about was losing my job. Being accused of something I hadn't done. The effect on my brothers. My mom." Blaze's jaw looked like it might shatter into a million pieces if I touched him. "I had to leave town. That was the only option. And I'm glad I did. I grew up."

Rage was a real and tangible thing. My twitching foot was shaking the bed. I wasn't sure how I'd be able to see Danette in town and not give her a piece of my mind. There was a C-word on the tip of my tongue that I never used, but I felt like this might be the one situation where it was warranted.

"There are better ways to grow up than having to leave town because of blackmail."

Blaze turned to me, his face softening as he took in my agitated state. "Annie, it was a long time ago. I'm over it."

I jumped straight up on the bed, nearly making Blaze fall over when the mattress shifted. I put my hands on my hips and wished I had clothes on. Naked Annie wasn't as tough looking. "But I'm not! I could kill that woman! Oh! I know! Meadow has a list of diabolical revenge scenarios. I can talk to her and—"

"Annie." Blaze came up on his good knee, pulling me down to lie next to him. He rolled, settling himself between my legs. He was smiling. I wanted to commit murder and he was smiling at me. With a hard-on pressing against my hip. I swear, men got off on the weirdest things. "Slow your roll, tiger."

I blew out a breath and tried to calm down. "I seriously don't like Danette."

Blaze's chuckle shook the bed and made me squirm underneath him. "I don't either and I'm tired of talking about her. That's just something I'll always carry with me. Now you know."

I ran my palm over his beard before running my fingers through his hair. "No, that's just it, Blaze. You don't have to carry it with you. At the end of the day, every hard thing either makes us bitter or better. It's your choice how to respond." Blaze had chosen bitter for so many years I wasn't sure if he could be any other way.

Blaze stared down at me for a long moment before dipping his head to brush his lips across mine. "I want to be better," he whispered.

He nudged my thighs further apart and I let him, pulling my knees up high over his hips. His erection tickled against my opening, asking to enter. His tongue flicked against my lip before plunging inside and exploring every corner. Finally, Blaze wasn't holding back any longer, and I wouldn't either. I'd give him all of me.

When he slid inside me once again, softly this time, his hands running over my skin reverently, I placed a line of kisses along his jaw. His fingers found mine, lacing us together as he moved slowly. Blaze was making love to me and I knew in an instant my heart would never be the same.

"You already are better," I whispered in his ear, right before the stars burst in front of my eyes and pleasure washed over me yet again. His name was the last word on my lips before I fell asleep in his arms.

CHAPTER TWENTY-THREE

laze

ANNIE'S ALARM woke me from the best dream I'd had since being back in Hell. She moaned and pulled away from me, slamming her hand down on her phone to stop the incessant beeping. Despite the early hour, I felt like a million bucks.

"Wait," I croaked, pulling her back and wrapping my arms around her warm body. I could stay all day in bed like this, but I knew she had patients waiting for her and I was damn proud of her. I placed a kiss on her shoulder. "I think we need to strategize how to tell Ben about us."

Annie froze, then lifted her head to stare at me. Fuck, she was pretty, even half asleep and a pillow crease across her cheek.

"Us?"

She was lying naked in my arms after I'd made love to her again sometime in the middle of the night and she wasn't sure there was an us? I was such an asshole.

I rolled her underneath me. "Annie McLachlin, will you be my girlfriend? Check yes or no. Wear my letterman's jacket."

A smile grew on her face until she was grinning so hard her eyes almost disappeared. "Hell, yes I will. To the girlfriend part. I don't see a letterman's jacket anywhere."

My grin felt like it matched hers. "Okay, then. Let's talk tonight over dinner and figure it out, yeah?"

She nodded and reached up to loop her arms around my neck and pull me down to her. I was expecting some sort of hot kiss from my girlfriend but what I got was a million fast pecks across my cheeks, jaw, eyelids, and nose. We were both laughing by the time I peeled away from her.

"Jesus. It's like being kissed awake by Tate," I teased her, slapping her naked ass as she climbed out of bed to get ready. "Wear the cat scrubs."

She looked at me over her shoulder while she dug around in her suitcase. "I was thinking the sloth ones."

I piled my hands behind my head. "No. I like your pussies."

She gave me a deadpan look, but the wobble of her lips gave her away. She ended up laughing as she pulled out the cat scrubs from the suitcase and headed for the bathroom for a quick shower. I had a full day of physical therapy, then a few new commands to teach Tate, and a coffee meeting with Callan that he'd set up a few days ago. He'd been surprisingly quiet since I'd been back to town. Where Ethan and Daxon showed up even when you didn't want them to, Callan was proving elusive. He kind of reminded me of me, which was like saying weak-ass tea reminded you of full-bodied coffee. The guy was usually the first to show up to help with a big ol' smile on his face. Silence was not normal.

I rolled out of bed and made Annie a scrambled egg and toast, forcing her to eat it before she left for the clinic. She packed one of her sandwiches for lunch and then was out the door before I could talk her into a quickie against the kitchen countertop. My phone dinged as I got ready for therapy.

Ethan: Since you can drive now, Blaze, want to meet us at The Tavern Friday for a beer with your brothers?

Daxon: Wait, are you still on crutches? Because that could kill our vibe with the ladies.

Ace: What are you talking about? Women love a wounded man.

Ethan: The invite was to visit with us, not to hit on women, stupid.

Daxon: We can hang out anywhere if it's just about shooting the shit. If we go to The Tavern, it's about hitting on women.

Callan: Is everything about hitting on women, Dax?

Daxon: Duh.

I shook my head and wondered how I was related to these losers.

Me: Sure. But I'm there to chat, not hit on women.

Daxon: Of course, because you already live with one.

Me: It's not like that.

Ethan: I don't know, dude. Annie beams like a thousand-watt bulb these days.

Daxon: Women don't beam unless they're getting dick.

Me: Dude, don't put Annie and dick in the same sentence ever again.

Ace: And women beam for many reasons, asshole.

Daxon: Whatever you gotta tell yourself, but women who get Hellman dick beam, bro. It's science.

I snorted and threw my phone down. I loved them, but mostly they were ridiculous. I must be in a hell of a good mood to agree to meet with them at The Tavern. It was gossip central on a Friday night with more ill-advised hookups happening on the dance floor than a late-night chapel in Vegas.

As I made the bed where Annie and I had nearly burned the sheets down last night, my gut clenched. What I had texted my brothers wasn't sitting well with me. I could act like Annie and I were a casual thing, but I knew the truth. Opening up to someone was damn near impossible for me, but telling Annie all about what happened with Dani, and all the embarrassing things I was accused of had felt...well, it had felt a lot like healing. Like maybe I could finally move past what had happened and not let the weight of those mistakes drag me down. How could I possibly think Annie and I were a casual hookup when she felt like the best fucking thing that had ever happened to me?

My phone vibrated again and I ignored it. Probably more bullshit from my brothers. It went off again in my pocket and I took it out in the off chance it was Annie texting me. It was an important woman, all right, but it wasn't Annie.

Mom: Family dinner Saturday night at my place since Ace and Callan are both off! Be there or I'll hunt you down and make you wish you'd listened to the woman who birthed you.

Ethan: I love you, but your invites need work, Ma.

I snorted. Wasn't that the truth. Mom was like a bull in a china shop, smiling and waving serenely amongst the wreckage.

We all dutifully texted back that we'd be there, me included.

Mom: Blaze, honey. Bring Annie so Addy isn't the only girl there.

Ethan: Umm. Aren't you a girl, Mom?

Mom: So glad you noticed. But I'm your mother, which is totally different. Besides, I just want Annie there so we can see how uncomfortable we can make those two.

Me: Mom...

Mom: What? You say you're not dating, so you should have nothing to worry about. Right, honey?

I shut my phone off and hustled to physical therapy. My mother was a menace and the only way to deal with her was with punishing my body in the gym and trying to forget about it.

I ENDED up late to Coffee with Callan. I'd sweated through my clothes so badly at physical therapy, I had to shower and change again at home. Then I realized my clean clothes were dwindling, so I threw them in the wash. Then I saw Annie had a stack of dirty clothes and so I threw them in too. However, over half of her clothes were hang dry, so I spent an inordinate amount of time laying her wet clothes over every available surface. Why couldn't women wear plain cotton like everyone else? Why did everything they owned have to be hang dry only?

Sitting down at the table in the corner of Coffee that Callan had reserved, I heaved out a sigh. "Women are little walking mysteries, man."

Callan snorted, running his hand through his sun-lightened hair. I was used to being around actors who dyed their hair, a habit none of my brothers had ever subscribed to, but now that I noticed it, Callan's looked a lot lighter than normal.

"Tell me about it."

"Do you put lemons in your hair?" I blurted out.

Callan scrunched up his face. "Fuck no. Are you supposed to?"

"I don't think so, but chicks do it to lighten their hair."

Twin spots of color hit Callan's cheeks and I nearly slid out of my chair. "You do use lemons!"

"Shh! Keep your voice down, dude." Callan leaned over the table, his broad shoulders stretching out his navy collared uniform shirt. I'd always been bigger than my younger brothers, but if I didn't get back in the gym soon, they were going to pass me by. "I don't use lemons, okay? But Cricket gave me some sort of shampoo she wanted me to try out for her salon. It's making my hair lighter."

I studied his hair, thinking of all the celebrity women I'd met who would like that kind of shampoo. "It's not brassy at all."

Callan rolled his eyes. "That's what Cricket said. Whatever the hell brassy means."

I shot him a grin. "So, Cricket, huh?" I'd been teasing him about his best friend for decades now. While all of us brothers had male best friends, leave it to a good guy like Callan to have a tiny blonde-haired female best friend.

He lifted one eyebrow. "So, Annie, huh?"

I narrowed my eyes at him. "Is that what you want to talk about?"

"No." Callan shoved one of the coffee cups toward me. "Black nitro coffee, just like Mom said you like it."

I actually did like that nitro shit, not going to lie. I took a sip and studied Callan over the rim. He looked serious, not the carefree, smiling guy he'd been when I left town a few years ago.

"Sorry I didn't make Annie's grand opening. Had to work a double."

I set the cup down. "No worries. How's work going?"

Callan shrugged. "It's good. No complaints there."

Exasperated, I leaned over the table to get in his face. "What the hell am I doing here, Callan?"

He just looked at me for a long moment and then laid his cards on the table. "I contacted our father and have a meeting with him next month. I wanted to see if you have an interest in coming with me."

I sat back in the chair and tried to digest that bomb. Our father was not a topic I talked about much because there was no reason to. He wasn't part of our lives and hadn't been for a long time. Why the fuck was Callan meeting with him?

"Ace know about this?"

Callan nodded once. "Yep."

"Having a hard time over here thinking he's on board with this." Ace and I had talked about our father only on rare occasions back in high school. We'd vowed to never let him back in our lives for the sake of the triplets. They shouldn't be around an asshole like him.

"Oh, he's not on board with it. Told me he wouldn't participate."

I nodded. "Can't say I blame him." I ran my thumb over the rim of the coffee mug. "Why, Callan?"

His gaze moved to stare out the window to my left. "I don't remember him at all."

I huffed. "That's a good thing."

Callan's gaze whipped over to me and I saw anger there. "No, it's not. I have no idea who my own father is. Just stories from

Mom when she actually talks about him which we all know is next to never. Shouldn't a man know who he comes from?"

I leaned across the table, forgetting all about our coffees or the other people in the coffee shop. "Let me tell you my last memory of our father. He and Mom were fighting while you triplets were crying and hanging on to Mom. He walked out of the house like all five of us were solely mom's responsibility. I ran after him and he slapped me across the face so hard I fell to the grass and my ears rang long after I went to bed that night. I was four years old, Callan. Is that the kind of father you want to get to know?"

Callan swallowed hard, indecision written all over his face. "I guess there's hearing about him being an asshole and then there's seeing it with my own two eyes."

I sat back, tamping down the anger that surfaced every time someone brought up Richard Hellman. He wasn't our father, but simply a sperm donor. He'd gone by Rich, but Ace and I liked to call him Dick. Seemed fitting.

"When you're seeing Dick with your own two eyes, make sure you also see the family he left us for. Five kids, Callan. He left all five of us, and Mom, just to start another family in another town."

Callan ran his thumb across a groove in the wood table. "Maybe he regrets that."

I shook my head. "Some things aren't forgivable, no matter how much the person might regret them."

Callan frowned. "You really believe that?"

I shrugged.

"I think everyone can be forgiven," Callan went on. "But I do agree with you that some things can never be forgotten."

"And I just think that's splitting hairs. I don't need someone else's apology to get closure. Slam the door and lose the key, Callan. It'll make life a hell of a lot easier."

"Or lonelier," he shot back.

"That's what I have you idiots for. And Mom. And Ben. And

now Annie." And fuck if that thought didn't make every rejected, lonely corner of my heart fill with something brighter and better than anything Dick could have offered me.

Callan smiled. "If Annie is on that list already, I'm happy for you. Will you need me as backup when Ben comes home?"

I groaned. "Shit. Not looking forward to that."

"Love's worth it."

My heart started pounding. I felt like I could jump right out of my skin. "Who said anything about love?"

"Your face did, jackass."

CHAPTER TWENTY-FOUR

nnie

MY LUNCH BREAK arrived before the anger bubbling in my head had time to dissipate. I'd SOS'd my friends before my first patient, requesting their presence at lunch. Thankfully, they all agreed, knowing I'd never requested their help before, which meant it had to be something huge.

"You have more cat hair on you than Yedda," Cricket said wryly, eyeing my scrubs with a little twist to her lips.

I tried to brush it off before I had a seat on the end of the park bench. Being a veterinarian was a messy job. Meadow and Addy had already tucked into their sandwiches. Cricket preferred fruit for lunch, no matter how much we tried to push a heavier meal on her. The girl could stand to gain a few pounds, but she just never had an appetite.

"So what's the emergency?" Meadow asked, getting right to the point. "Are you sore from all the sex?"

My face instantly flamed. "Jesus, Meadow. The things that come out of your mouth."

She just shrugged with zero shame. "As your best friend, I would be disappointed if you weren't sore. I mean, the Hellman boys have a reputation. Isn't that right, Addy?"

Addy nearly spit out her bite of lunch. "Um, yeah. I have a salve for that though."

I patted her knee which was covered by some kind of patchwork skirt that should have looked ridiculous, but only made her look more beautiful. "I'll let you know if I need it, thank you."

I tried to take a bite of the turkey and avocado on focaccia bread sandwich I'd made for myself this morning. It tasted like dirt. I put it back on the butcher paper and decided I needed to spill my guts before I could possibly eat.

"Okay, here it is. Blaze's ex is not only a raving bitch, but she's a criminal." All heads swiveled in my direction, lunch forgotten.

"Danette?" Meadow asked.

I nodded, wondering if maybe telling them was only opening a can of worms I'd regret later. But they were my best friends. As much as they loved gossip, if I asked them to keep it a secret, they would. And this was too much to keep to myself.

"Yep. Blaze told me some things in confidence, but basically, it comes down to the fact that he saw her do things while they were together that were illegal. When he confronted her, she threatened him and he left town."

There was silence as they all looked at each other in shock. Meadow finally broke the silence.

"Does Blaze want to do anything about it now?"

I shook my head, anger coursing through my veins that had nowhere to go. "No! And it's ridiculous! She's still out policing the streets and who knows what else she's gotten up to in the years since!" I jumped up from the bench, needing to move. "I have to do something!"

Addy put her hand on my arm. "Whoa, lady. You seem very upset about this."

My eyes nearly bugged out of my head. "I am! It's wrong!"

Cricket stood up too, putting her arm around my shoulder. "I get that, but it's Blaze's decision, right? If he just wants to let it go, then you need to also."

I opened my mouth to object, but Meadow beat me to it. "My question is why are you so upset? Me thinks you have feelings that go deeper than an affection to what most certainly must be a lovely dick. Am I right?"

And there went my face again. Damn, I hated being a ginger sometimes.

Cricket hooted right in my ear and I shrugged her arm off me. "Yes, okay? I like the guy. A lot." The girls all squealed in unison, tugging at the smile that kept wanting to form on my face. "He asked me to be his girlfriend today."

"Oh my God, this is huge!" Cricket shouted.

"That's what she said!" Meadow squealed.

We dissolved into a pile of happy giggles. When we settled down, I sat and took a huge bite of my sandwich. I was still mad about Danette, but at least it was down to a low simmer instead of a boil.

"So Ben's okay with it?" Addy asked sweetly.

My stomach dropped and the sandwich lost its appeal again. "Um, well. He doesn't know yet." I turned to them. "Which means I need you ladies to stay quiet about everything I've talked about today. Okay?"

Their smiles were gone. In its place was concern. Maybe a touch of pity.

"Oh, honey," Addy said, her hand rubbing circles on my back.

"It's not ideal, I know," I said weakly.

Meadow plopped her sandwich down. "Yeah, I see why you're nervous, but nobody should be putting limits on your relationship. Not even a big brother. Ben will have to put on his big boy pants and suck it up."

I cringed. "It's just he's done so much for me and I feel like I've betrayed him."

"By dating a good guy?" Cricket asked. "I mean, Blaze is his best friend, so clearly he thinks he's a good guy."

Addy shook her head. "Men don't reason like that. He'll see it as Blaze breaking his trust."

I nodded, dread lining my stomach. "Exactly."

Meadow, ever the optimist about love now that she'd found Judd, threw her arm in the air. "Then you'll just have to weather the storm and show him you two are good for each other!"

I thought about it, getting behind the idea the more I thought about it. Ben might be a butthead at first, but he'd come around. He couldn't stay mad at his sister and best friend forever, right?

We finished up lunch, and as I headed back to the clinic, I felt better for spilling my guts to my best friends. They'd left me with an optimism I needed. Blaze and I were the real deal. Yes, this relationship was new and therefore shaky, but we'd weather this storm. I knew we would. I believed in us.

My phone dinged later that afternoon and I pulled it out of my pocket between a Yorkie who needed her anal glands expressed—ah, the glamorous life of a veterinarian—and a canary who wasn't eating her daily seeds.

Grandma Donna: Call me tonight, my lovely! I want to hear how the clinic is going.

I sucked in a deep breath and thought about my response. I knew what Grandma Donna wanted and it wasn't to check in on my business. It was a chance for her to grill me about Blaze. And I didn't feel like I could tell her. The fewer people who knew about us, the better. Until Ben knew, I felt weird telling everyone else.

In the end, I ended up pocketing my phone and ignoring Grandma's text. It wasn't nice and it certainly wasn't the mature route, but it was all I could do until I'd talked to Blaze and formulated a plan for telling Ben about us.

I was cleaning the back exam room at the end of the day when I heard the little bell above the front door ring out.

"I'll be right there!" I called out. I stored the disinfectant under the cabinet and made my way to the front. Two dogs ran in circles in the lobby as I approached. I looked left and right. Then behind the check in desk.

"Hello?"

Not a single human was in the clinic. Just me and two dogs I'd never seen before. Both of them were Doberman pinschers, possibly just full grown based on their size. They looked a touch on the lean side, a few rows of ribs showing that should have been covered by bulky muscle.

"Hello, beautiful puppies. Who's your owner?" I bent down and petted them both after they'd sniffed my hands and decided I was to be trusted. They were sweet dogs, sitting when I pushed their behinds down. They followed me through the clinic as I checked to see if they were chipped—they weren't—or had any medical problems, and then gave them treats from my cabinet below the check-in desk.

Of course, the first person I thought of was Blaze.

Me: Any chance you want to train a couple of Doberman pinschers while I track down their owner? I think they're a brother and sister.

His answer was immediate.

Blaze: Hell yes. Are they at your clinic now?

Me: Yep. Someone just dropped them off and left. They're sweet pups.

Blaze: I'll be right over with my SUV. And I'll call Ethan to install some security cameras.

I wrinkled my nose, not liking the idea of needing them in this small town I'd grown up in. But as the dogs ran around my clinic and checked out every corner sans owner, I knew it was a good idea. Blaze, true to his word, showed up ten minutes later. He swooped into the clinic and pulled me in for a kiss that made my knees weak before he even took notice of the two dogs jumping against our legs for attention. I loved that Blaze was so focused, especially when that dark gaze was focused on me.

We got them home safely and I tried my hand at making spaghetti while Blaze worked with the new dogs and mediated their interactions with Tate. By the time we sat down to eat, the three canines were lying down in a row in the living room, quietly getting along.

"You're like the dog whisperer, you know."

Blaze wiped his mouth with a napkin. "I don't know about that."

"Come on. You're amazing with them. It's okay to toot your own horn."

Blaze's lips twitched. I realized I was addicted to making that happen. His frown was like a siren call to say or do something that would make him break out in a rare smile.

"I was thinking because of their mostly light brown color, if we can't find their owner, we could name them Sugar and Spice."

I nodded, liking those names. "Keep with the food theme?"

Blaze shrugged. "I should probably find them new owners soon. This isn't my house and I can't imagine Ben would want to come home to find a full kennel in his backyard."

Unspoken was the issue of Ben finding Blaze and me cozy together. Ben would overlook the dogs, but he'd never overlook his best friend dating his little sister.

I cleared my throat. "About that...I think we should—"

A cacophony of barking and snarls cut me off. Blaze jumped up and hustled into the living room and I followed behind. He got in the middle of the tussle while I shouted for him to be careful. We didn't know the temperament of the new dogs yet. And young dogs tended to bite when flustered.

"Aha!" Blaze pulled something from the swarm, holding it up over his head. "They're fighting over a toy."

I looked up to see a light blue shark toy. "Oh my God!"

Blaze brought it over to me, studying it intently. I tried to snatch it from his hands, mortification making me desperate. It flew out of his hands and I bobbled it like an idiot. One of the dogs leapt through the air and caught it in his mouth like a damn Frisbee. I ran after him, yelling about him being a bad boy. Blaze helped me corner him against the couch. Then Blaze pounced, grabbing the toy from the dog's mouth and walking toward the kitchen with it. I followed, trying to dart around his broad back and snatch it back.

He must have found the little button against the dorsal fin. The one that started the vibration. It let out a steady buzz, one I was very familiar with. My friends and I had each bought one at The Hardware Store during a bachelorette party six months ago. The mouth of the shark was a silicone suction cup thingy that was surprisingly lifelike.

"Holy shit," he muttered.

I buried my face in my hands.

The dogs, seeing that their fun was over, went back to lying down in the living room. I heard a sputter and then a chuckle, which turned into a full belly laugh. I peeked one eye open to see Blaze nearly doubled over by the refrigerator, laughing hysterically as he stared at my toy called The Shark Bite.

"It's not that funny," I groused.

Blaze wiped at his eyes, barely able to breathe. "It...really...is."

His uninhibited laugh made my lips tug upward. He sounded like the teen I remembered. The one who would howl with laughter with my brother and the shenanigans they got up to. The boy who let joy flow unfiltered.

Before long, my laugh joined in. I snatched the toy from his hands and pretended the shark was about to bite his face. Blaze just laughed harder, batting away my toy, but snagging his hands on my hips and tugging me closer. I came willingly even though he was laughing at me. It was at my expense, but I didn't really care if it could help him heal. Grandma Donna had always said that laughter was the best medicine. And I had to admit, it was kind of funny to find your dogs fighting over your vibrator.

Blaze finally settled enough to kiss my cheek. "How about you go take a shower and I'll wash up Jaws."

"It's okay. I'll just stick him back in my suitcase." The less Blaze handled my vibrator, the better.

Blaze's hands crept around to grab my ass. "Nope. I have plans for you and that shark tonight, baby."

And suddenly my mortification fled, leaving a breathlessness that spelled pleasure in my future.

CHAPTER TWENTY-FIVE

laze

SUGAR AND SPICE were turning out to be the best damn training dogs ever. They picked up on commands faster than Tate, seeming eager to do more each day. They had a lot of energy, which made sense when Annie figured out they were probably only ten months old. They had another month or two before they were fully grown, with all the rambunctiousness of puppies, but once I gave them work to do, they jumped in with enthusiasm.

"Sit."

Both rumps hit the floor and I fed them a tiny treat. The bell over the door at Annie's clinic rang out and all three of our heads turned to see old man Lenny standing there looking awkward. A bead of sweat ran down his forehead even though it wasn't particularly warm out yet.

"You okay, Lenny?" I asked, moving a little closer.

He ran his hands down his flannel shirt and seemed a bit

confused. He glanced at me, but focused in on the cushioned chairs in the waiting room. He shuffled over and nearly collapsed into one.

Sugar let out a whine and ran over, disobeying my sit command.

"Sugar!" I lunged for her, but all she did was sit by Lenny's feet and put a paw up on his knee, the whining picking up steam.

"Sorry, Lenny. She's new to me and not quite trained."

Lenny grumbled out something I couldn't make out, but leaned forward to put a gnarled hand on her head. He gave her a few strokes and then looked up at me.

"I need a dog."

I sat in the chair next to him. "What for?"

Lenny scratched at his jaw, looking a little out of sorts. "I had a little Pomeranian, but she passed a few months ago. She was such a good little dog. Didn't realize how much I came to rely on her while living alone, you know. I figured maybe I'd get a cat as they're easier to take care of, but I took one step into Yedda's place and nearly sneezed my head off. Allergic, I guess."

Annie's tennis shoes came squeaking down the hall and she stopped short when she saw me with Lenny.

"Hey, Lenny." Her smile faded as she took him in. "Are you feeling okay?"

Lenny batted a hand through the air, never taking his other hand off Sugar's head. "Getting old is for the birds, darlin'. Avoid it if you can. Doctor told me last week I have diabetes. Can you believe that? I do yoga three days a week and go for walks every day. How the hell can I have diabetes?"

Annie sat on the other side of Lenny. "Well, diabetes is becoming more and more common. Did the doctor send you to a nutritionist?"

Lenny flapped his lips. "What do they know that I don't? I've lived seventy-seven years and suddenly don't know how to eat?"

Annie had a patient smile that made me want to pick her up out of that chair and take her home with me. "Well, they know a hell of a lot about food when you have a medical condition, Lenny. You need to go see the nutritionist. You don't look quite right."

Sugar let out another whine and she pawed at Lenny's knee. An idea hit me. I'd just finished one of the modules of the course I was taking on dog training that could apply here.

"Did you know you can teach a dog to detect a blood sugar swing?"

Lenny's head swiveled in my direction. "You can?"

I nodded. "Sure. They can detect changes in your breath. Trained properly, they can even wake you up in the middle of the night if your blood sugar gets too low. Maybe you could get a dog like that."

Lenny considered my words, but then patted Sugar's head. "But I like this dog."

Annie interjected. "Blaze, maybe you could work with Sugar and see if she could learn how to do that?"

Lenny spun in his chair so fast I pulled my bad leg back to get out of his way. "Would you help me, Blaze?"

I shrugged. "Sure. But I have to warn you, I've never trained a dog to do that, so I'm not sure I'll know how. And it takes years before they're reliable."

Lenny ran his tongue over his dentures. "Well, I don't intend to up and die anytime soon. Tell you what. You try to train Sugar and I'll go to that nutritionist. Between the two of us learning a new trick or two, maybe we can get a handle on this diabetes thing."

I put my hand out and Lenny shook it. "You got yourself a deal."

Annie beamed at the two of us, her proud smile making my chest seem to expand to double its size. She seemed to believe I could do it, which only made me want to try that much harder.

"Oh, wait." Lenny frowned, taking in Spice, who sat in the same spot the whole time, eyeing us with curiosity. "What about that one?"

Annie hopped to her feet to pet Spice. "It's actually better to separate littermates, especially when undergoing rigorous training like you're talking about. We have an adoption event coming up. We'll find a great home for Spice too. Maybe these two could have some playdates though so they don't miss each other."

Lenny frowned. "Sure. Just don't adopt him out to Poppy. That woman has flirted with me for years. Scares me, honestly. She's what we called a man-eater in my day. She'll chew you up and spit you out before you even know what's happening. Did I ever tell you about the time I stumbled into a cave by the water and found her in a, well, let's just say a compromising situation?" His bushy eyebrows waggled and I lost my appetite.

I grimaced and got to my feet. "I just remembered I have an appointment to get to. Sorry to rush off."

Annie gave me a look of death for leaving her with Lenny and his rambling story. "Where are you going, mister?"

I hedged toward the door. "I have that thing with my brothers."

Annie looked at the watch on her wrist. "That's at six."

Lenny's head swiveled back and forth as we sparred. "Yeah, well. I have to get ready."

Annie put her hands on her hips. "Blaze Hellman, you get your ass back here and help Lenny home."

I bit my bottom lip and thought it through. I didn't want to piss off Annie, but I really didn't want to hear that story about Poppy either. Maybe I could walk Lenny home and distract him with the dogs.

"Okay, fine." I came back over and held out my hand for Lenny. "Let's see if Sugar will walk nicely on a leash for you."

Lenny gave me a wide grin. "You can buy me lunch first and then we'll get to that walk."

I was being hustled by an old man and my girlfriend, but based on the way Annie was eyeing me with appreciation shining out of her blue eyes, I'd allow it to happen. A happy Annie was worth it.

"Forty-Diner or it's no deal."

Lenny took my hand and stood. "Will you poke my finger and check my sugars before we eat?"

I glared at him. "You're pushing it, Lenny."

He gave me an impish grin and walked out of the clinic, looking a thousand times better than when he walked in.

Yep. I was getting hustled, all right.

Annie kissed me goodbye and all was right with my world again.

"WHAT DO you mean you can only have one beer?" Daxon looked ready to throw punches over my declaration as I sat down in one of the wooden chairs around the sticky table at The Tavern.

The place hadn't changed much from when I used to try to sneak in here. The floor was real wood, scraped from heels, boots, and tussles that caused furniture to be rearranged. Nugget poured out pints from behind the bar while a pretty new bartender kept all the orders coming in.

"I'm trying to rehab from an injury, remember?" I groused, irritated that I even needed to defend my position. Since when did my little brothers become the beer police?

"They do say alcohol is a toxin. Lord knows I've seen enough nasty accidents because of it." Callan clapped me on the shoulder.

Ace finally made an appearance, sliding into the last empty chair and smacking the table. "What did I miss?"

"Blaze is a teetotaler now," Daxon blurted.

I rolled my eyes and tried to remember why I agreed to come

tonight when I could have been in bed with Annie, showing her new and inventive ways to use that shark bite toy.

"I have limits and boundaries. It's a concept you should explore when you've matured enough," I shot back.

"Damn. Just like old times." Ethan took a swig of beer and grinned like an idiot with foam in his mustache.

Ace raised his arm and caught Nugget's eye. Then he turned back to Daxon. "You know you're looking a little beefier these days. You lifting weights?"

I scrutinized Daxon, realizing he filled out his shirt a bit snugger than what I remembered. Shit, I needed to push harder in the gym. I couldn't let my little brother out bench me. That went against all laws of big brothers.

Surprisingly, the guy looked a little embarrassed at the attention. "Yeah, been hitting the gym a bit more recently. That's all."

Ethan sputtered and Callan chuckled.

"What?" Ace and I looked between the triplets. They always seemed to have their own fucking language that left Ace and me in the dark.

Ethan put his frosted mug of beer down on the table. "I think poor Dax is sick of women taking one look at his ass and recognizing him from his modeling days. Wants to go incognito."

Daxon rolled his eyes, but looked around the room as if he wanted to be anywhere but here, discussing his modeling.

I bit back a smile. "I remember seeing a bus go by when I first moved to LA. Had your ass right on it in those washed-out jeans. Billboard size. Nearly pissed my pants laughing so hard."

"Fuck off," Dax muttered.

"Come on. The money had to be good, right?" Callan said, ever the peacemaker.

Nugget came over with another round of beers, but I pushed mine over to Daxon. I wanted all my faculties about me. Not for rehab purposes like I said. I wanted to go home to my woman and get her naked without feeling like the alcohol was fogging up my abilities.

"Yes, the money was great. It gave me the cash to open my business and get it profitable quick. But I'm ready to leave that behind. Okay?"

Ace nodded. "Okay, man. We won't mention your pretty ass again."

Daxon glared at him while we all laughed, but we dropped the subject. The conversation turned to work and what we were all up to. By the time I was nearly done with my beer, I'd relaxed and remembered why I missed my brothers. They were an all-right bunch.

"So, how's living with Annie?" Ethan asked out of the blue. All heads swiveled in my direction and I shifted on the hard wooden chair.

"Going good."

Dax made a weird noise that sounded like a fucking bird call. "Going good? Really? That's your answer?"

"I think what he means is that we've never seen you smile more." Ace nudged my elbow. "And Annie sure seems happy."

I thought about lying. Telling them we were just friends was even on the tip of my tongue, but I just couldn't do it anymore. Not when we were actually dating and I was pretty sure I was developing some serious feelings where she was concerned.

I put my elbows on the table and leaned in. "I'll punch you right in the nuts if you share this, but yeah. We're dating. And it's going really good. Like, real good."

"Congrats, man." Callan was the first to quit gaping over my announcement.

"Does Mom know?" Ethan piped in.

"No. Not really. No one knows. We're keeping it a secret until Ben is back and we can tell him together."

"Oh fuck. I would literally pay to see that." Daxon's face lit up. "You think he'll throw a punch? Ben's quiet, but he can be unpredictable, you know."

"Thanks for that," I replied wryly. "I'm not sure how he'll

react, but finding out from someone other than Annie or me would be worse, so keep this between us, okay?"

"You got it. Our lips are sealed." Ace looked around the table one by one. "Right, guys?"

They all grumbled their agreement and I trusted them to keep their mouths shut. I couldn't fuck this up. My lifelong friendship with Ben was on the line.

"Hey, boys!" A feminine holler came over my left shoulder. Some girl with too much perfume and a desire to show as much skin as possible while still being dressed was eyeing each of us, two quieter friends wedged in on either side of her. "How about a dance before the place gets packed?"

Daxon immediately stood up with a grin that was all flirt. "I was just waiting for the prettiest girl in the place to ask." He took the woman's hand and led her off to the dance floor, probably making plans already to take her home. The guy certainly had a way about him when it came to the ladies.

The friends stood there awkwardly in our circle. Ace and I made eye contact and shrugged. We had no interest in dancing with either one of them. Callan jumped to his feet and shot one of them a wide smile.

"And what's your name?" He started up conversation and moved the taller one to the dance floor, putting her out of her misery.

"Care to dance?" the last woman standing asked me, her voice soft and hesitant. I felt for her. Wasn't easy to go up to a group of men and risk rejection. But I also had no interest in dancing with her.

"Sorry. Normally I would, but...I can't."

She nodded and smiled shyly. "I get it. You have a girlfriend?"

I swallowed hard. "Yeah. Something like that."

Fear pounded through my veins. Hell was known for spreading gossip like wildfire. Even kind of mentioning a girl-friend was asking for trouble. I'd better get home to Annie and figure out what we were going to tell Ben. Sooner rather than later.

"I, on the other hand, do not have a kind-of girlfriend," Ethan said, drawing her attention over to him.

He stood and the woman moved to his side. The two of them headed for the dance floor, heads bent together as they chatted.

I shook my head. "He and Callan might be the nicest guys I know."

Nugget came over to deliver another round of beer, his weathered face creased in a perpetual frown. "Nice guys finish last."

Ace sat back in his chair watching our baby brothers. "I guess we'll see, won't we?"

I left soon after, not wanting another beer and worried I'd have to turn down more dances, therefore increasing my chances of being gossiped about. And I wanted to get home to Annie. She'd become an addiction flowing through my veins. I didn't think I could sleep if I didn't spend some time touching her skin, hearing her talk about her day, or see the flaming color of her hair spread across my pillow.

I found her with an audience of three dogs watching her try to put up new shelves in the living room. Right next to the curtains Ethan had fixed last week. This time, she was using the nail gun, which was the right tool for the job, but the top shelf was crooked. So crooked if you put a ball on it, it would roll right off.

"Now I probably should have used a thingy that sees if it's level, but sometimes eyeballing it works too." She was talking to the dogs over her shoulder and hadn't seen me yet. I bit back a smile. The woman was crazy. Crazy wonderful. "Now it's time for shelf number two."

She turned to grab the wood shelf and I saw she'd put on safety goggles. The bulky kind you'd use in a science lab. She jumped and looked right at me, startled.

"Blaze!"

The goggles had smooshed her eyes and nose, making her face look like an alien. The strap around the back of her head had caught on some hair, and a handful of it stood straight up from her head. She was a delightful mess.

And I had a feeling I was head over ass in love with her.

"Annie." I muttered her name like a prayer. A request for the universe to grant me this woman every day for the rest of my life.

"I'm putting up shelves! Want to watch?" She grabbed the nail gun and I got a little nervous.

"What is with you and home improvements?"

She shrugged, trying to smile, but the goggles bent her cheeks and top lip at a weird angle. "I just like to do nice things for people."

I took a few steps into the room and took the nail gun from her hands. I needed to straighten out that top shelf before attempting the second shelf. "Are you sure that's all it is?"

She frowned and I had to dip my head down to kiss her, goggles and all. Fuck, she was adorable.

"Are you sure you don't feel the need to pay Ben back for letting you stay here?" I asked softly.

"Are you psychoanalyzing me, Blaze?" She cocked a hip out to the side, and I heeded the warning signal.

I gripped her goggles with both hands and pulled them away from her face. They let out a suction noise when I finally got them off. Took a few minutes to get her hair untangled from the strap, but I got it done.

"I'm absolutely not analyzing you. I just want to make sure you understand that family does favors because they love you, not because they want you to pay them back." Ben was a lucky bastard to have Annie in his life. He didn't need fucking shelves as payback.

Annie frowned some more, looking ridiculous and adorable with lines dug into her skin from the goggles. I relented.

"How about you make me one of your famous sandwiches with everything on it and I'll finish up these shelves?"

It would take at least an hour to redo what she'd done, but if my girl wanted shelves up to thank her brother, I'd put in the effort.

"Only if you wear the goggles so you don't put an eye out."

I kissed her nose. "Deal."

CHAPTER TWENTY-SIX

nnie

"I THINK I should be the one to tell him, don't you?" I slid the straps of my sundress over my shoulders, looking in the full-length mirror at where Blaze was supposed to be getting dressed. We were due at his mom's house for dinner in ten minutes and were on the verge of being late. Blaze had wanted to take a shower with me. You know, to save water. Instead of dressing though, he was frozen in place, staring at me.

"Blaze?" I turned, the turquoise flowered dress spinning around my thighs that were just starting to pick up a bit of color from the late summer sun. Redheads didn't really tan. We just burned and returned to a shade on the ghostly spectrum.

"Are you..." He cleared his throat. "Are you wearing that to dinner?"

I looked down at the dress. "Yeah. Why?"

Blaze swallowed hard and flopped down on the bed dramatically. "I'm never going to be able to keep my hands off you."

I sputtered out a laugh. "We're going to your mother's!"

"And?"

I came over and flicked his leg. "Behave yourself. And you didn't answer my question."

That got his attention. He sat up, that scowl I'd come to love back on his face. "No. Absolutely not. I need to be the one to tell him or he'll see it as a betrayal of our friendship. The bro code was broken, Annie."

I rolled my eyes. "Stupid bro code."

Blaze stood and shrugged. "Can't fight gravity, baby." He took my hand and pulled me toward the door. "Now let's get dinner over with so I can strip you out of that dress."

It was entirely his fault that I showed up at Nikki's house with a red face. Blaze had taken liberties with the hem of my dress while he drove. How he could stay on the road and still find the exact spot that made my lungs spasm was probably a Hellman brother trait. They were good with their hands.

The front door swung open as soon as we climbed out of Blaze's SUV. I didn't even have time to take a deep breath or fix my thong that Blaze had pushed aside. One of my girl flaps was free as a bird, which was a hell of a way to go to your secret boyfriend's mother's house for family dinner. The chafing might kill me before the embarrassment.

"Come in, my little secret lovebirds!" Nikki shouted loudly enough to alert the entire neighborhood.

"Jeez, Mom," Blaze muttered, putting his hand on my lower back and pushing me up the porch stairs and through the doorway.

Nikki gave me a hug, then Blaze, talking a mile a minute. I couldn't stop smiling, feeling like I could really get along with Nikki. A stampede that shook the house started in the living room. Turned out to only be the rest of the Hellman brothers coming over to say hello. As a child with only one quiet older brother, I wasn't used to the noise level.

"Annie!"

That was Ethan, coming over to pick me up in a bear hug and

spin me around. He was already chuckling when he set me down, shooting a wink at Blaze.

Addy pulled me away from Ethan and Ace shook my hand like a normal person. Callan gave me a quick hug and moved on. Of course, Daxon couldn't be outshined by Ethan, so he sidled up to my side and put his arm around me smelling of cologne and sawdust. He kept up a steady barrage of questions, but all I could focus on was needing to excuse myself to the bathroom to fix my underwear.

Blaze wedged himself between Daxon and me. "Let the woman breathe, you freaks."

"Ahh, Blaze doesn't like us touching his woman," Daxon pouted.

Nikki reached up and flicked Daxon's earlobe. "You promised not to tease him."

Daxon grabbed his ear and moved back. "I did not! You asked me not to, but I never agreed."

Nikki put her hands on her ample hips, a streak of magenta in her hair today that seemed to be purposely matched to her bright pink tennis shoes. "You watch yourself, young man. I made pie, but you won't get one damn bite if you keep up the attitude."

"How about we just sit and eat, huh?" Blaze grumbled, his face looking like a storm cloud in the heat of summer.

"I'll be right there. Bathroom," I murmured and hightailed it into the living room.

Addy followed me, pointing down the hall to the bathroom. Thank goodness I had one normal person here with me. Taking a deep breath and pulling that thong back in place was almost as nice as the orgasm Blaze had given me coming over here. I washed my hands with a bar of soap shaped like a flamingo. It was almost too cute to use, but I had a feeling Nikki had more just like it.

When I came out of the bathroom, Addy was leaning against the opposite wall waiting for me. "Based on that permanent blush on your cheeks, shall I assume things are going well in the Blaze department?"

I was grinning before I realized it. "Very well."

Addy's face went soft, her eyes rounded. "Did our little Annie catch feelings?"

I nodded, taking a deep breath. I hadn't said it out loud. Hell, I hadn't even been brave enough to think it through, but I could see myself falling in love with Blaze. Very, very easily.

"Well, I think he's caught the same feelings. He couldn't take his eyes off you. Thought he might start a fight with the way he was glaring at Daxon and Ethan for touching you."

I giggled, realizing the overprotective thing was hot as hell. "Let's just hope things don't go sideways when Ben comes home."

"I believe that love always prevails." Addy put her arm around me with that comforting sentiment and we walked into the dining room together.

The thing with Ben was like a black cloud hanging over my head, but just for tonight, I was going to let myself envision a future with Blaze. A future that held weekly family dinners and brothers that treated me like one of them. I didn't have a big family growing up. It was just Ben and Grandma Donna. They were fabulous and I wouldn't trade them for the world, but an orphan tends to have secret dreams of a big happy family. And the Hellmans were big alright. There was so much testosterone shoved into one room it was no wonder Nikki wanted another woman to attend dinner to balance things out.

We made it all the way through to dessert with lots of friendly conversation flying around the table before Nikki let herself ask the questions she'd been holding back.

"So, give it to me straight. What's the deal with you two?" She waved her fork between Blaze and me. The table went quiet. My throat closed and even the bump of Blaze's knee against mine under the table wasn't enough to get me talking. Imagine that. Me, Annie McLachlin, had lost the ability to speak.

"Well, Mom." Blaze pushed his half-eaten plate of apple pie away from him. "We're officially dating."

Nikki smiled like we told her Christmas was now going to be celebrated twice a year. She set her fork down and clasped her hands below her chin.

"I'm so happy," she said softly. Something about the sincerity and approval in her voice made my eyes well up.

Blaze put his arm around me and I trained my gaze on the tablecloth. I would not cry at the Hellman family dinner.

"I'd appreciate your discretion though until we can tell Ben."

And that dried up my tears in a heartbeat.

"We'll all keep our mouths shut. You can count on that. When do you plan to tell him?" Nikki asked kindly.

I raised my head. "He should be coming home any day now. We'll do it first thing. I just didn't want to do it over the phone."

Ace blew out a breath. "Thank God someone realizes some things shouldn't be done over the phone. Did you know Polly *texted* me that there was a fire in the dumpster behind the T-Spot? Pick up the phone and call 9-1-1. Don't text!" Ace shook his head. "People these days."

And just like that, the conversation flowed in other directions, giving me a second to swallow and get the heat to dissipate from my cheeks. Blaze's thumb stroked back and forth over my shoulder, as if he knew how uncomfortable I'd become when Ben was brought up.

"Speaking of ridiculous," Ethan piped up. "Did you see that a lady was paddleboarding just a few miles south of here a week ago and got into some trouble?"

Callan threw down his napkin on the table. "I got called out on that one. No injuries other than a concussion from the board hitting her as she tried to escape."

"Escape what?" Addy said, nose wrinkled.

"A shark!" Daxon exclaimed.

Blaze and I both looked at each other, our brains clearly thinking of the same light blue shark toy. He bit his lip and I rolled mine inward. Nope. It was no use. I burst out laughing and Blaze followed a second later. Pretty soon we were both howling with laughter and the table had gone quiet again.

"What's so funny?" Ethan asked, a ready smile on his face.

It was an inside joke. No way was I sharing about my vibrator with Blaze's brothers and his mother.

A yelp had our laughs drying up immediately. All heads turned to see Nikki crying, her hands pressed to her face.

"Mom? Are you *crying?*" Blaze asked, looking to his brothers for help. They all shrugged and waited out the crying fit.

"I'm sorry, Mom. I know I shouldn't have taken that girl home with me, but she swore she wasn't from around here. How was I supposed to know she was Mrs. Trudowski's granddaughter?" Daxon looked around at us, his hands splayed wide, eyes innocent.

Addy sighed and said what we were all thinking. "Why are you like this, Dax?"

Nikki raised her head, her cheeks wet with tears. She'd hate to know it, but her mascara had smudged, making her look a little like a raccoon.

"That's not why I'm crying, Daxon, but you and I will be speaking about that later." She turned her red eyes to Blaze. "I'm crying because I've missed the sound of your laugh, son."

Blaze's shoulders slumped, and damn it all to hell, I was officially crying at the Hellman family dinner. Blaze jumped out of his chair and came around to hug his mom, murmuring something low in her ear. I caught Addy's eye and she was using her napkin to wipe her eyes. She made a face and I made it right back.

I'd caught feelings all right.

I was in love with Blaze and this whole crazy family.

THE SOUND of the zipper giving on the back of my dress seemed to echo in the bedroom. Blaze's mouth trailed down my spine, leaving open-mouthed kisses that gave me the shivers.

"You are so beautiful," he said softly, letting the dress pool at my feet before spinning me around. His hands trailed over my breasts, down my stomach, and between my legs. "I need to be inside that hot pussy, Annie."

"I won't stop you," I answered on a whisper. I sat on the bed and scooted backward. I let my knees open for him. I'd already lost my underwear on the ride home from dinner.

Blaze grunted, looking at me like he hadn't eaten a damn thing at dinner and needed to feast on my body instead. He stripped off his shirt, then his jeans, his heavy-lidded gaze never leaving me. He climbed onto the bed and hovered over me. I opened my legs wider and he sank into me like we belonged together. He slid inside without breaking eye contact, the whole thing more intense than anything I'd ever experienced before. He didn't even stop for a condom, which seemed to be some sort of statement. Like he'd made a decision about us in his head.

"Annie," he breathed, moving in and out of me so slowly I was going to lose my mind. "How is this so good?"

I ran my hands through his hair, pulling him closer so I could kiss him. "I think I've been wanting that dick since I ran into you naked from the shower."

He grinned, like I knew he would, but sobered quickly. "It's more than that. You're absolutely everything."

My heart soared. A confession of that magnitude from tight-lipped Blaze was all the confirmation I needed.

"I love you."

It was simply a verbal manifestation of everything that was happening in my heart. Of the tenderness that already existed between us. Of the future I envisioned with this man.

Blaze didn't answer, but his eyes squeezed shut and his body trembled.

"Annie, Annie, Annie." He kept saying my name, in time with

his increasingly intense thrusts, his hands holding so tight I could barely breathe. The orgasm hit hard and fast, pulling me under like it always did with him. He followed right after, his hot release seeping out between us. He didn't move. Just blew his overheated breath against my skin where his head lay on my chest. He should have been too heavy, but I couldn't push him away. When the anxieties of my one-sided confession of love and the return of my brother threatened to ruin the moment, Blaze's weight was like a blanket pulling me down to slumber.

Sometime later my phone vibrated with an incoming text, but I was already asleep and didn't hear it.

CHAPTER TWENTY-SEVEN

laze

I WATCHED the sun rise through the blinds we forgot to close the night before. I'd lost my cool watching Annie in that damn dress all night at my mom's house where I couldn't touch her like I wanted. When we got back to Ben's, I'd forgotten everything but getting my hands on the woman I was crazy for.

It was more than that though. As the sun traveled higher in the sky, I admitted what had been pressing against my rib cage for days, if not weeks now. I was in love with Annie.

And she was in love with me.

As much as it scared me to admit to something that could blow up my friendship with Ben, I had to put it into words. Annie deserved nothing less. She'd had the courage to say those words to me last night, not even blinking an eye when I hadn't said it back. She put up with far too much from everyone, putting herself last. I would not be one of the people that took her for granted.

Annie finally stirred, letting out a soft groan and rolling into my side without even opening her eyes. I wasn't going to do anything to wake her. The woman had been working her ass off at her clinic. She deserved one morning a week where she didn't have to get up to the sound of the alarm clock. When her fingers began to twitch along my stomach where her hand lay, I peeked down at her. I counted the freckles on the right side of her cheekbone, hoping they'd never fade as she got older. Faces in Los Angeles had been so boring with the same puffed-up lips, highlighted cheekbones, fake lashes, and drawn-in eyebrows. Annie's face was both beautiful and interesting.

Her eyelids fluttered and suddenly those blue eyes were staring up at me. Her mouth tilted up into a smile and I realized I'd break every bone in my body and lose my career over and over again if only it led me to this exact moment with Annie.

"Morning, gorgeous," I whispered.

"Morning," she croaked back, then crossed her eyes comically.

I cracked a smile and ran my fingertips down her bare arm. "Been waiting for you to wake up, sleepyhead."

She frowned. "It's Sunday, right?"

"Yeah, but I had something to say."

She let out a yawn, hiding her face in my side. "What's that?"

"Annie." I waited until she looked back up at me. I had to do this right. "Remember what you said to me last night?"

Her eyes immediately focused, her body tensing against me. "Um, yeah?"

I reached up to cup her face, my thumb running along her jawline. "Well, I didn't get a chance to say it back, but I want you to know I love you too."

She sucked in a deep breath, her eyes lighting up. "You do?"

I nodded against the pillow. "I absolutely do."

Annie smiled so brilliantly Hell wouldn't need the sun today to light up the place. Her fingers walked down lower, finding the erection I'd woken up to every morning since I moved in and she'd been somewhere in this house. I grunted as she took a firm hold of it.

"This is cause for celebration, don't you think?"

I rolled so that I was above her, my hips settling in between her thighs—incidentally, my favorite place to be. Dipping my head, I kissed her like I'd been wanting to all morning.

"I love you, Annie."

Her eyes stared into my soul. "I love you too."

"What the fuck?"

A voice from the doorway of the bedroom had my heart seizing in my chest. All three dogs ran from the corner of the room where they'd been sleeping to bark and sniff at the intruder. So much for them being watch dogs.

Although this wasn't an intruder. This was his house.

Ben stood in the doorway, a suitcase at his feet and an expression that was a mix of anger, disbelief, and pure, unadulterated rage. Seconds ticked by, all of us frozen except for the dogs scrambling around the room wondering why no one was acknowledging them. Ben held a white bakery bag in his free hand, looking exactly like my best friend, but aiming an expression my way I'd never seen before.

"Ben!" Annie finally gasped, scrambling to make sure the sheets were pulled high enough to cover her.

"Shit." The word wasn't even out of my mouth before Ben turned on his heel and marched down the hallway. I slid out of bed and lunged for my jeans from the night before. My heart was thundering so loudly I wasn't sure if I'd lost my hearing. "Stay here. I'll talk to him."

Annie also scrambled out of bed, running around the room looking for something to wear. "Wait!"

But I couldn't wait. Every second was precious and I had to stop Ben before he misconstrued this as something it wasn't. This wasn't a casual hookup. I intended to buy Annie a ring at the first available opportunity. Like maybe around lunchtime today.

"Fuck, fuck, fuck." I couldn't believe this was happening. The absolute worst way for Ben to find out about me and Annie.

"Ben!" I ran down the hallway into the living room as best I could on a leg that needed stretches and warmups before it could even attempt to move that quickly. Desperate times called for desperate measures.

I caught up to him right as he put his hand on the front door to leave. He still had his suitcase rolling behind him.

"Ben, wait! I can explain."

He spun around, his thick glasses literally fogging up. Fuck. The guy was pissed. He threw the white bag at my chest and I barely caught it. "Because of our lifelong friendship, I'll give you exactly ten minutes to get your shit out of my house."

"Ben—"

"I swear to all that's holy, if you don't get yourself and your shit out of my sight, I will rearrange your face. Rehabbing your leg will be the last thing you care about. Are we clear?"

I hung my head, unable to continue looking at the anger and hurt on my best friend's face. "Crystal."

I heard the door open, the wheels scrabbled across the doorway, and then the door closed with a slam. I let the white bag drop and ran my hands through my hair, pulling on the strands so hard it gave me some other pain to think about. Anything to dull the ache in my gut that I'd just ruined a lifelong friendship with one of the best guys on this planet.

"Ben!" Annie came running to the door and ripped it open, now dressed in one of my T-shirts and a pair of cutoff jean shorts. She ran down the porch steps and made it to Ben as he stood by his bright red convertible sports car. "Wait, Benji."

Ben's head came up, but his gaze darted back up to me standing in the doorway, his eyes narrowing. Annie put her hands on his arms and drew his attention back.

"Don't leave angry, Ben. This isn't how I wanted you to find out and I'm sorry that it happened this way. I wanted—"

"The whole town is talking about you two." Ben's voice

sounded hollow. "Stopped to get muffins for—" He cut off as if
he couldn't even force himself to say my name. "Anyway,
everyone was talking about my little sister with my best friend. I
thought they were crazy. Surely I wouldn't be the last one to
know, right? Surely my little sister and my best friend wouldn't
go behind my back, in my house, in my bed—"

Ben's voice was escalating, cutting off suddenly as he looked
around. "This isn't the place to discuss this. And I want that
fucker out of my house. Immediately." He was back to glaring
at me.

Annie tried to turn him away, but he wouldn't budge, not
even for her. "It's not his fault, Ben. Please, let me explain."

"It's a matter of violating the brother code of ethics, Annie.
You wouldn't understand." He shrugged her hands off of him and
threw his suitcase in the car. "Get him out of here. Then we can
talk."

And with that, he got in the car and literally peeled out of
the driveway, leaving tire tracks. Shit. I'd tried to get him to peel
out when he first bought the thing with his piles of cash and he
wouldn't do it.

Annie watched him drive down the street, only turning to
come in the house when his taillights disappeared around the
corner. She moved slower than me, stopping in the doorway
where I stood. When she lifted her head, tears blurred her eyes.
She looked like she'd crack into a thousand pieces if I so much as
touched her.

"Annie," I croaked, not sure anything could be said to fix this.
I'd been so worried about ruining my friendship with Ben,
without even considering what this would do to Annie's relationship with her brother. I was just another asshole in her life,
taking what I wanted from her without considering her sacrifice.

I took a step back and considered my options. Ben wanted
me gone, and I'd give that to him. Annie wanted her brother
back, and I could give that to her too. I'd take the blame. All of
the blame. Ben would direct his anger at me and forgive her.

I hooked my thumb over my shoulder. "I should probably go."

Annie swiped angrily at her cheeks where tears had begun to fall. "No! Why?"

I took another step back when my arms itched to pull her into my chest and dry her tears. "He wants me gone. We were wrong to do this. Here."

Annie took a step toward me, alarm written all over her face. "Wrong to do this? Or wrong to do this here? Because that's two totally different things, Blaze."

I shook my head, looking around the stark house that had become a home with Annie in it. I couldn't do this to her. Sure, she said she loved me, but her love for Ben had existed every day of her whole damn life. If one of us had to go for there to be peace in her life, it had to be me. It might literally kill me, but she'd thank me eventually.

"Wrong to do this, period." I chanced a glance at her, determined now to make her see that this was the only way.

Annie's face went ghostly white, twin rivers of tears parting her freckles. Her lower lip trembled when she opened her mouth. "I refuse to believe two people loving each other is wrong."

"How can something be right when it hurts the people we love?" I countered.

Annie's lips went flat as she pressed them together. I nodded once and spun away to grab my shit. I didn't have much anyway. Would only take me a minute or two to shove my clothes in my bag and do the drive of shame back to Mom's house. I could fall apart later. Find my spot in the familiar wallow I thought I'd left behind.

The door to the bathroom slammed shut while I was in the guest bedroom grabbing my clothes. Annie, apparently, was hiding out. I wasn't sure what protocol called for here, but saying my goodbyes through the door didn't seem right. Nothing about this seemed right. I'd ignored my instincts which told me touching Annie in the first place was wrong. I'd ignored my instincts and look where that got me. Back at rock bottom, but this time I had heartbreak of a different kind to kick me while I was down.

"Come on, guys." I whistled out the side of my mouth and all three dogs came running. I got them loaded in the SUV and climbed behind the wheel. I gave one last glance to the house that had come to mean so much to me. Now those memories were tainted by the look of betrayal on Ben's face and devastation on Annie's.

"Way to go, fucker. You hurt both McLachlins in one go."

I fired up the engine and turned the wheel to head to Mom's. Pretty sure her grilled cheese wasn't going to be enough to heal me this time.

CHAPTER TWENTY-EIGHT

nnie

I THREW my phone down on the couch. Ben wasn't answering my calls. Blaze was on my shit list and I couldn't bear to call or text him right now. The dogs were gone. All that was left was the silence that would slowly kill me if I didn't get out of here. After the first tears fell while Blaze basically said everything beautiful between us was dirty and wrong, I'd felt numb. My cheeks were dry and my heart felt hollow. I knew I probably should have felt something. Rage, sadness, confusion. But all I had was a weird numbness that felt an awful lot like that time I drank too much cough medicine in college. My nose went tingly and it felt like my head was floating above my body.

Before the tidal wave of sadness hit me, I decided to follow Blaze's lead and grabbed all my shit, shoving it into my bag and throwing it into my car. I just couldn't bear to look around Ben's house, seeing the imprint Blaze had left on it. Grandma Donna's it was.

My stupid car backfired twice on the way over to her house,

which only made me think of Blaze. He'd be giving me grumpy side-eye right now if he were here. I shook my head and gritted my teeth. Nope. I wasn't going to think of him right now. I screeched to a halt in front of Grandma's place and left my bag inside the car. I'd always just walked in the front door before, but since Juan Carlos had come on the scene, I'd learned my lesson.

I knocked. "Grandma? Are you home?" I glanced around the porch, wondering what day it was. Hell, I didn't even know what time it was. I reached for my back pocket and realized I left my phone at Ben's. I was a mess.

The door swung open and Juan Carlos stood there with a five o'clock shadow, a Bloody Mary, a pair of boxers with hot dogs all over them, and the silk robe I'd gotten Grandma Donna two Christmases ago. It was a lot to behold on any day, but especially today.

"Annie? Are you okay?" His accent was over the top, but it was the genuine concern in his voice that had my face crumpling. Before I knew it, I was wrapped in his arms, inhaling his cologne and chest hair.

"Oh, there, there, little Annie. It can't be all that bad, can it?" Juan Carlos kept up a steady croon while I sobbed. We must have shuffled while he swayed me side to side because next thing I knew, I was being spun into Grandma's arms somewhere in the front living room of the house. She got me settled on the couch where I'd watched hours of television as a kid while she made dinner every night.

By the time the sobs faded and my eyes felt like they'd swollen shut, I'd soaked through a spot on Grandma's shoulder. A tissue appeared in front of my face, a hairy hand holding it.

"Thank you, Juan Carlos," I managed to say without spewing snot everywhere.

Grandma waited until I'd dried my face and blew my nose. She kept her arm around me, looking up at Juan Carlos. "Do you mind giving us girls some alone time this morning?"

"Juan Carlos will give you all the time you want, baby." He

dipped down and kissed her. I turned my head away. As lovely as Juan Carlos had been to me, I didn't need to see the smooching from a front-row seat.

Grandma settled into the couch and so did I, waiting until Juan Carlos got dressed and said he was heading for the store to buy us crab legs for dinner. Why crab legs? Who knew, but I wasn't in the state of mind to question his dinner choices.

"Tell me everything."

I sagged against the cushions, feeling older than Grandma suddenly. How did the best morning ever get so jacked up?

"Well, Blaze told me he loved me. Ben came home to find us in bed together. His bed." I cringed. Damn. No wonder Ben had gone nuclear. "And then Blaze said he regrets everything and walked out. So, yeah. Everything pretty much blew up today and everyone's mad at each other."

Grandma Donna blinked, fiddling with the reading glasses that hung from her neck. "Wow."

I huffed a laugh that held no humor. "You're telling me."

"Well, I can't imagine Ben staying mad at you, honey. He's probably directing all his anger at Blaze, so I would start there. Explain that you're in love with the boy and maybe those two can patch things up."

I shook my head. "It's not that easy, Grandma. You didn't see Ben's face. He's angry, yes. But he's also really hurt. He gave his best friend a place to stay and what did he do to pay him back? He slept with his sister! I slept with his best friend! It's all a mess."

Grandma frowned. "Excuse me?"

"What?"

"You didn't sleep with his best friend."

"I most certainly did. Just jumped right on that pleasure train. Choo-choo!" Yep. I'd officially entered the stage of grief where my sense of humor had jumped the rails.

Grandma sighed. "You don't understand my point. Sure, you slept with Blaze." She nudged me with her elbow and shot me a wink. "Congrats on that, by the way. I'm sure it was magnificent." She patted her hair and kept right on going. "But you don't need to put it so cheaply. You fell in love. Ben should be ecstatic that you're in a steady relationship with a good man. And there is no payback."

I wrinkled my nose, ignoring the part about falling in love with a good man. I wasn't ready to touch the part where Blaze called that a mistake. "Huh?"

"Why are you always trying to pay people back for simple kindness, Annie boo Bannie?" Grandma jumped off the couch with surprising agility. Maybe all that acrobatic sex with Juan Carlos was working out for her. "Remember how you used to set your alarm early before school and make my sandwich for work? I kept trying to tell you that you didn't need to do that. I was the adult. I had to set my alarm for before the crack of dawn to beat you to the kitchen."

I folded my arms across my chest. "You said you loved my sandwiches."

Grandma flapped her arms. "I did! But I didn't want your sandwich because you felt like you *owed* me. Listen carefully, child. You didn't then, nor do you now, owe me a goddamn thing!"

"But—but you raised us. When you were done raising kids. You even had to change jobs to accommodate our school schedule. You didn't even date again until we graduated."

Grandma's eyes turned to lasers that tried to incinerate me. "I chose to do those things because I wanted to! You are my granddaughter! I'd walk through the fires of hell in bare feet every day if it meant you benefitted. Never have I ever asked you for payback, and frankly, I'm insulted you think I'd accept your payback."

I hopped to my feet. I didn't think I'd ever heard Grandma yell like this. Getting this excited probably wasn't good for her heart at her age. "Okay. I hear you. Not sure I agree with you, but I was just trying to make your life easier, in return for your kindness. That's all."

Grandma let out a sigh that would have blown a smaller woman over. "Listen. I don't want to add to your trying day, but all I'm saying is that we all make choices about how we want to live. Those choices are mine and mine alone. Your choices are yours and yours alone. If you want to love Blaze, then who cares what Ben thinks. He'll get over it, or he won't, but that will be his choice. Quit looking for permission. Or to pay people back. You are not a burden, Annie boo Bannie." Grandma put her hands on my cheeks. "Watching that redheaded ball-of-energy toddler turn into the passionate, intelligent, stubborn woman before me was the privilege of my lifetime. You are a blessing in every way. Now go find your own blessings and don't let them go for anything."

With that, she walked out of the room, muttering under her breath about life wasting youth on the young people. My eyes were overflowing again. I flopped back on the couch and tried to parcel through all her statements while I swiped at my cheeks. Blaze had said something similar, that Ben didn't need me to do little things around the house to pay him back. I guess I just thought of those acts as a kind thing to do, but in reality, I was feeling like I owed people for helping me. I thought about my friends. I did nice things for them all the time too, but I didn't expect them to pay me back. That would be weird if Shelby, for example, was keeping a tally of every coffee I bought her and feeling like she needed to reciprocate.

I sat up straight, a sudden realization hitting me. I'd stopped Blaze from doing what he thought was right in calling Ben. Blaze had wanted to call right when he and I first got together, but I'd stopped him. All because I didn't want to disappoint Ben when he'd done so much for me over the years. And based on Ben's face this morning, all he really wanted from me was honesty.

Covering my face with my hands, I let out a groan. I'd royally fucked this whole thing up. If I hadn't stopped Blaze, Ben would have been pissed at first, but he would have appreciated the honesty and maybe given us the chance to talk things out. Now, Ben was not only angry we were together, but he felt betrayed by our silence.

I ran out of the house, calling to Grandma Donna that I'd be back. My car grumbled about it, but I made it back to Ben's in record time. My phone was still on the couch where I'd left it and Ben was nowhere to be found. I shot off a text to Blaze. I was determined to make things right. Not because I owed Ben or owed Blaze, but because I was a grown-ass woman who wasn't afraid to face the hard conversations.

Me: Hey. Can we talk, please?

I waited not-so-patiently, my knee jumping up and down as I sat on the couch. I didn't even realize my thumbnail was in my mouth until my teeth had nearly chewed it down to the quick.

"Shit!" I sat on my hand and waited some more.

Finally it vibrated.

Blaze: I need some space, Annie.

I rolled my eyes, even as my heart squeezed. Typical Blaze.

Me: Sure. But I must warn you. I won't wait around forever. I need to know you're still in this with me.

I hit send and shoved the phone in my pocket. I deserved someone who would fight for me. Just like I'd fight for Blaze. The front door opened and I held my breath.

"Annie?" Ben's hesitant voice sent butterflies swirling.

It was time to fight for what I wanted.

I walked to the door and saw him roll his suitcase in. He shut the door and looked up at me. He looked exhausted. Bags under his eyes that even his thick glasses couldn't conceal.

"Hey."

"Hey," he answered coldly. The bag of pastries he'd thrown at Blaze was still on the floor. "I have to warn you. I'm not in a good mood. Maybe we should talk later."

Old Annie would have slunk away and given him his space because it was what he needed. But what New Annie needed was to speak her mind without worrying about repercussions I couldn't control.

"Actually, I need to say something right now. Blaze and I love each other. What you saw earlier was an unfortunate way to find out about us, and for that, I'm sorry. But I won't apologize for loving him."

Ben yanked his hand through his dark hair. "I didn't find out by seeing you in bed together. Everyone in town knows. I heard about it from Poppy as soon as I parked downtown. Then Dante asked how you two were doing when I placed my pastry order. Everyone fucking knew but me." His voice was rising. "How do you think that made me feel, Annie? My own sister!"

Tears in my eyes were making him appear wobbly. "I'm sorry! I didn't intend to keep it a secret, but you've been gone for so long."

"Oh, so now it's my fault?"

"No! That's not what I meant. I just thought telling you in person was the right thing to do. Now I see that Blaze's idea of telling you straight away would have been better."

"Don't even talk to me about Blaze right now." Ben's jaw went hard as granite.

"Listen, I love him and he loves me and it's not ideal. I know. But it's real and we have to deal with it. All three of us."

Ben wouldn't even look me in the eye. "I just can't get past how my best friend, the guy I've known my whole life, would take advantage of my little sister while I'm out of town in my own goddamn house. He's clearly not the guy I thought he was."

I took a step forward, risking putting my hand on his arm. He flinched, but didn't push me away. "He didn't take advantage of me, Ben. I'm a grown woman. Capable of making grown-up decisions."

Ben swung his gaze back to me, and instead of anger, I saw sadness. "Without Mom and Dad, I'm the guy who watched out for you, Annie. I always will watch out for you. I can't just shut that off."

My heart felt ripped in two. "I'm not asking you to. I'm just asking you to hear me out. To know that I made this choice and wasn't coerced in any way. To simply give Blaze and me a chance."

Ben shook his head slowly. "I don't know if I can."

My throat felt thick. "At least don't give me an answer until you've given it some time. Please?"

He stood there studying me for several tense minutes. "Fine." He walked away, tossing over his shoulder right before he got to the hallway to the two bedrooms, "I'd prefer it if you still stayed here with me. But for fuck's sake, wash the damn sheets."

"Okay," I called after him, feeling anything but okay.

Ben was talking to me, even wanted me to live there with him, but things were far from okay between us. I still didn't know where I stood with Blaze either, but I'd keep fighting for what I wanted. Because Grandma Donna was right. I was a goddamn blessing, not a burden and I deserved a man who knew it. If Blaze ran from me like he did after things blew up with Danette, there was nothing I could do to keep him.

I just hoped he'd stay and talk this time.

That I was worth it to work things through.

CHAPTER TWENTY-NINE

laze

"I CAN SMELL you from the front door."

Daxon's annoying voice cut through my dark musings. I tossed the stick Tate had been playing with for the last hour while I licked my wounds in silence. He tore across the green grass I'd cut this morning. My little brother was an asshole and I didn't need his bullshit adding to all the thoughts swirling in my head.

"Fuck off."

There wasn't much heat behind it. I couldn't seem to gather much energy for anything these days except for training the dogs. And I did shower. Daily. But only because Mom put her foot down and told me she'd boot me out of her house if I didn't obey the very basics of human hygiene rules.

Daxon plopped down on the steps of the back porch right next to me, his shoulder nudging mine. "Have you talked to either of them?"

An avalanche of feelings pressed down on my shoulders.

Anger at myself for fucking things up with both Ben and Annie. Pain from missing Annie like she was a missing limb. Nothing worked in my life without her. Confusion over whether I'd done the right thing. Shame for walking away from her when I probably should have fought harder to stay by her side. And then that same feeling I got when I was probably eight years old and I'd wanted to play with Ace and his friends. They'd ridden their bikes faster than me, leaving me in their dust. I came to a stop on the road alone, my lungs heaving and my chest aching from being ditched. Ben and Annie were off having fun without me. They'd left me behind. I was no longer part of their lives and based on their silence the last two weeks, they were happier without me.

The screen door creaked open behind us. "Well, at least he's not high."

I wanted to laugh at that, but the humor wouldn't come. Ace sat down on my other side. When he and Addy had gone through some things last year, he'd hit rock bottom by getting high with her dad. I kind of saw the appeal, though whiskey would have been my poison of choice.

"Maybe we should have brought beer."

I turned and saw Ethan and Callan in the doorway too. I rolled my eyes and turned back to stare out at the backyard, not even seeing the rustle of the leaves in the trees, or the squirrels chasing each other at the edge of the lawn.

"What the hell is this? Some kind of brotherly intervention?"

No one answered right away which gave me all the answers I needed. Fucking brothers. Always in your business about everything. You just want to be left alone and they poked their noses in. Tate came running back and dropped the stick at my feet before visiting each of my brothers for a scratch behind the ears. At least somebody was happy to see them.

"Listen," Ace began, always the official spokesperson of the group. "We've given you two weeks and things haven't improved."

"Yeah, no shit."

Ace continued, undeterred by my bad mood. "So we thought you might need an outlet. Let's all head to the beach for a bonfire tonight. Beer, shooting the shit, and absolutely no women. What do you say?"

I rolled that around in my head. It actually did sound kind of good. Other than training Sugar and Spice at their new homes and physical therapy, I hadn't left the house. Maybe faking it for a bit might help me to actually make it, if the saying held true.

"Fine." I dipped my head and hoped that was the end of the intervention. As far as interventions went, it wasn't too painful.

"You aren't going to run away to LA like you did before, right?" That was from Ethan, the sensitive one of the pack.

I turned and saw him eyeing me as if he really was worried about that. "Dude. No. I'm done with LA."

He let out a breath like he'd been holding it. "Okay, good. I was worried you'd run again."

I frowned. "Run again?" Far as I knew, none of them were aware of why I'd left the first time.

Callan shrugged above me. "We don't know the details because you don't tell us anything, but we were able to piece together that something happened at work that caused you to run."

"You were gone for years, bro," Daxon said with a huff. "You're the king of running."

I was flabbergasted. I had no idea they saw me moving as running away. I'd told them I had a job opportunity in Hollywood, and I did. Kind of. I guess I didn't think my leaving really affected them that much.

"We're just really glad to have you back and hate to think that this thing with Ben and Annie would make you leave again." Callan clapped his hand on my shoulder.

"You guys think I'm a runner?" That was meant to be a question in my head, but it came out of my mouth.

"You remember what you did after our biological donor left?" Ace asked.

My back stiffened. I hated talking about our father. "Yeah, I begged him to stay and he gave me a handprint across my cheek."

Ace shook his head, his voice gentling. "You walked back in the house and went straight to that dilapidated tree house." He pointed at the pile of rotting wood and rope that lay neglected around one of the largest trees in the backyard. "You slept there for six straight nights. Not even Mom could get you back in the house."

I searched my brain but couldn't come up with that memory. I must have blacked it out as some sort of survival mechanism during an emotional time in my life. That was the only explanation for it.

"Why did I come back in?" My voice was rough. I tried to clear my throat, but it was stuck as if I'd swallowed glue.

"Ben came over on the second night and slept there with you until he could convince you to come back inside. Told you he was getting bit to death by mosquitoes and you finally came in."

A giant fist of emotion squeezed my ribs and wouldn't let go. Ben. Of course.

My brothers left, one by one, and still I stared at that old tree house. Vague flashes of memories flitted through my brain, but try as I might, I couldn't grasp exactly what had happened that week after our father left. But Ace was older than me and remembered more than I did. If he said Ben stayed with me in that old fort, then that's what happened.

The rest of the day passed in a blur of throwing sticks for Tate and trying to eat the grilled cheese Mom made me. I felt like I just might crawl out of my skin. I missed Annie and Ben so much I physically ached with it. Ben knew me better than I knew myself, having been there for me my whole life, but Annie was the one I envisioned the rest of my life with. Not that Ben wouldn't be part of my future either, but I couldn't imagine not loving Annie for the rest of our lives. Not being able to watch her run from place to place with her incessant enthusiasm. To not hear her sweet voice as the soundtrack to my life's story.

When seven o'clock rolled around, I headed for the beach, parking at that same spot where Dani had harassed Annie and me. My brothers weren't there yet, but that was fine with me. I could use a little silence before they descended. Maybe staring at the ocean waves would give me a sense of peace that had eluded me these past two weeks.

When I got down the cliff and hit sand, my leg wasn't screaming at me, which showed how much the physical therapy was helping. I came around the large rock face and saw the bonfire going already. A lone figure stood next to it.

Ben.

I came to a halt and almost turned right back around, but something about Ace's story about the tree fort made me stay. Ben had been my best friend before we even knew what being best friends really meant. I wasn't going to hide out in my tree fort—aka Mom's house—this time around. I wasn't a hurt little boy any longer. I trudged forward, heart in my throat as his head lifted and I saw the fire reflected in the lenses of his glasses.

"Blaze."

"Ben." I came to a halt a few feet away, unsure how to say what needed to be said.

He glanced around at the empty beach. "Did you put this together?"

I shook my head, instantly knowing what happened here. "Nope. My brothers said we were getting together. I assume they said the same to you?"

The corner of his lips tilted upward. "They always were nosy motherfuckers."

I smirked. "Yup."

His attempt at a smile fled quickly, replaced by a frown.

"Listen, Ben. I'm sorry."

He huffed air out of his nose. "For what exactly?"

I swallowed hard. "For a few things, but not everything. I'm sorry for not telling you about my feelings for Annie right away. I'm sorry for breaking your trust. I'm sorry you found out the way you did. But I'm not sorry for loving Annie."

His head came up sharply. "Don't."

"Don't what?"

Ben looked like he was gearing up to punch me. "Don't you dare say you love her. Love isn't something you hide. You don't keep a side chick a secret and call it love. Don't you dare cheapen her like that."

Now I wanted to throw a punch. "Side chick? Who the fuck said anything about a side chick?"

Ben scoffed and turned around, talking with his back to me like he couldn't stand to see me. "Just get the hell away from me, Blaze. You can't fuck around with my sister and then offer up a quick apology and think everything's okay again. You betrayed my trust and hurt my sister." He spun back around, angrier than I'd ever seen him. "I've always defended you! When anyone grumbled about your bad attitude, I apologized for you and smoothed things over. Told them that under the frown you were a good guy. Then you ran away for years, barely keeping in touch with me. And when you come back you immediately fuck my sister? Who the fuck even are you, Blaze Hellman?"

I was stunned by the hurt in his eyes. The way the anger came out in the volume of his voice. Ben was clearly done with me.

He stomped off, leaving me there alone. The flames from the bonfire danced in the breeze. I stared at them until they died down so low I was shaking with cold. I blinked and looked around, realizing it had gotten late. I slowly made my way back up the cliff in what was left of the moonlight.

If my brothers had thought a meeting with Ben would help smooth things over, they were dead wrong. I made it home in a numb fog, Ben's words echoing over and over in my head. Tate greeted me when I came through Mom's front door, but I didn't have the heart to bend down and pet him. If I did, I might just slide to the floor and never get back up. Instead, I flopped down on my old bed and stared at the ceiling, deep in thought. I was still awake when the sun came up the next morning.

I hadn't figured out how to mend things with Ben, but I'd come to a few conclusions. I had a lot of wrongs to make right. I'd finally hit rock bottom of this epic wallow and had the bruises to show for it. Like a phoenix rising, I wasn't the same man I'd been just the day before. I was going to step out of this wallow with a new outlook on life. A new purpose. A new way of handling the shit that life inevitably sent my way.

And I could only hope Annie would still be in love with the new Blaze Hellman.

CHAPTER THIRTY

nnie

"I DON'T KNOW if you've ever met my daughter, but if this turtle dies, she's going to raise hell." Oakley leaned over the examination table where their family turtle moved his head left and right in slow motion. "I can't handle a three-year-old breakdown over the death of a reptile right now. I'm due with our third baby any day now."

I kind of understood the urge to rage over the health of a turtle. It didn't take much to set me off these days. Either I sobbed uncontrollably or I ranted until I was hoarse. There was no in between. Even my friends were starting to avoid me now. If I didn't get my shit together, I'd tank my new business before it had even gotten off the ground.

Stupid Hellmans and their stupid handsome genes.

I put my hand on Oakley's arm to calm her down. I didn't need her going into early labor in my exam room. I knew animals, not humans.

"Mr. Peaches is a young box turtle. He'll probably live at least fifteen to twenty more years." I pointed at the lump of turtle on my table. "His lethargy is due to his toenails being too long. He can't get around. Let's clip them so he can move without pain and he should be good as new."

"Oh thank God." Oakley slumped into the seat behind her. "As a cop, you think you've seen it all. And then you have kids."

I chuckled and got out my equipment to fix this turtle right up. "Can I ask you a hypothetical question, Oakley?"

She began to rub the huge belly that protruded under the Auburn Hill Police Department T-shirt she wore instead of an official uniform shirt. She'd been working behind a desk during her pregnancy, barking orders at her officers just like her father had when he was chief of police in town.

"Sure. I'm officially off the clock, so ask away."

I started clipping Mr. Peaches' nails, wondering if I was making a huge mistake talking to Oakley about something that had nothing to do with me. But Addy had instilled in my brain that there were no coincidences in life. The universe had conspired to put Oakley in my path. I didn't know about all that, but I was going to use that as my excuse if this next conversation ever came back to bite me in the ass. Plus it was my nature to jump in and help and it was all I could do these last two weeks not to rush over to Blaze and try to make things right.

"So, let's say an officer is breaking the law. Would you want to know about that?"

Oakley's hand stilled, her voice sharp as a tack. "Always. Even if it's something as benign as jaywalking. I might not do anything about it if it's minor like that, but I still want to know."

There was an awkward silence, only broken by the dull ping of each toenail getting clipped. Mr. Peaches' beady eyes slow-blinked at me. My heart felt like it might jump right out of my chest. Should I say what I really wanted to say? Or did I keep the secret and let Danette get away with it?

"Is there something you'd like to report to me, Annie?"

I straightened, not trusting myself to keep clipping nails

while my hand was shaking. I looked at Oakley and she gave me a slight dip of the head, as if prompting me to speak my mind. The part of me that jumped in to help in every situation was getting antsy.

"Okay, here's the thing. I know something, but it has nothing to do with me and I don't know if the parties involved want me to bring this to your attention."

Oakley scooted forward in the chair, arms and legs flailing for a bit before she got to her feet. "How about you leave names out for now?"

I brightened. "Oh, that's a good idea. Okay, so you didn't get this from me, but someone I know knows that one of your officers has taken things out of the evidence room."

Oakley frowned. "Taken things out. As in, stolen?"

I nodded. "Yes. And when this person I know confronted her. Um, I mean them. They threatened them. Blackmailed them, basically." Dammit, this was a mess. I shouldn't have opened my mouth. Tattletale's remorse.

Oakley took a step closer, her belly just brushing my arm. "Annie McLachlin, is this about Danette?"

I gasped, covering my mouth with the toenail clippers. I'd have to disinfect my mouth later. "How did you know?"

Oakley's face went hard and I realized I would never want to be on her bad side. "She's already under investigation. Would this person you know be willing to testify against her? If they are, we could get her immediately placed on leave, arrested, and tried in a court of law."

The butterflies took flight. Holy shit. She'd done more than what Blaze knew about. "Uh, well, I'm not sure. There was the whole blackmailing thing."

Oakley put her hand on my arm, firm but gentle. "Talk to Blaze. See if he'll come forward. We could really use the extra information."

I nodded and moved away to keep clipping Mr. Peaches' nails. My heart hammered away, knowing that Oakley knew even if I hadn't come right out and said what this was all about. I wasn't even talking to Blaze right now. How could I possibly talk to him about the Danette situation? Although, the pet adoption event was this weekend, and despite our differences right now, he'd promised to help facilitate the event. If he actually showed up, maybe I could talk to him then. But honestly, I had more personal things to discuss with him. Like, were we truly over?

He'd left me hanging for over two weeks now and the pain was dulling enough that anger had taken over. My rants were becoming epic, if I did say so myself. But I'd taken Grandma Donna's words to heart. I was amazing and deserving of love. I wanted to rush over to Blaze because I hated having someone out there mad at me. It was my nature to fix things, but I couldn't fix this. I had to give Blaze time to decide if he wanted to mend things with me.

I went about the rest of the week in a fog, wondering if I'd said too much to Oakley or not enough. Wondering if I should reach back out to Blaze, but putting the phone down every time and remembering my pride. I'd told him to get in touch with me when he was ready.

I guess I just hadn't realized he might never be ready.

Sunday morning dawned bright without a single rain cloud on the horizon. The animal shelters from Blueball and surrounding towns had set up tents in the park downtown. As I parked along Main Street, I saw vans starting to unload all the stray canines, their barks and whines echoing across the grass. My heart ached seeing how many of them there were. As much as I'd been dreading today because of the situation with Blaze, I was glad to be a part of such a needed event.

Lucy came running over with clipboard in hand, already looking like she'd had at least two nitro coffees. I barely got out of the car before she was tugging me toward my own booth in the park.

"After each dog is adopted and we've done the paperwork,

we'll send them to your booth. Do you have all you need to do an initial exam?"

I could barely keep up with her long legs eating up the grass and I was used to walking fast. "Yes. I'll check for all major diseases and offer a discount on further things they might need like vaccinations or procedures. I also have the name of a pet groomer in Blueball they can go to, if need be."

"Excellent." Lucy finally came to a stop by my booth. "Though I hate to send business to that town."

I held back my eye roll. Everyone was so quick to hate on Blueball just because they beat us in sports most of the time. It was a lovely town. With a horrid name.

"Now where's Blaze?" Lucy looked around, oblivious to the way his name had caused all the blood to drain from my extremities.

"Uh, I don't know. I'm sure he'll be here soon," I said weakly.

Lucy spun toward me, studying me closely. I didn't like that look on her face. "Trouble in paradise?"

I got busy setting up my table for exams, trying to avoid her scrutiny. "No trouble." I bent down to get the box of equipment I'd need. "No paradise either," I grumbled to myself.

"What's that, dear? Maybe I should— Oh wait, there he is!"

My head popped up and I nearly dropped the box on my foot. There, on the other side of the park, wearing dark jeans and a polo shirt in a royal-purple color, with Tate trotting by his side, was the one person who could shred my heart. As evidenced by the loss of electrolytes from all the crying these last two weeks. His beard was trimmed close in the way I liked. He barely had a limp any longer, his leg muscles filling those jeans in a way that made every female in a fifty-foot radius turn and look. Damn, he was beautiful. He pulled at my heartstrings and ovaries in equal measure.

"I know that look," Lucy said quietly. "You love him. And based on the way he hasn't taken his eyes off you since he arrived, he loves you too."

I couldn't even find words to correct her. To let her in on the fact that things were not good between us. She moved away, probably running off to yell at someone about something, but I barely noticed. All I could do was stare at Blaze as he approached. He walked all the way up to my booth, stopping three feet away. I soaked in the sight of him like a woman who hadn't had water in days.

"Annie."

His deep voice washed over me, making goose bumps break out along my arms. He looked good. Tired maybe, but good. So fucking good. The ache in my chest that had started up when he walked out that day at Ben's house came back full force. I grabbed the table to stay on my feet.

I opened my mouth to beg him to work things out with me, but Lucy's voice on the bullhorn cut me off. Just as well.

"All right, ladies and gentlemen. We have a slew of puppies and full-grown dogs looking for their forever homes. Please make your way to the first booth."

Blaze's gaze hadn't left mine, his dark eyes cataloging everything about me. I'd worn my cat scrubs, hoping he'd see them and be reminded of a time when things had been good between us.

"Blaze Hellman, are you here?" Lucy's voice blared again.

Blaze's eyebrow lifted. He hitched his head in the direction of the first tent. "I better get over there. Can we talk after?"

"Yes!" I pounced, the word out of my mouth before I could even attempt to act cool. I cleared my throat. "For sure. Definitely after."

He nodded and walked off, Tate giving me one longing glance over his shoulder before obeying Blaze's command to walk with him. I watched the two of them all the way across the grass, letting myself roll around in the pleasure of simply looking at the man I was clearly still head over heels for.

"That man's a specimen," Meadow muttered.

I jumped to see her at my side. "When did you get here?"

She shook her head at me. "I've been calling your name but you were too busy eye-fucking that Hellman boy."

I flushed, but didn't deny it. "He's not a boy."

Meadow cracked up. "And you should be fucking him for real, not just with your eyes."

I elbowed her and shushed her as a family walked by, two little kids jumping for joy at the prospect of adopting a new pet today. I didn't get another glimpse of Blaze for the next hour. My tent was inundated with pets wanting their free checkup. Having not done an adoption event before, I wasn't sure what a successful one looked like in terms of numbers, but it seemed like every single dog that had been driven here today from the animal shelters was going to get a new home.

I'd just passed a long-haired Yorkie to their new owner's arms when Lucy's voice cut in on the bullhorn again.

"We have only ten dogs left, folks! If you're looking to adopt, now's the time!"

I didn't have anyone waiting for an exam and I couldn't wait any longer. "Will you man my booth, Meadow?"

She shot me a wink. "Only if it's because you're going to get your man candy."

"I have to go to the bathroom actually."

Her face fell and I sputtered out a laugh. "I'm teasing you, silly."

She glared at me, but pushed me out of the booth. "Go before I have to listen to another rant session, or God forbid, you actually do cry a river and flood our poor little town."

I snorted, but quickly began to give myself a pep talk in my head as I walked over to the booths at the front. I heard his voice before I saw him. I came around the corner of his tent and saw a group of people gathered around Blaze, watching him give commands to Tate. That sweet little puppy we found on the side of the road performed like a trained elephant at the circus.

"Can you help me with my dog too?" one lady asked as she clutched her newly adopted Chihuahua to her chest.

"Sure. Sit, Tate." Blaze reached for a business card on the table behind him and handed it to her. I kept hidden behind the corner of the tent, watching him with tears in my eyes. He was doing it. He was putting himself out there and making a career out of what he loved to do. I wanted to rush to his side and throw my arms around him.

But I couldn't do that. Not yet. Not until I could tell him that my brother wouldn't stop us from being together. I had to be brave like Blaze. I backed away from the tent quietly, turning and running through the crowd in a frenzy until I caught sight of Ben's dark brown hair that glowed red in the morning sun.

"Ben!"

He turned around and I kept running, grabbing his arm and dragging him behind the public bathrooms with me. I was out of breath, but I couldn't wait for a better time. He had been avoiding me the last two weeks, hoping we wouldn't have to have this conversation.

"Can this wait, Annie? I have—"

"No!" I crossed my arms over my chest. "I'm done walking on eggshells around you. Done avoiding the topic that needs to be discussed."

Ben dropped his head toward his chest, letting out a deep sigh. "Fine."

I nodded. "Fine. Okay. Good. So, Blaze and I. I'm going to try to make it work with him whether you're on board or not. I can't live like this any longer."

His head came up, his dark eyebrows drawn together. "What do you mean?"

I wanted to knock some sense into him. "I'm miserable without him, Ben! I can't eat. I can't sleep. I can't focus on my job when I'm wondering how he's doing. Have you really not noticed?"

Ben rubbed the back of his neck. "I guess I thought you'd get over it."

I shook my head. "Get over it? Get over the fact that the one man in the whole world that I love wants nothing to do with me because of you? My own brother is stopping me from being happy and you think I'll just get over it? Are you kidding me right now?"

He grabbed my arm and pulled us closer to the brick wall of the bathrooms. "Shh. Keep your voice down. I'm sorry. I guess I thought you'd get over your infatuation soon enough."

I yanked my arm back. "I'm not infatuated with him, Ben. I love him! Pull your head out of your ass or I will go around you. I love you too, but I won't let you stop me from being happy."

I took a step to walk away, but Ben reached out again and pulled me back. "I'm sorry, Annie. Really. I am. I talked to Blaze two nights ago."

That stopped me in my tracks. "You did?"

Ben nodded. "I did. And it went badly." He cringed. "Mostly because I accused him of being a terrible person after he said he loved you."

I nearly melted on the spot. "He said that?"

"He said he loved you and I didn't believe him. You said you loved him and I didn't believe you. But based on the way you two have been moping around, maybe I'm the one who's gotten this all wrong."

"You did get it wrong, dumbass."

His eyes twinkled and I knew we'd be okay. "Hey!"

I flicked him in the chest. "For being a genius, you sure are dumb sometimes."

He chuckled and pulled me in for a hug. "When it comes to love, yes. I agree. I'm a dumbass." He pushed me away to look at me earnestly, his hands on my arms. "But I won't stand in your way any longer. If you want to be with Blaze, I won't try to stop you."

Hope was like a drug in my veins. "Really? You promise?"

"I promise. In fact, I'll go talk to him right now."

I threw my arms around my brother and squeezed him tight. "Thank God I don't have to disown you."

He laughed some more and then got serious. "I really am sorry. Let me try to set things straight with Blaze, okay?"

I let go to beam up at him. "Okay."

And for the first time in a long while, things really were starting to look okay.

CHAPTER THIRTY-ONE

laze

"CAN you teach him to fetch me a beer?"

Irritation was my new friend. I had to walk away from Annie when looking at her was the first thing in weeks to make my heart rate calm. Just seeing those freckles across her cheeks was enough to tell my entire central nervous system that all was well. All the worries I'd focused on had faded away. All the guilt for hurting my best friend got pushed to the corner of my brain where I could see that he and I would move past this, given enough time and effort. But then Lucy's voice had blared through the bullhorn and irritation had been my companion ever since.

"Sure, but maybe we can start with more useful commands."

The guy standing before me scratched the top of his head and pursed his lips, looking down at the two-year-old Sheltie he'd just adopted. I stepped forward to snatch that poor dog right out of his hands and demand she get adopted by someone far more capable of appreciating her as man's best friend, not a servant, when Jack came pushing through the crowd standing around my tent.

"Blaze!" Jack had Spice on a leash, looking haggard yet smiling.

I left the annoying guy's side and rushed over to pet Spice. I'd gotten to know Jack, his wife, and even their six-month-old daughter during my trainings at their house. Spice had integrated with their family perfectly. Or so I thought.

I put a hand on the distressed man's shoulder. "Is everything okay?"

Jack swallowed hard and caught his breath. "You'll never believe what happened last night! Spice saved our baby's life!"

The crowd gasped and so did I. "What happened?"

"Kara's in the hospital right now. They wanted to keep Lacey overnight, just to check her out."

Cold dread lined my gut. Had Spice bitten the baby? You just never knew sometimes with rescued dogs. Something could have triggered aggression.

"Spice kept nudging her door open and going in her room." Jack was saying. "I pulled him back out like three times. I mean, we all know you don't wake up a sleeping six-month-old."

A woman in the crowd behind me wholeheartedly agreed.

"So, the fourth time he went in there, I followed him, thinking maybe there was something in her room, but he just went right up to her crib and whined. He sat there and wouldn't let me pull him away. I had this weird feeling in my gut, so I checked on Lacey."

Jack choked up and I squeezed his shoulder to let him know it was okay. I couldn't imagine what had happened, but if it made Jack this frantic, it had to have been something huge.

"She'd stopped breathing, Blaze." Jack scrubbed a hand across his eyes. "Her lips looked gray. I called 9-1-1 and they whisked her away. She, huh, had something stuck in her throat. Must have had it clutched in her little hand when we put her down for bed and we didn't notice."

"Spice noticed!" someone in the crowd offered. A cheer went up.

Jack lifted his head and nodded, looking at me with tears in his eyes. The man looked exhausted, but exhilarated.

"She's okay?" I asked quietly.

Jack nodded again and then he suddenly flung his arms around me in a bear hug. "She's okay because of Spice. He saved her life."

I whacked him on the back a few times, feeling like maybe I needed that hug too. When we stepped apart, I wasn't ashamed to admit that I was a bit misty eyed just like Jack. When I decided to train dogs for a living, I hadn't expected this. I thought I might get a few dogs that could help people, but saving a life? I wasn't sure what to do with all of that.

"I'll come by the house this week and check up on you all. Give Kara and Lacey my love."

Jack clapped me on the shoulder again before bending down to pet Spice. I'd have one hell of a treat for that pup when I came for the next lesson. Everyone crowded around me, demanding business cards and wanting to know how soon I could come train their dogs. Business was booming, but all I could think about was finding Annie after this event and seeing if we could work things out. What good was a booming business if I didn't have Annie to come home to every night? My plan to turn my life around centered around her.

When the crowd finally dissipated and I was able to tear down my tent, Annie was nowhere to be found. Instead, I found Ben. He was leaning against a huge oak tree, watching me like some kind of creep. I tried to read the expression on his face, but he wasn't giving me anything.

"Heard you're the new town hero," he called out finally.

I lifted the table and the case the tent folded into, ready to head to my car. "Suppose so. Feels kind of weird."

Ben pushed away from the tree and came over slowly. "Why is it weird?"

I shrugged best I could loaded down with stuff. "The hero worship was always directed at Ace."

"How about you follow me home? I think we have some things to discuss."

As much as I wanted that, I wasn't in the mood to be ripped a new asshole again. I'd said I was sorry and there wasn't much else to say. Ben must have seen the hesitation as he was quick to continue.

"Or maybe I have some things I need to say. More than what I may have said the other night."

I looked away at the park, seeing most of the tents already deconstructed and the people gone home. "Not sure I can take much more of that."

Ben sighed. "Just come over." And then he walked away.

I shook my head at his back. The fucker knew I'd come over. Ben had meant too much to me over the years to turn my back on him. I tried to squash down the hope that tried to pop its head up at his invitation. He probably just wanted to play whack-a-mole with my face being his own personal punching bag.

I threw my stuff in the back of my SUV and headed to his house, my heart doing some weird fast rhythm, followed by skipping a beat when I thought about my chances of seeing Annie. I'd heard she was still living with Ben.

The front door was ajar when I came up the porch stairs. I closed one eye and prepared for a fist to be flying into my face as I pushed the door open. When nothing happened, I went inside and closed the door behind me. "Hello?"

Ben came out of the kitchen with a beer in each hand, setting both down on the little table where I'd had so many meals with Annie. "Have a seat."

I did, sitting and wishing things were back to the way they used to be. Ben and I could spend hours together, talking or silent, and not have this horrible tension between us. I still felt guilt for being the one to cause this tension, but the last few days I'd come to the conclusion that I wanted Annie more than I wanted Ben's approval. If only I could find Annie and tell her.

Ben had a seat in the chair opposite me and the thing let out a creak. I instantly thought of the day Annie had sat on my lap in her barely there pajamas and tried to seduce me. Fuck, I missed her.

"You win."

I stared at Ben for a couple beats and then frowned. "Excuse me?"

He took a swig of beer and then set the bottle down. "I said you win. I've seen how depressed Annie is and I don't like it. She claims to love your sorry ass."

My hope-mole popped his head up again, this time refusing to be whacked down. "Well, that's mighty convenient because I love her too."

Ben grimaced. "That's going to take some getting used to. But I won't stand in your way any longer. If you truly love her and treat her like she deserves, then I have no beef with you."

I hopped to my feet, shoving the chair back. "Really?"

Ben tried to keep frowning, but his mouth kept dancing around a smile. "Yeah, really. But again, only if you have good intentions."

I spread my arms wide, my hope-moles multiplying and popping their heads up everywhere. "I intend to marry her as soon as she'll let me."

Ben smiled then. Full-out, blinding smile like I remembered from all those years growing up together. "I guess we're going to be brothers, then. For real."

"Fuck yeah." I leaned down and hugged him, nearly tilting him back and knocking him over. His chair gave out a mighty creak and gave it up, dumping his ass on the floor in an explosion of splinters. I nearly went down with him, catching myself on the table at the last second.

"What the fuck?" Ben looked around at the chair in pieces.

I cringed, remembering that I'd intended to glue that chair

back together after Annie sat on my lap and we cracked it during our make-out session. I had a feeling I ought to keep that little detail to myself. Ben grabbed my hand and I hauled him up.

"You think Annie still loves me? Because I walked out on her, thinking I was doing the right thing. It's been a few weeks."

Ben kicked the pieces of the chair out of the way, muttering under his breath about cheap furniture. At my question, he turned to me with a look I often gave my little brothers when they asked stupid questions.

"You may be the new town hero, but you've always been my sister's hero. Of course she still loves you, you dumbass."

Warmth seeped into every square inch of my chest. I still had a shot.

"Is she here?"

Ben shook his head. "Nah. Meadow distracted her with dinner when I told her I wanted to talk to you."

I nodded, brain spinning with possibilities. "Good. I need to put together a plan."

"A plan?"

I playfully punched him in the arm. "I gotta win the girl back, dumbass."

As soon as I got back to Mom's house to formulate my plan to win Annie back, all my brothers were there, Addy included. I dropped my box and tent right by the front door, eyeing the fine china on the dining room table.

"What's all this?"

"Dude, family dinner. Didn't you read the text?" Daxon asked.

I cringed. "Totally."

"You didn't read it," Ethan stated correctly.

Mom came out of the kitchen folding a takeout bag from a new barbecue place in Blueball. At least she wasn't cooking. That boded well for our digestion later tonight.

"Hi, darling. You're just in time."

I gave her a hug. "Planned it that way."

Callan snorted behind me, but didn't out me. We all filed to our seats around the table and waited while Mom put a huge platter of brisket in the center of the table, along with corn on the cob, and cornbread.

"You aren't growling," Ace said as soon as Mom took a seat and we began to dig in.

I looked up and realized he was talking to me. "Huh?"

"You've been a grumpy asshole the last few weeks. You seem almost happy today. Did you talk to Annie?" Callan continued.

I shook my head. "Not yet. But I just came from Ben's. Apparently he's cool with me and Annie dating now."

"Praise the Lord!" Mom beamed at me from the head of the table.

"Ah-ha." Daxon grinned evilly. "So it's time for your wake-up crawl."

I slathered butter on my cornbread, realizing I was starving. I hadn't eaten much lately. Too deep in my wallow to care about food. "What the fuck is that?"

"Language!" Mom tittered right before munching down a row on the buttery ear of corn in her hands.

"Sorry, Mom."

"It's where you wake the fu—eff up and realize you love the girl and can't live without her," Ethan explained like I was a two-year-old.

"Then you crawl on your knees for forgiveness. A wake-up crawl," Ace finished.

"Don't you remember Ace when he begged Addy to forgive him for being a dumbass?" Ethan asked.

Ace threw an ear of corn at him and Mom muttered about us always ruining her tablecloths.

"Dude, I was in LA."

Callan rolled his eyes, his mouth full of meat. "Great. Since you don't know what you're doing, we're all going to have to help you figure it out. You can't mess this up. This is your one shot to get her back."

I put down the rest of the cornbread, nerves making me rethink the plan I'd been formulating in my head the last few days. "I've got a plan."

Ethan shook his head. "It probably stinks."

"It doesn't." At least I didn't think so.

Addy reached across the table and put her hand on mine. "How about we talk after dinner? I'm one of Annie's best friends. I can help you if you need it, but I'm sure what you have planned is going to be just fine."

"Thank you for believing in me, Addy." I glared at my brothers.

But secretly I was thanking my lucky stars for Addy and her guidance. Maybe my idea did suck. What the hell did I know about groveling? Or women in general? Next to nothing, that's what. I just knew I loved Annie and would do anything to get her back. Anything.

CHAPTER THIRTY-TWO

nnie

ADDY: I've got coffee in the car. Pick you up in ten?

Me: Where are we going? Do I need to dress nice?

Sunday was my one day off. I was planning to spend it in sweats and ratty hair piled on top of my head, but Addy had texted me last night about hanging out with her. I almost turned her down, but agreed at the last minute. My motivation came more from wanting to grill her about the Hellman boys and maybe get some advice on what to do with Blaze. He said at the adoption event that he wanted to talk to me, but then Ben had wanted to talk to him first. I thought Blaze would be knocking down my door this morning if he still wanted to be with me. The fact that he wasn't made me want to stay in my sweats and eat my weight in chocolate.

Addy: Doesn't matter where we're going. Don't you always deserve to look nice?

I rolled my eyes. From my precarious perch on the slippery slide into depression, I didn't think looking nice was much of a priority. But then I thought about running into Blaze in town and how horrible it would be to get turned down by the man I loved while also looking like I hadn't showered in days. If he was officially breaking up with me, I planned to leave him with a lasting impression that I was most definitely the one who got away.

I grabbed a brush and got the snarls out of my hair. A swipe of mascara and some lip gloss and my face was good to go. It was too cold these days for a cute sundress, so I found my favorite ripped jeans and threw on a blue blouse with a daring neckline. One pushup bra later and I was feeling like a million bucks. Maybe Addy was right.

The honk from the curb had me running outside with my purse trailing behind me. I climbed into Ace's truck—Addy still hadn't bought her own car...something about reducing her carbon footprint—and gulped down that sweet nectar. Addy waited me out, knowing how important caffeine was for me in the morning. How she got up and just meditated before starting her day was something of a miracle. Or she was an alien life form.

"Can I head out now?" she asked dryly.

I swirled the remaining coffee and smacked my lips. "Yes. I'm officially ready for whatever."

"Glad to hear it," she mumbled.

She kept up a steady stream of conversation about her latest yoga class—done in the dark in the woods behind her house with only a single headlamp per participant—before parking at the cliffs. I rubbed my fingers over the pang in my rib cage. I'd had such a good time here with Blaze. Well, before the run-in with Danette.

Addy climbed out and handed me a thick stack of blankets. "Can you take these down and I'll get the bag of food out of the back?"

"Sure." I grabbed the blankets and trotted off, figuring I could handle a day at the beach with my friend if I really focused. I wouldn't look at that exact spot where Blaze's leg gave out and he put his arm on me for support. Or the spot where he kissed me and it felt like my head floated away into the clouds.

I turned the corner by the rock face, bracing myself for the very spot where Blaze and I had talked about grief and how I'd never felt more connected to another human being. But the pain never came. Just shock.

Blaze was standing right there by the unlit fire pit, looking all kinds of delicious in a T-shirt and jeans. He held a huge bouquet of roses of all colors. Tate was sitting by his feet, his tail swooshing back and forth behind him as soon as he caught sight of me.

"Blaze." My voice was weak and so were my knees. I dropped the blankets to the sand.

"Annie."

Blaze pointed to me and Tate took off, covering the distance between us and sitting directly in front of me, which was certainly something Blaze had trained him to do.

"Good boy, Tate," Blaze crooned. "He has a note for you, Annie."

I tore my gaze away from Blaze and pet Tate, pulling a rolled-up piece of paper from his collar. I glanced back at Blaze, wondering what was going on.

"Read it," Blaze urged.

I smoothed out the paper, seeing Blaze's handwriting in what could only be described as a love letter. My heart, the one that loved every romantic comedy movie that had ever been made, gave a long sigh.

My dearest Annie,

I am attempting to write this letter as I know I'm not good with words. I have so many things to tell you and yet I know it will come out wrong. I love you, Annie. Truly, wholly, and forever. I thought I could walk away from you and things would go back to the way they were before. What an idiot, right? I know now that I'm permanently changed from living with you. I don't even see the world the same way since you talked your way into my life.

I let out a teary laugh at that. Even while apologizing and telling me he loved me, Blaze was able to rib me about my incessant talking.

I thought having a steady and successful career would be what would make me feel accomplished in life. Apparently, I had a huge lesson to learn. None of that matters without you, Annie. I've become a better man simply by loving you. I once lectured you about not doing favors for Ben because you thought you owed him. Well, I thought I owed the world. I thought because my father left me, I wasn't worthy. That I had to be successful in my career to prove my worth. Silly, really, that the actions of someone else could leave a permanent stain on me. Thank you for showing me that even as a broken, limping, angry man, I was worthy. You always made me feel ten feet tall even when I couldn't stand up without crutches.

I'm sorry for walking away from you. I'm sorry for taking so long to understand that it's you. It's always been you. I can't run from you because you are the very best parts of me. I don't deserve it, but I'd very much like it if you could find it in your heart to forgive me.

I love you.

Blaze

My heart had already found an abundance of forgiveness. Thank God the letter ended because my eyes were too full of tears to read it anyway. I bounded over Tate and ran across the sand, throwing myself into Blaze's arms. He caught me, like I knew he always would, holding me so tight I could barely breathe.

"I'm sorry too. It's been killing me to stay away. I love you too." I rattled off everything that had been bottled up in me these last few weeks, peppering his face with kisses in between breaths. "I hate being away from you. Ben shouldn't be an issue between us. Not when we love each other. And I hate being away from your family too. I even miss your grumpiness."

Blaze's chuckle finally got me to shut my mouth. He was

grinning at me, his face smashed between my hands on his cheeks. "I have missed you so much."

I had to get this last thing out before I lost my courage. "Blaze. You need to know that I would give up a relationship with Ben for you. You are so worthy of love. Worthy of someone fighting for you. Worthy of someone staying, no matter what."

Blaze stared at me for a long time, both of us just breathing and fighting back tears. His eyes closed, looking like he was in pain. I opened my mouth to say something, anything that would make him feel better, but he opened his eyes again and all I saw was love. Acceptance. Trust.

I sucked in a deep breath and willed my tears to stop. Blaze dipped his head and kissed me, his lips brushing across mine repeatedly as if to savor me. Then he deepened the kiss and my hands slid into his hair. I thought I might be dreaming. Surely feeling this euphoric could only happen in my dreams.

Blaze pulled back too soon. "We should talk things out."

I made a face. "God no. Forget talking."

He cracked a smile again and my ovaries whimpered. "My Annie doesn't want to talk?"

I pulled his head down and kissed him again. Just because I could. "I like the way you say my Annie."

"You are, aren't you?" he whispered against my lips.

"Always."

He slanted his head and captured my mouth. We didn't come up for air until Tate butted his head against our thighs, breaking us apart. Blaze pressed his forehead to mine, breathing heavy.

"He's right. We should sit on those blankets I asked Addy to bring and talk things out."

I blinked, trying to get my brain to work properly. These Hellman boys could kiss a girl senseless.

"Oh yeah, Addy!" I let go of Blaze's hair and stepped back, looking around in bewilderment. "Did she leave?"

Blaze took my hand in his and tugged us over to where I'd dropped the blankets. He spread them out and held out his hand to assist me. We sat across from each other, knees touching, fingers interlaced with each other.

"I asked her to bring you here. There's so much I need to tell you."

"I need to talk to you too." I had to tell him about my conversation with Oakley. I needed to apologize for breaking his confidence.

He squeezed my fingers. "Mind if I go first?" At my nod, he continued. "I went to see Captain Oakley two days ago."

I gasped and felt the blood drain from my face. Blaze only shot me a knowing grin.

"Yes, I know that you talked to her. You didn't name names, but I filled her in on everything I saw. Dani is officially on unpaid leave while they put together their investigation."

"Oh, Blaze. I'm sorry for talking to Oakley, but I hated how Danette ran you out of town."

"That's just it. She didn't run me out. I chose to leave. Running away was my default when bad things happened. I needed time to process, and yes, probably to wallow a little. But running was the bravest thing I could do at the time. I wasn't equipped at twenty years old to face the situation. I'm older and slightly wiser now. Which is why I went to Oakley."

"I'm proud of you. I can only imagine how hard that was to do."

Blaze let go of one of my hands to run his hand along my jawline. He pushed some hair behind my ear. "You had every right to be angry at me for the things I said and yet you went to Oakley anyway. You cared more about righting that wrong for me than your own pain. Your love is a gift, Annie."

I blushed, trying hard to accept the compliment and not brush it away. "I love you, so yeah, I wanted to make things right for you."

"And I love you. I'm not running anymore. I don't give a shit about Dani or what anyone thinks. You're what matters."

I got to my knees and crawled over his lap, settling my legs on either side of his hips. I was tired of the space between us. I never wanted to be away from this man again. My arms wound around his neck and I looked into his warm brown eyes.

"How private is this beach, you think?"

His eyes lit up and I could have sworn something moved underneath me. "Annie McLachlin, are you proposing what I think you're proposing?"

I ran my nose along his, my lips desperate for his kiss. "If you're thinking dirty, sandy sex on the beach, then yes."

He grabbed my hips and ground against me. Yep. He was most certainly on the same page as me. Tate let out a whine from two feet away. We both looked over at him, his tongue lolling out the side of his mouth. He gave an excited bark, knowing he had our attention. His tail flicked sand left and right as it began to wag.

We both started laughing and soon we couldn't stop. I was getting cock blocked by the rescue dog I'd come to love.

"Maybe this isn't the best venue," I muttered finally.

Blaze squeezed my waist. "Let's go look at houses."

I pulled back, my mouth dropped open. "What?"

His smile was patient, like he was waiting for me to catch up. "We love each other. I'm in it forever, aren't you?"

"Well, yes."

"Then let's go look for a house to rent. Move in with me, Annie."

I blinked in the early morning sunshine, thinking that through. It was perfect, really. I was living with my brother. Blaze was living with his mom. At this rate, we'd never be able to have sex again.

I jumped off his lap and scrambled to my feet. "Let's go look at houses."

Blaze laughed, coming to his feet and brushing the sand off my jeans. I must have had a lot of sand on my ass based on the amount of time he spent on that spot. "I figured you'd see it my way."

I frowned then, thinking of my nearly empty bank account. All I had was tied up in my clinic. "Wait. I might have to ask Ben for a loan."

Blaze picked up the blankets and shook his head at me. "I've got money saved for a down payment."

I opened my mouth to say I'd pay him back, but he cut me off.

"And I swear if you say you'll pay me back, I might have to spank you. We're in this together, okay? And another thing, I don't care if you try to put others' needs before your own and go to ludicrous lengths to pay people back. I love you no matter what ridiculous rules you make up in your head. You are worthy, too, Annie. And I'll be by your side until you figure that out."

Well, crap. I just fell even deeper in love with Blaze. With tears in my eyes, I made the motion of zipping my lips and throwing away the key.

"Just the way I like you," Blaze muttered under his breath as he turned to walk up the cliff. At the last second, his lips twitched.

My jaw dropped. "Hey!"

His laughter trailed off into the wind as I scrambled up the hillside after him. Joke was on him though. I had the best view of his muscled ass.

EPILOGUE

ix Months Later

Blaze

"SIT, SMOKY." The Dalmatian Ace had brought into the fire station sat on his haunches, looking at me with eager eyes, ready for the next command. Ace had hired me to work with him the last month and he was already making huge progress.

"Too bad you didn't follow in your brother's footsteps. Blaze is a perfect fireman's name." Joe, a fellow firefighter, tipped his head at me as he passed through the kitchen at the fire station.

I cracked a smile. I did that a lot recently. "It's a little too on the nose if you ask me."

Joe shrugged. "Yeah, you're right. It's like a stripper named Candy. No one wants to be a cliche."

"Exactly." I looked down at the dog. "Smoky, fetch Joe a bottle."

The lanky Dalmatian immediately ran to the refrigerator in

the kitchen and used a paw to open the door. He returned with a bottle of water in his mouth, depositing it at Joe's feet.

"Good boy, Smoky." I gave him one of the tiny treats I kept in a pouch around my waist while Joe gave him a good rub behind the ears.

Dalmatians were no longer needed to help fight fires or clear roads ahead of the rigs, but they served as an important part of the team. I wanted Smoky to not only provide emotional support but to offer minor conveniences for the crew when they came back to the station tired from a long call. So far, the boys had gravitated toward Smoky since day one.

"I'm done for the day. Tell Ace I'll see him next week?" Joe and I fist-bumped and I hustled to my car. I had a hot date with a redhead tonight.

Annie thought we were going out to dinner after a long week for both of us. Our businesses were booming, which was great, but it meant we had to sneak in time with each other wherever we could. As much as I wanted to take Annie out to show her off to the world, I mostly just wanted her all to myself. Especially tonight.

I got the last candle lit right as I heard the front door open. The house we'd rented was small. Just a two bedroom close to the ocean with a nice backyard for Tate. Figured we could save our money and buy a bigger place later. For the first time in a long while, I had a lot of plans for the future.

"Blaze?"

I came around the corner of the living room, smiling when I saw Annie standing inside the front door in the new cat scrubs I'd gotten her. This pair had the famous Grumpy Cat face all over them. "Hey, gorgeous."

Annie put her bag down, toed off her shoes, and looked around at the white candles on nearly every surface. "Hi. Are we trying to get a visit from the fire station?"

I came forward and tugged on her hand, pulling her into the house. The trail of red rose petals started in the living room and led to our bedroom where I'd lit another ridiculous amount of candles. Mom had not been too happy when I ransacked her rose garden earlier today. I'd also run this whole date idea past Addy a few days ago, getting her stamp of approval. And an extra fire extinguisher from Ace, just in case.

"Oh my gosh!" Annie gasped, her mouth curved into a soft smile. "What in the world?"

I pulled her into the bedroom, watching her face as she took in the chocolate-covered strawberries and champagne on the nightstand.

"I thought we should celebrate."

Annie kept looking around in amazement. "What are we celebrating? Oh shoot, is it the anniversary of something? Did I forget?"

Poor thing looked panicked. She had no idea what I had planned for her tonight. "No. Nothing like that. I just like celebrating you. Your clinic. Us. It's a lot to celebrate, is it not?"

Annie stepped into me, looping her arms around my neck. "Why yes it is." I stopped her from reaching up to kiss me.

"The pussies have to go."

She stuck her lower lip out. "I thought you liked my pussies?"

"Oh I do." I reached for the hem of her shirt and pulled it over her head. "But I really like the wet one underneath your scrubs."

Annie's neck and cheeks took on that blush that never ceased to appear when I started talking dirty to her. She pushed the pants down her hips and stepped out of them, kicking them aside and leaving her in the black lace panty and bra set she bought for my birthday a few months ago. The woman knew the way to my heart.

I pointed to her chest. "That has to go."

Annie held my stare as she reached around her back and unclasped the bra. It fell to the floor, leaving her gorgeous tits to my hungry gaze. I had every freckle across every inch of her body memorized.

"That too." My voice was hoarse. In the back of my mind, I wondered when the sight of Annie's naked body would stop taking my breath away. Six months together, and if anything, I was more in awe.

Annie shimmied out of her panties, leaving them on the floor as she stepped closer to me. "I feel like you're a bit overdressed, Mr. Hellman."

I trailed a single finger across her collarbone, down between her breasts, over her stomach, and from hip to hip. Her skin puckered and quivered as I moved.

"I feel like I could make you come with just a finger."

Annie's breath was already coming faster. "Is that a dare?"

I leaned down and sniffed along her neck, careful not to actually touch her. "It's a promise."

The finger came back up to coast along her torso, finding one nipple and making it stand at attention before giving the same attention to the other. Annie moaned my name and I grinned down at her.

"Why so quiet?" I taunted her.

Her eyes were already dilated, her head tipped back in invitation. I wanted to kiss her. To taste those lips and lose myself in her, but I had a promise to fulfill first. My finger swooped lower, parting her and finding her clit already swollen for me.

"Blaze!" Annie gasped, her body swaying into me.

"Ah, ah, ah." I moved back just a fraction of an inch, refusing to touch any other part of her. I was thoroughly invested in this experiment now. Annie was soaked, promising I would win this bet if I just gave it a bit more time and attention.

I slid one finger inside of her, biting back my own groan at the heat that surrounded me. My cock jumped inside my jeans, thinking he could get in on that action. I pulled back out, finding the nub my teeth and tongue had come to memorize these last six months. Keeping up a steady rhythm around and across and then back down to dip back inside, Annie was soon chanting my name. Her hands grabbed my wrist and held me over her clit, her hips desperate for release as she ground against my finger. She bit her bottom lip and I watched her eyes roll back in her head. She gasped my name one more time as her whole body clenched. Her nails bit into my wrist with a flash of pain, but I didn't care. Watching her fall apart was the best part of my day.

Her eyes finally fluttered back open and her grip on me relaxed. "Wow. One finger, huh? That must be some kind of record."

I smiled smugly even as I had to push back on the desire that had me wanting to spill myself into my pants. Fuck, that was hot. Everything about Annie turned me on. Damn inconvenient when we both had jobs that required us leaving our house every day.

Annie stepped back and turned to the bed. "If you get naked, I'll feed you those strawberries."

I only got my pants off and one strawberry in my mouth before Annie was bent over the bed and I was plunging into her from behind. I wasn't a total ass. I'd fed her two strawberries, one of which was currently in her mouth and distorting her moans.

"Fuck, how does this get better every time?" I said between gritted teeth. My T-shirt kept getting in the way each time I thrust into her. I pulled it off with one hand, tossing it to the floor. The feel of the tiny ring of metal against my chest as I moved made me smile, even as I panted. Annie hadn't seen it yet, just like I planned.

Annie groaned again, pushing her hips back as if she couldn't get enough of me. The feeling was mutual. She was small, but she took my cock like she was made for me. Every night as I held her close and we drifted off to sleep, I knew she was. A woman more perfect for me had simply never been born. She filled the dark corners of my life, reminding me that the world was a beautiful place simply because she was in it.

A crescendo of barks broke the sound of our heavy breathing. Annie's phone. It must be in the pocket of her scrubs that were now sprawled over the end of the bed.

Annie's back flexed, as if she were going to get up and get it. I pushed a palm down on her back. "Leave it."

"Just...let me...turn it off."

She reached an arm out for the pants, her hand disappearing in the pocket. I reached too, getting my magical finger back on her clit. She yelped when I hit the jackpot. I grinned and slid almost all the way out, loving the way my dick looked covered in her desire for me.

"Hello?" came a distant voice.

It was not Annie's.

We both froze. Then I looked over at her scrubs and realized Annie had answered the fucking thing instead of turning it off.

I slapped her ass quietly and she bit back another yelp. "Answer her," I whispered, smoothing my hand over her hip.

"Hello?" she answered loudly, sounding out of breath and an octave too high for normal.

"Hey, Annie. Sorry to bother you. Are you around? Could you help me tonight? I have a huge order to load in the van and I just need a second set of hands for like five minutes."

It was Shelby, the florist next door to Annie's clinic. Annie propped herself on her elbows, all too eager to help a fellow human. I decided messing with Annie was exactly what she needed. There was a time and place for helping someone and when I was buried deep inside her was not the time. I slammed back into her and she collapsed face-first into the mattress with a stifled groan. I reached around again and strummed across her clit. I felt her tighten around me, her legs quivering against mine.

"Annie?" I heard Shelby call.

"Y-yes. Sure," Annie called out.

I pulled out of her and slammed back in, grinning down at her. She let out a groan and scrambled for the phone, smashing the screen and maybe hanging up if we were lucky, right before she chucked the phone out the bedroom door.

"You're evil," she called over her shoulder, but then backed her ass up and ground against me. Ah, my girl liked it when I teased her.

But I was done teasing. Done taking it slow. And done holding back. My speed increased and instinct took over, requiring that I plunge into her warmth over and over again like an animal out of control. Her legs gave out and she collapsed against the bed. I followed her, pinning her beneath me. She turned her face to the side to gasp for breath, her red strands of hair a mess across her cheek.

"Fuck, Annie, I love you." I couldn't make myself go slow. Couldn't even get my hands to leave her shoulders where I held her down to the bed. Lights popped behind my eyelids and then Annie was screaming, clamping down on me so tight I wasn't sure if I could have pulled out even if I wanted to. And I sure as hell didn't want to. I buried myself as deep as I could go and exploded. Pain and pleasure of equal measure curled up my body and had me flat against her back, holding on for dear life.

Time passed and the sweat between us began to cool. I blinked my eyes and realized I was probably crushing her. That had not been part of my plan for tonight.

I tried to roll off of her and she groaned. "Don't go."

I pulled out and rolled her so she was on her back. Holding myself above her on my arms, I looked down at her closed eyes. "Did I unalive you?"

She moaned and lazily brought her hands up to wrap around my shoulders. The ring on the chain around my neck tickled along her breastbone. She peeled one eye open and looked down. The other eye flew open.

"What's that?"

I grabbed the ring and held it between us. "Oh, you mean this?"

Annie's eyes were wide open now. They flew to me, shock and confusion written all over her face. "Where'd you get that?"

I shrugged like it wasn't a big deal. "Got it from Grandma Donna last week. It's your mom's wedding ring."

Annie was back to gulping for breath. "I know. But how...why do you have it?"

"Figured if I was going to ask you to marry me, I should give you a ring that means something to you. So what do you think, Annie McLachlin? Will you marry me?"

Annie went positively still. Then she was a blur of motion, pushing me off of her and sitting up, grabbing the comforter and not quite covering her breasts.

"Are you serious?"

I bit back a smile. Her hair was a fucking mess and I'd left a mark on the side of her neck that probably wasn't going to be gone by tomorrow, but she was the most gorgeous woman I'd ever seen. And if she'd just say yes, she'd be all mine. Forever.

I got up, aware that proposing naked maybe wasn't my best idea, but it was too late to rethink it. I came around to her side of the bed and knelt down on one knee. My Annie deserved this to be done right.

"Annie. I've always loved you, even when we were kids. That love blossomed into something else this last year. Something beautiful and wonderful and even a bit magical. I don't deserve you, but I want you just the same. Please marry me so I can spend the rest of my life showing you how special you are. So I can spoil you with all the good things in life. So I can make it my mission to make you smile every single day of your life. Plus your sandwiches are fucking works of art."

Annie managed a laugh, tears swimming in her eyes. "Yes, Blaze. Hell yes, I'll make you sandwiches for the rest of your life."

I tackled her onto the bed, letting out a whoop that was sure to get the neighbors grumbling. I heard Tate whine from the back porch where I'd set him up for the evening. Tate and a house full of candles was not a good combination.

I lifted the chain from my neck and slid the ring off. "I already bought a new wedding band to go along with this one, but I thought you'd want to have something of your mom's with you always."

I slid the antique diamond engagement ring on Annie's finger as a tear slid down her cheek. I'd learned over the last few months that many times those tears were happy ones and not to freak out.

"I love it. And I love you. So much." Annie got up on both knees and wrapped her arms around my neck in a death grip. "I can't believe Grandma Donna didn't tell me."

I chuckled into her neck as we held on to each other. "She also tried to convince me to buy assless chaps, but I had to turn her down gently. Juan Carlos is just too much of a man for me, I guess."

Annie tossed her head back and laughed so loud my ears rang. Her phone began to bark again from wherever it had landed in the hallway. I'd almost forgotten about Shelby calling.

I groaned, knowing Annie would want to help her, even if the timing was damn inconvenient. "You should probably go."

Annie swiveled her hips over my dick. Even spent, the damn thing lifted his head, sensing things weren't done for the night. "No way. I live here now."

I twisted us so she was underneath me. "We have time for a quickie. And then I'll go with you to help her."

"My hero," Annie whispered right before I claimed her lips and made love to my fiancée.

BONUS EPILOGUE

laze

"I SWEAR I won't take more than ten minutes to get ready!" Annie yelled, the slamming of the front door highlighting the lie.

She was home late from work again, the life of a veterinarian requiring long hours and being willing to jump up in the middle of the night to help an ailing animal. Annie was good at it. Exceptional, really. I was just grumpy about having to share her all the time.

I waited for her to burst into our bedroom at warp speed. When she did, she froze, her mouth dropping open. She had to quit staring at me like that or we'd be really late to Ace and Addy's wedding rehearsal. I cocked an eyebrow at her.

"You gonna stare or get ready?"

We were both in the wedding and therefore couldn't be fashionably late. I shivered to think of the blistering Mom would give me for holding up her eldest's rehearsal. Or the payback when it came time for my own wedding. If it was up to me, I'd just go to city hall and do the dang thing, but my girl wanted the white dress and all the fancy stuff. And I'd turn myself inside out giving her exactly what she wanted for the rest of her life.

Annie cleared her throat. "Damn. Warn a girl before you put on a suit, Blaze Hellman. That kind of thing could cause early heart failure." She leaned in, as if she meant to kiss me, but I spun away in the nick of time.

"Nuh-uh. If you kiss me, we won't make it at all."

She stuck her bottom lip out. "Well, now I don't want to go."

I smacked her ass and walked out of the room. "Nine minutes left."

She yelped, the sound of the closet opening and drawers being pillaged following me out to the living room where I waited for her. She came out only two minutes late, her feet in wedges that made me instantly develop a weird foot fetish, a short frilly dress in lavender, and her hair twisted in some strange updo girls learn at birth so they can distract us boys.

"Fuck."

She put her hands on her hips. "Seriously, Blaze? That's all you have to say?"

I stood and adjusted the front of my pants. "I have a lot of things to say. None of them appropriate when I'm going to kiss my mother with this mouth in five minutes."

Her sultry smile had me calculating exactly when we could leave the rehearsal and not piss off my family. I groaned and put my hand on her low back to usher her out the door. Too fucking long. That was how long we had to stay.

The Peacock B&B came into view and we parked right next to Callan's dump of a truck. That thing was his original set of wheels from when he turned sixteen. You'd think he'd trade up now that he was a working professional and living on his own, but you'd be wrong. The guy had a soft spot for it and couldn't move on.

"You're here!" Addy squealed and ran down the aisle to hug Annie and me as soon as we stepped through the iron gate to the left of the lobby. The grounds of the bed-and-breakfast were dotted with mature trees and flowers everywhere you looked. Addy's feet were bare and there was a flower crown on top of her long blonde hair. She positively beamed.

Ace came down the aisle at a slower pace, clapping me on the back as we hugged. We were the last couple of the wedding party to arrive. Mom gave me the hairy eyeball, but didn't say a word. Daxon did some lewd motion with his hips when Mom turned her back, but that was Daxon for you. Always getting in a dig where he could. I rolled my eyes and took my place on the groom's side. Annie took her place on Addy's side with Meadow and Cricket. She shot me a smile that meant everything was right in my world.

The rehearsal was short, everyone complying with the instructions from Amelia Jackson, one of the owners of the B&B. Ace looked so happy he could burst. I'd never seen him so comfortable in his own skin. If I hadn't been so distracted with watching Annie's every move, I would have congratulated him on being the best damn big brother a guy could ask for. As it was, it went without saying. When we hugged it out at the end of the rehearsal, he knew how I felt.

Dinner was served at the little restaurant attached to the B&B. We all sat down, the door opening again to let in a guy I didn't recognize. Callan, who sat on my left, bristled.

"Hey, Alistair!" Cricket jumped up from her chair across the table and ran to give him a kiss. "Glad you could make it."

I noticed Callan looked away before the two actually kissed, a move that had me interested in his business. Us boys had been teasing him for two decades about his friendship with Cricket. Those two had met on the first day of kindergarten and had become fast friends. Time nor maturity seemed to make a dent in their best friend status.

Annie's knee hit mine under the table. I dutifully leaned her way and she whispered in my ear, "There's something going on here."

I whispered back, "That's what I was thinking."

And if I knew Annie at all, she was going to get to the bottom of this uncomfortable silence that had descended over Callan as Alistair had a seat directly across from us. It didn't take long for everyone at the table to realize there was an issue. Callan didn't say a peep all through the appetizers and the main entree. It wasn't until dessert was served that he finally had had enough.

"You don't need that dessert, Crick." Alistair leaned over the woman and shoved her plate of cake away from her.

"Crick?" Callan said quietly but with so much vehemence it sounded like a whip cracking. The table went quiet, sensing danger.

Alistair turned his sleazy smile on Callan. "Yeah, we have nicknames for each other."

Callan eyed the cake that should have been Cricket's. "Maybe you should think harder on that one. And let her eat her dessert if she wants to."

Alistair took a healthy swig of his fourth—or fifth, I'd lost count—glass of wine. "She doesn't need it. She told me just yesterday she's trying to eat better."

Callan's eyes squinted dangerously. "So now you're her food police?"

"Callan, it's fine," Cricket said quietly. "I do want to eat better."

"You're like a size two," Meadow said with an unamused chuckle.

"Won't be if she eats cake all the time," Alistair answered, digging his own grave. I was an idiot around women most times, but even I knew that wasn't the right thing to say.

Callan lurched forward in his chair and I moved quick to put my hand on his chest. "Let's not do this here. It's Ace and Addy's night."

I said it as quietly as I could. Personally, I'd have loved to get in on a fight that involved bashing in Alistair's smug face. But this was not the appropriate time. I felt Callan relax, one muscle at a time. When I was sure he wouldn't leap across the table, I let him go.

"As a plant lover, are you satisfied with the floral arrangements for tomorrow?" Annie directed the question to my mother down the long table by a few seats.

Mom shot her a relieved smile. "Shelby has outdone herself. You should see how she wrangled all those wildflowers!"

"And she's making me a special flower crown," Addy chimed in, successfully changing the topic of discussion at the table. "It'll be all white to match my dress."

The conversation flowed naturally after that, but Callan continued to eye Alistair and Cricket. After dinner, we milled about chatting, and even then he kept glancing over at Cricket in the corner where she was looking to have a heated discussion with her boyfriend.

"Lover's spat?" I asked lightly.

Callan nodded. "That guy's an asshole."

Ace leaned away from his future bride to give his opinion. "What the hell is she doing with him? Cricket's too good for him."

"I know. I keep telling her that but she doesn't want to hear it. Says he's sweet when it's just them." Callan's face was darker than a thundercloud.

Ethan swirled the ice around in his glass. "Maybe we need an intervention."

Daxon snorted. "Maybe what she needs is for Callan to remember he has a pair of balls and tell her how he feels."

Callan jumped so fast I didn't have a chance to hold him back this time. He had Daxon shoved up against the wall, the two of them breathing fire at each other.

"Boys!" Mom hustled over, putting her face between them. "Stop it right now. I did not raise you to act like barnyard animals."

They stayed that way for another moment or two, then Callan let go of him. Daxon straightened his shirt collar, smirking because he didn't have one ounce of good sense in his damn head. Mom backhanded his chest.

"Stop that."

"What?" he yelped.

"Your face isn't helping. Leave your brother alone or I swear I'll get the Love Shirt."

Daxon's face drained of color. "Damn, you're tough."

Mom sniffed. "Don't you forget it."

Annie turned to me wide eyed. "What's the Love Shirt?"

Ace and I chuckled, glad the crisis had been averted. For now.

"Mom would stuff two of us into one of Dad's old T-shirts. Made us stay adjoined like that for hours if we were acting like jackasses," I explained to Annie.

"Which happened a lot," Ace chimed in.

Callan wandered off to the bar, but I watched him closely. He pointed at Alistair's back and chatted with the bartender. Then he slipped the guy a folded-up bill before coming back to our group.

Not long after, Alistair left Cricket's side and headed for the bar. The dude was drinking way too much. I wondered if I should call a ride for him right now.

"He's watering them down," Callan said quietly, watching the asshole order another drink while winking at one of the female servers clearing the table.

Annie darted around me and wrapped her arms around Callan. "You're a good man, Callan Hellman."

She pulled back and thank fuck she did because I did not need to see her wrapped around another man, even if the other man was my brother.

"Cricket's one of my best friends, but this guy has got her all messed up. Thank you for watching out for her."

Callan looked at Annie and I saw something flash in his eyes that he'd never let me see before. Pain. The soul-crushing kind that haunts you day and night. I knew that look because I'd seen it in the mirror every time I looked at myself after running away from Hell and Dani and that whole mess.

"I've been watching out for her since we were kids. Second nature now." Callan tried to pass it off, but we could all tell he was affected.

I pulled Annie back into my side, feeling remorse for teasing Callan about Cricket in the past. There were one-sided feelings going on there that he wasn't admitting to. If loving Annie while keeping it a secret from her brother was torture, imagine loving a woman your whole life and never saying anything? Pure fucking hell.

Putting my arm around Callan's shoulders, I pulled him into me. "Let's go have a beer after this whole wedding business is over, okay?"

He looked over at me, lines of tension on his face when there was usually an easygoing smile. "Sounds good."

Callan walked away from us, heading for Cricket. He whispered something in her ear. She shook her head and Alistair got between them.

"I can get her home, Hellman. Why don't you find your own girl?" Alistair was talking so loudly we could all hear him.

Callan pulled himself up, refusing to look at Alistair. "Find a safe ride home, Cricket. See you tomorrow."

Cricket gave him a sad smile, nodding. Callan walked out of the restaurant without a backward glance.

"Damn," I muttered. Annie tightened her arm around my waist.

"He'll figure it out," Mom said quietly, watching her son walk to his beat-up truck. "The rest of y'all need to stay out of it."

"Yes, ma'am," we all grumbled.

It was a damn lie and Mom knew it. No way were we going to let one of us suffer when we could do something about it.

"Let's all go home and rest up for tomorrow, huh?" Ace injected happiness into his voice, though I was sure it didn't take much to put it there. He was head over heels in love with Addy.

Back in my car with Annie by my side, I pulled up my text messages and made a group chat with my brothers. Minus Callan.

Me: Tomorrow we celebrate Ace and Addy. The day after that we figure out how to help Callan. Agreed?

Daxon: Fuck yes.

Ethan: I'm in.

Ace: Agreed.

With that decided, I put the phone away, drove my Annie home, and showed her exactly how grateful I was for her love. Much later that night we pulled the covers over us and attempted to get some shut-eye before the wedding craziness began.

"I can't wait to marry you and be yours forever," I whispered to the top of her head as she drifted off to sleep. I'd made my way through hell all the way to heaven with Annie in my arms.

ALSO BY MARIKA RAY

All Steamy RomComs Set in Hell:

Grumpy As Hell - Hellman Brothers #1

***

Ridin' Solo - Sisters From Hell #1

One Night Bride - Sisters From Hell #2

Smarty Pants - Sisters From Hell #3

Ex Best Thing - Sisters From Hell #4

***

Love Bank - Jobs From Hell #1

Uber Bossy - Jobs From Hell #2

Unfriend Me - Jobs From Hell #3

Side Hustle - Jobs From Hell #4

Man Glitter - Jobs From Hell Novella - Grab it FREE here!

***

Backroom Boy - Standalone

Steamy RomComs:

The Missing Ingredient - Reality of Love #1

Mom-Com - Reality of Love #2

Desperately Seeking Househusbands - Reality of Love #3

***

Happy New You - Standalone

Sweet RomCom with Delancey Stewart:

Texting With the Enemy - Digital Dating #1

While You Were Texting - Digital Dating #2

Save the Last Text - Digital Dating #3

How to Lose a Girl in 10 Texts - Digital Dating #4

<u>Sweet Romances:</u>

The Marriage Sham - Standalone

***

The Widower's Girlfriend-Faking It #1

Home Run Fiancé - Faking It #2

Guarding the Princess - Faking It #3

***

Lines We Cross - Nickel Bay Brothers #1

Perfectly Imperfect Us - Nickel Bay Brothers #2

<u>Steamy Beach Romance:</u>

1) Sweet Dreams - Beach Squad #1

2) Love on the Defense - Beach Squad #2

3) Barefoot Chaos - Beach Squad #3

* Novella - Handcuffed Hussy

4) Beach Babe Billionaire- Beach Squad #4

5) Brighter Than the Boss - Beach Squad #5

* Novella - Christmas Eve Do-Over

ACKNOWLEDGMENTS

Thank you so much for reading Bro Code Hell!

Special thanks to Jennifer Olson for the incredible Cover Design and for the hours cover model searching that were so incredibly tedious. lol Thank you to Judy Zweifel for triple checking this manuscript and making it shine as usual.

To my Rays of Sunshine: you give me life. <3

ABOUT THE AUTHOR

Marika Ray is a USA Today bestselling author, writing small town RomCom to make your heart explode and bring a smile to your face. All her books come with a money-back guarantee that you'll laugh at least once with every book.

Marika spends her time behind a computer crafting stories, walking along the beach, and making healthy food for her kids and husband whether they like it or not. Prior to writing novels, Marika held various jobs in the finance industry, with private start-up companies, and then in health & fitness. Cats may have nine lives, but Marika believes everyone should have nine careers to keep things spicy.

If you'd like to know more about Marika or the other novels she's currently writing, please find her in her private Reader Group.

If you want to take your stalking to the next level, here are other legal-ish places you can find Marika:

Join her Newsletter -
http://bit.ly/MarikaRayNews

Amazon - https://www.amazon.com/author/marikaray

Goodreads - https://www.goodreads.com/author/show/16856659.Marika_Ray

Bookbub - https://www.bookbub.com/authors/marika-ray

TikTok - https://vm.tiktok.com/ZMJvnQ2Cv